THE MISFITS

A PSYCHOLOGICAL DARK ROMANCE

SHANDI BOYES

COPYRIGHT

Editing: Nicki @ Swish Design & Editing
Proof: Kaylene @ Swish Design & Editing
Second Proof: Chavonne Eklund
Cover Design: SSB Covers & Design
Published: Skye High Publishing

DEDICATION

To the misfits in all of us.

This one is for you.

Shandi xx

ALSO BY SHANDI BOYES

Sugar and Spice (Cormack & Harlow)

Lady In Waiting (Regan & Alex #1)

Man in Queue (Regan & Alex #2)

Couple on Hold(Regan & Alex #3)

Enigma: The Wedding (Isaac and Isabelle)

Silent Vigilante (Brandon and Melody #1)

Hushed Guardian (Brandon & Melody #2)

Quiet Protector (Brandon & Melody #3)

Enigma: An Isaac Retelling

Twisted Lies (Jae & CJ)

Bound Series

Chains (Marcus & Cleo #1)

Links(Marcus & Cleo #2)

Bound(Marcus & Cleo #3)

Restrain(Marcus & Cleo #4)

The Misfits

Russian Mob Chronicles

Nikolai: A Mafia Prince Romance (Nikolai & Justine #1)

Nikolai: Taking Back What's Mine (Nikolai & Justine #2)

Nikolai: What's Left of Me(Nikolai & Justine #3)

Nikolai: Mine to Protect(Nikolai & Justine #4)

Asher: My Russian Revenge (Asher & Zariah)

Nikolai: Through the Devil's Eyes(Nikolai & Justine #5)

Trey (Trey & K)

The Italian Cartel

Dimitri

Roxanne

Reign

Mafia Ties (Novella)

Maddox

Demi

Rocco

Clover

Smith

RomCom Standalones

Just Playin' (Elvis & Willow)

Ain't Happenin' (Lorenzo & Skylar)

The Drop Zone (Colby & Jamie)

Very Unlikely (Brand New Couple)

Short Stories - Newsletter Downloads

Christmas Trio (Wesley, Andrew & Mallory -- short story)

Falling For A Stranger (Short Story)

Coming Soon

Jack Carson

WANT TO STAY IN TOUCH?

Facebook: facebook.com/authorshandi

Tiktok: https://www.tiktok.com/@authorshandiboyes

Instagram: instagram.com/authorshandi

Email: authorshandi@gmail.com

Reader's Group: bit.ly/ShandiBookBabes

Website: authorshandi.com

Newsletter: https://www.subscribepage.com/AuthorShandi

FOREWORD

Dear Reader,

This is your warning. This isn't my standard type of writing. It still has suspense and intrigue. It is just in a twisted, warped way. If you want hearts and flowers, this isn't the book for you.

Dexter roared.

I listened.

Enjoy the ride.

Shandi xx

PROLOGUE
DEXTER

"*A*ttempted murder, also referred to as Murder One, is when one, say the defendant, commits the heinous act of murder. Is that correct?"

My heart thumps my ribs when Cleo, the key witness at my trial, strays her wide eyes to mine. They're the color of baked clay —bright and entrancing but utterly lifeless.

The last part of my assessment makes my cock swell. The broken are the most beautiful. They are fractured souls left defenseless to the people who don't understand the beauty of their cracks.

I see past the damage. Past their wilted, pained looks. I see the exquisiteness behind the ugliness because the strength required to fix the broken is nothing less than miraculous. It separates men into two groups—cowards and gods.

I belong to the latter.

My pulse rages in my ears when Cleo licks her cracked lips. Her most subtle movement reminds me of their plumpness. Full enough to sink my teeth into, but not so pudgy they can't hide her aloofness when she wordlessly consults with the DA. She's hopeful he'll advise her how the man sitting behind him wants her to answer.

Although annoyed she's seeking *his* opinion, I'm not shocked at her ability to express herself without words. We've communicated the same way many times during the three weeks of my trial. Her sneaky glances when she loses *his* unforgiving glare and the alteration of her scent when I'm near proves she's watching me as closely as I'm monitoring her.

That's why I am defending myself. I don't need pompous, insolent men telling me I'm "misconstruing the facts." I can't misread the way Cleo's pulse quickens when she captures my steel-blue gaze or the sweat that mists her brow when my watch has her squirming in her seat. She isn't panicked about my undivided attention. If her needy gaze isn't witnessed by the man who *wrongly* believes he owns her, she's thrilled by it.

The most beautiful things in the world cannot be seen or heard. They are felt. Whether it is an invisible pull or the stars aligning just right, when you find your other half, you never give up the hunt until they are yours.

I erased the evidence of Cleo's betrayal.

I forgave her for her error in judgment.

Now we have this last hurdle to jump, then we'll be free to be with one another.

This trial isn't Cleo's choice. *He* forced her into it. I can't say I blame him. Who wouldn't be threatened by my looks and unreachable wealth? I don't just have the brains. I also have the brawn.

I could have had Cleo eating out of my palm years ago, but a change in game plan added an additional thrill. My relationship with Shelley, my last little pet, was exhilarating. It occurred at a rate three times the speed of my usual liaisons, but with the thrill of the hunt weakened by the ease of the game, the spark fueling our connection soon dwindled.

I tried to re-ignite the flame—I gave it everything I had—but her death ended our game before I could woo her with my god-like stamina and cunning intellect.

News of Shelley's demise rocked me in a way I've never experienced. Seeing the life in her eyes vanish at the hands of another man was not a game I had ever fielded. When you are responsible for relighting the flame in one's eyes, it's only right that you're the one who extinguishes it.

Cleo's dad stole that right from me.

When his car veered across a patch of black ice and crashed into Shelley's vehicle head-on, he took my game and flipped it on its head.

He also awakened a beast.

I was raised believing I had complete control. He proved I didn't.

The fall from my tower was eye-opening and painstakingly long.

I will admit, I was lost the week following Shelley's death.

Power isn't something that is given.

You take it.

You steal it.

You go to the ends of the earth to find it.

But at no time do you have it stolen from you.

For the first time in twenty-four years, the devil beat me at my game. He snatched the prize out from beneath my nose. He played me for a fool.

So it was only fair I returned the favor.

The game Cleo and I are playing is long, but the prize will be worthy. She's even more broken now than when I stumbled onto her at her brother's funeral. You see, her father's wrongdoing didn't just claim Shelley's life. It saw himself, his wife, and his only son take the same blackened path I plan for his two remaining offspring to eventually walk.

Cleo's eyes are wet from the tears she shed when questioned about the death of her unborn child, the contents of her nose precariously pools in the crevices of her nostrils when the jury is shown photographic evidence of the fresh scar in her lower abdomen, and her hands shake when she's forced to point to me when asked who 'allegedly' assaulted her.

Her frightened response is beautiful—utterly breathtaking.

And she is also mine.

Desperate to break the fog our eight weeks of absence has caused, I step into her line of sight, blocking *him* from her view. The veins in her neck throb as her pulse quickens. She's so pleased to have secured my devotion, she struggles to breathe.

Every ragged gasp she takes doubles the thickness of the blood in my veins.

I understand her struggle.

I feel her pain.

So I will once again save her from her nightmare.

"Is that correct?" I ask again, my voice raspier than earlier. Her sneaky glances do that to me. They make me unstable but in a way I can't help but encourage.

The doctors say I have obsessive-compulsive tendencies driven by an unbalanced family environment. They don't know what they're talking about. I am not insane, mentally unstable, or psychotic. I am a man who knows what he wants, and I don't stop hunting until I get it.

Upon spotting the faint bob of the DA's head, Cleo mimics his movements. She doesn't enjoy disappointing me, but our lengthy absence since my arrest in her home has jumbled her mind.

She'll soon learn that *he* is not the rule maker.

He isn't half the man I am.

I am the god who saved her from hell.

He is the coward.

"So, if I am being accused of murder, who is the victim?" I turn to face the jurors. Half their expressions are as ashen as Cleo's. The other half is a cross between confused and angry. "The DA stated many times that the charges brought forward are for grievous bodily harm, deprivation of liberty, assault, and murder one, but the victim's identity has not been brought forward. How can that be?"

The jurors follow my gaze back to Cleo. She straightens in her chair the instant she spots my narrowed glare. I'm not overly angry at her, but some penance must be paid for the wrongs she's committed. Even after being publicly humiliated in front of millions, she still ran back to *him.* That's why I had no choice but to react the way I did. Her inability to see how stupid he makes her look is why I did what I did. I am guilty of what I am accused. I pierced Cleo's stomach with a knife, killing her unborn baby, but I am not a murderer.

Not a convicted one, anyway.

"Who is the victim, Cleo?"

Her throaty groan as she strives to hold in her tears rolls through me like liquid ecstasy. It's heaven to my ears, the equivalent of an afternoon swim on a scorching hot day.

I stop relishing her nearly choked response when the DA shouts, "Objection, Your Honor! The accused is well aware of the victim's identity. It's been stated multiple times during preliminary hearings and is documented in the evidence we handed to him weeks ago."

He stands from his chair, hopeful a bit of height will bolster his appeal.

He should sit the fuck down because height isn't his only

disadvantage. His failure to recognize my brilliance is another downfall. He is an amateur dabbling in a world where he doesn't belong.

I am the master.

He is a mere pawn.

I return my focus to the judge, who's glaring at me over his half-rimmed spectacles before speculating, "The opinions of a jury often change during cross-examination due to doubt being cast on the witness. I am not saying Ms. Garcia lied during her earlier testimony, but perhaps if her answers aren't coerced by the DA, she will freely express herself."

"What are you saying, Mr. Elias?" the judge asks while pushing his glasses back up his blackhead-covered nose. "Do you believe the witness has been coached to give false testimony?"

The worry in his voice hums through me. "Yes, Your Honor, that is *precisely* what I am implying. But Ms. Garcia hasn't merely been coached. She's been brainwashed as well."

The jury gasps in sync, but the ruckus is barely heard over Cleo's loud gulp. She knows what's coming, that I am once again freeing her from his trap.

"Do you have any proof of this?"

While nodding at the judge's question, I make my way to the desk I've sat behind grinding my teeth for the past three weeks. I flip through numerous pages of text until I come to the evidence the DA failed to lodge. "Deprivation of liberty. Harassment. Cyber-stalking. Credible threat to cause harm. Rape." For each sentence I deliver, I hand proof of the crimes associated with them to the bailiff. "*He* hacked her computer. *He* harassed her at her place of employment. *He* cyberstalked her for months before *he* raped her under the guise of an exchange in power."

The judge's bushy brows shoot up his face when he scans the evidence presented before him. The images are horrid, ones I'm certain Cleo would never like publicized, and although I don't want to hurt her, to free her from his madness, I need to expose *him* as the monster he is.

"As you can see, Your Honor, I'm not in any of those photos because I am not a monster who hides his face to ensure his crimes remain unprosecuted. I'm merely a byproduct of his madness. An innocent caught up in a world run by violent, heinous men."

I add an affluent edge to my voice. It's the tone I generally use when surrounded by my father's associates. He taught me well. I play the game so perfectly the judge is soon eating out of my hand. "I did not hurt the complainant, Your Honor. I was merely trying to save her from that. From him. If that makes me a terrible man, so be it. I'd rather rot in jail as an honorable man than be a spineless one."

I refuse to look at *him*, but I know I've secured his utmost attention. I can feel his black-as-death eyes burning a hole in the back of my head. Smell his aversion thickening the air. How? The putrid scent seeping from his pores is as repulsive as mine. The hate blackening his blood is just as tainted, and his world just as violent. He simply hides his evilness by referring to it as his 'lifestyle.' That's why he is a coward, and I am a god. I don't require a contract to exert power nor a safe word.

I give an order.

You follow it.

The rules don't get any simpler than that.

When the judge requests the bailiff to hand my evidence to Cleo, her hand shoots up to clamp her mouth. I take a few moments to relish the stream of moisture gliding down her cheeks before I dart from my chair to block *him* from her view.

He brainwashed her for months. It's time to even the playing field.

My girl is strong, but my pull is even stronger than that.

She cannot resist me.

For every step I take toward Cleo, the fire in her eyes grows. The temptress I feed off like a vampire drinks blood is striving to break free. She wants me to save her. She wants to come home.

"I didn't kill your baby, did I, Cleo?"

Her earthy brown hair falls from her shoulders when she shakes her head. Her strength as the woman behind the mask resurrects from the tomb *he* placed her in is cock-thickening.

I suck in a lung-filling breath like the devil did while claiming the throne in heaven when Cleo confirms, "You didn't kill my baby, Dexter."

The jury members' stunned gasps are loud, but they're nothing compared to the painful groan *he* emits.

He knows he is losing.

He shouldn't be surprised.

No one can compete with me.

I take a step back when Cleo faintly murmurs, "You killed *our* baby. The baby I created with Marcus. The baby I plan one day to still have with him."

Her words are barely whispers, but one of them bombards me with an immense amount of violence—*his name*. It resurrects the devil I struggle to contain. The sadistic villain who maims without regret and smiles while sliding a knife into a pregnant woman's womb. He is the evil spawn my father loves, and my mother hated. He is the runaway, the misfit. Marcus Everett's worst nightmare.

He is the true me.

He is Dexter Elias.

"No!" I shake my head the way I did when the doctors ran off their long list of diagnoses to my mother ten years ago. "I didn't kill your baby! I killed *his* baby! I fixed *his* mistake! I took back what is mine!"

"I'm not yours. I'm Marcus's!"

Cleo doesn't whisper her confirmation.

She shouts it for the world to hear.

When I step closer to her, wanting her to swallow her lies, the bailiff wedges himself between us. His stance makes my jaw tick with fury and causes something inside me to snap. For years, I watched Cleo from afar. I held my place until the time was right, but not anymore. I'm tired of following the rules, but even more than that, I'm sick to death of ungrateful women who don't know their place.

Years ago, my father taught my mother a lesson, and now I must do the same to Cleo.

The bailiff's shoulders are double the width of mine, the difference in our heights is highly notable, but it doesn't stop him hitting the ground like a bag of shit when I toss him to the side. I'm up in Cleo's face faster than I can snap my fingers. The pounding of the batons on my back and the roar of the man who wrongly believes he owns her don't deter me in the slightest. It is just her and I. The woman who isn't close to paying for her father's atonement.

Cleo's father took away my one true love. For that alone, I should have slaughtered his entire family.

I would have if Cleo didn't spark my interest. The longer I watched her, the brighter a new plan became. I didn't need immediate revenge. I needed entertainment.

For the past four years, Cleo gave me that and so much more. It was enough—until Marcus entered the equation.

I don't back away when challenged, but he wasn't merely threatening to call "checkmate." He tried to swipe all the pieces from the chessboard, and that's when my game plan changed. My interest in Cleo switched to something greater than revenge. We reached a mutual understanding. We connected. We were more than strangers, but Marcus destroyed any possibility of us finding our happily ever after. He tainted her with lies and made her a woman undeserving of love.

He ruined her.

And although I tried to save her from the madness, she didn't listen.

She still isn't listening.

"After everything I did for you, you still want to have his bastard child?" I eat my words twice when they bounce off Cleo's tear-stained face before ramming back down my throat.

Clearly brainwashed, Cleo nods, which should be impossible with how hard I am clutching her face.

As anger envelops me, my grip doubles. Just like Stephen, I consider snapping her neck now. It would make her death clean and painless, but unfortunately for them both, my father never taught me leniency.

Stephen betrayed me. He paid for his stupidity with his life.

When Cleo betrayed me, I gave her my forgiveness.

I will not make the same mistake twice.

"No, please, no." Cleo's lips tremble as she tries to yank away from me. I'm not going to kiss her as her eyes are begging me to do. I'm going to issue her one last promise, one I intend to keep even if it kills me.

The hairs on her neck prickle when I snarl, "I saved your child from the depths of hell by stopping it from turning out like him... and perhaps even a little like me." The smile that arrives with my last sentence doesn't suit the callousness of my words.

Cleo's breaths quiver when I squash my lips to her ear. My smile is so broad my teeth graze her fleshly skin sufficiently enough for the seductive scent of her blood to linger in my nostrils. "I promise to save any future children you have as well. We don't want any misfit bastards left lying around."

I only see the quickest flare of alarm dart through her eyes before a strike to the back of my head forces me to succumb to blackness, but it is more than enough. It will feed my appetite for revenge for the next several years, only growing in intensity for every year we spend apart.

The weak request forgiveness.

The strong seek revenge.

I'm the strongest I've ever been.

1

DEXTER

Three Years Later…

"Come on in, Dexter, don't be shy." When my greeter's smile grows, the whiteness of her teeth makes me want to gag. "We're all friends here."

She gestures to the dozen-plus people sitting in a circular pattern around her. They're gleaming at her like she's the sun, the moon, and the Earth all rolled into one.

I'm looking at her in wonderment as well, *wondering if her blood will run as red as her lipstick.*

I slump into a vacant chair, unsatisfied about my first taste of group counseling but preferring it over the other option. With my outburst three years ago awarding me a seven-year stint in a psychiatric hospital for the criminally insane, I either play nice with these weirdos or get transferred back to the maximum-security hospital where I was originally incarcerated.

I'd prefer neither option, but since the staff at this hospital don't carefully monitor their patients to make sure they're not skipping meds, I plaster a fake smile on my face then peer up at the counselor.

Although she's hitting close to retirement age, my smile affects her the same way it does every red-blooded female. Her eyelids flutter as her hand lifts to fan her cheeks. Her roused response has me jotting down a mental note for future exploration. My dick withers at the thought of getting close to her, but my brain power is wondrous. It can make anything bend to its will—even my cock.

As the counselor gives a rundown on how our sessions will work, I scan the room. There are the standard misfits you find in every psych ward. The nervous twitcher sits two spaces up, talking to himself. The cutter is next to him, her wounds so fresh I can smell her blood, and the remaining seventy-five percent are so doped out on mind-numbing medication, they don't realize they're awake.

That leaves only two space cadets remaining. The demure wallflower sitting in the furthest corner of the room and me. Just like me, she's wearing a bright pink wrist bracelet, announcing she's new to this facility. Unlike me, she's so detached from the group, she's not even part of the original circle. She's a demented kink in a completely fucked-up group of people.

I laugh, amused by my inner monologue. It isn't a smart thing to do. Laughter in a place like this is never well-received. Here, you only laugh for two reasons. You're either low on meds or high on meds—there is no in-between.

"Wow, can you see that? Pretty fireflies."

I wave my hand in front of my face, pretending there are hundreds of butt-lit bugs in front of me. There aren't, but the stupid fuckers tripping on meds don't know that. They are so doped up the simplest movement represents a Martian landing on earth. They smile with glee, our counseling session over before it truly began.

The only patient not seeking invisible insects is the brunette I mentioned earlier. She's watching the freaks with as much concern as the counselor. She just isn't taking notes.

Well, not handwritten ones, anyway.

When she notices I've spotted the rapid flicker of her diamond-shaped eyes, she drops them to the floor. Usually, I'd follow suit, but since she's a patient and not a counselor, I keep my eyes locked on her.

She's pretty, in a dorky, psychopathic type of way. Her mousy-brown hair is pulled back in a low ponytail, her skin is pasty white, and her cheeks are hollow and lifeless. If we had met anywhere but here, I would assume her lack of color is natural, but since we're surrounded by fuckwits with half a brain, I'll confidently declare she's been locked up for a while—perhaps even longer than me.

An average man wouldn't look twice at a woman with an extensive list of mental illnesses. Unfortunately for all involved, I'm anything but ordinary. Just wanting to unearth the cause of her long incarceration has me studying her more intensely.

Although she has a slim build, her curves are sweltering enough to keep her list of favors with the guards high. The generous swell of her breasts has my dick's attention—more due to lack of use than attraction—but it's interested all the same.

Ninety-five percent of the guards at my last placement were male. The other five percent were either gay or in a 'committed relationship,' so the only favors I received were ones that cost money. They were beneficial, but they never got me close to unlocked doors.

I don't see that being an issue for this unknown brunette. With my money and her looks, I've unlocked a treasure trove. Most notably—a one-way ticket out of Crazyville.

Just as my eyes drop to the moderate hem of the brunette's floral dress, a pair of black polished shoes enter my peripheral vision. "No firefly catching today, Mr. Elias?"

My teeth crunch as my eyes lift. They take in plain black pants, a buttoned-up white shirt, and a wonky-ass smile on the way. Warden Bryce *tsks* under his breath when my clear, undiluted eyes stop on his. With their perusal of the brunette making them the purest they've been the past decade, he's confident my earlier laugh was a side effect of low-dosage drugs.

He's right—regrettably.

"Open up." He croons his short demand like he's going to feed me his cock instead of the medication he's been forcing down my throat three times a day since I arrived at Meadow Fields four weeks ago.

Although I've been seeking an out for my predicament since the day I was incarcerated, I'd rather rot in hell than suck a man's cock for freedom, so you can be assured the only way Bryce's cock will ever be in my mouth will be when I'm biting it off in retaliation for his numerous silent insinuations.

Such as, "Lift the tongue, Dexter. I need to make sure you've swallowed like a good boy."

I work my jaw side to side to calm my anger before sticking out my tongue and swiveling it around. It's the fight of my life not to yank Bryce's pen out of his pocket and stab it into his neck when his thighs press together at the sight of my wiggling tongue.

What the fuck is he? A girl?

Happy I've performed like an obedient puppy, he gives my shoulder a gentle pat. "Good boy. All gobbled up just the way I like it." His statement is as sexually suggestive as it sounds. "Until tonight." He saves his frisky wink until he spins on his heels, but it doesn't stop me from seeing it.

I wait until he's halfway across the room before forcing the mind-numbing tablets out of my stomach. It's a hard task with how dry Bryce's attention made my throat, but I keep silently heaving until I'm clasping three little red pills and two giant white ones in my palm.

I've played the part of a perfect patient for too long to let a cock-gobbler ruin my plan. He isn't lacing me up on meds because he believes they will bring me one step closer to society. He wants me so out of my mind he can play with my periwinkler without chastisement.

I'll never let that happen.

I'd slit his throat with a blunt knife before I'd let him ride me.

With a cough to hide the pings of the tablets' wholeness, I peg them to the furthest corner of the room. Usually, I'd put them in my pocket, but I was caught skipping meds last week.

It didn't end well.

This is the safer option because when forced between interrogating twenty psychotic patients and letting one go without medication for a few hours, most counselors veer toward the latter —even ones as hopeful as Bryce.

Confident the tablets are far enough away from me to evade suspicion, I return my eyes front and center. On their way, I catch the inquisitive glare of a pretty pair of hazel eyes. It's the demure mouse. Little Ms. Sunshine in a fucked-up world.

I expect her to rat me out, to advise the counselors of my inability to follow procedures.

She does no such thing. She keeps her head bowed and her suspicious gaze on the down-low.

I had wondered earlier if I found an ally. Now I know without a doubt. I've been on Bryce's radar since I walked in the door, so

I'm confident the guards not as light-footed as him spotted this brunette just as quickly. Not because she's outstandingly beautiful with a smile that outshines the sun, but because at one stage in his life, every man wants to bed a psycho.

The rumors are true. Psychotic women are just as crazy in the sack as they are outside of it.

You can take my word on that.

2

DEXTER

"*I*s this seat taken?"

The still unnamed brunette sheepishly lifts her eyes to mine. They're more unique than first perceived two weeks ago. More gold flecks are mottled throughout the green than I realized.

This will work well—very, *very* well.

Although Little Ms. Skitzo doesn't answer me, I fill the empty seat next to her. We're on a thirty-minute allotment of free time. It is an experiment the counselors thought would help 'clear the congestion from our minds.'

The only thing it's helping is my escape plan.

When I lean in close to the brunette's side, the hairs on her nape prickle from my nearness. That's not unusual. My attention does that to both men and women. The women want to fuck me. The men want to be me.

Sometimes it's hard being this brilliant.

"What's your name? Have you been here long?" My back molars crunch together. It sounds as if I'm striving for a date, not a pawn to be discarded like trash the instant I get what I want. "Do you want to play a little game? Show the professionals their years of study weren't squandered?"

My sick and twisted game hits a snag when the brunette shuffles her chair away from me. I'd feign hurt about her rejection if it didn't expose a vault load of information. One scrape of her chair and three guards' eyes popped up. One pair belongs to Bryce—he doesn't count—but the other two give away fascinating clues. They aren't eyeing me with worry. They're warning me to back off. Their slitted gazes and tense jaws assure me of this, not to mention the jealousy flaring out their nostrils.

They're reacting *exactly* as hoped.

Never one to back away when challenged—and interested to see how far I can push the boundaries—I scoot my chair closer to the brunette. Probably a little too close when the scent of her shampoo streams through my nostrils. It isn't the smell of the shampoo supplied in every penitentiary three states over. It is fresh and fruity—almost enticing.

"Your hair smells pretty. Did someone gift you fancy shampoo? Was it one of the guards?" Because my first comment isn't a lie, it covers up the interrogative nature of my questions.

Silence. Nothing but dead silence greets me.

I'm not even sure she's breathing since she is so still.

Her frozen-in-fear stance is even more alluring than her zesty shampoo. I like that she's a hard nut to crack. I've been void of stimuli for years, so my brain is well overdue to flex its muscles.

Outside this environment, I'd be on my game, but this is different. I'm not being forced to act like an ordinary man. She already knows I'm fucked in the head, or I wouldn't be here, so shouldn't that make the game easier?

"Why are you so quiet? Are you doped up on meds?" I pinch

her chin between my thumb and index finger then return her eyes to mine.

She comes without too much protest, revealing she's more submissive than first perceived.

Another impressive development in my campaign.

If you can look past the infinite number of secrets in her pretty eyes, they are clear, almost lucid—*for a psycho.* She's not tripping on personality-stripping drugs. This is who she is—plain and demure.

She will learn well.

I drop my hand from her face as if it scorched me when a deep voice says, "Step back, Mr. Elias. We don't touch people without permission. Bryce said you know that better than anyone."

Lee laughs like he's funny—like he isn't five seconds from losing an eye. It's a pathetic attempt to act as if he doesn't want to beat me to a pulp for touching what he *believes* is his.

Lee is like all ill-informed men. He thinks machoism outranks intelligence. In some cases, it might, but nothing compares to deeply mind-fucking someone.

Not even real fucking can compare to that.

Deciding to test a theory, I say, "I wasn't touching her without permission. She wanted my hands on her. She likes it. Don't you, sweetheart? You love my big, strong fingers stroking that little freckle on the inside of your thigh."

As the brunette's eyes rocket to mine, her pupils expand into giant black orbs. She isn't shocked about my finger's figure-eight pattern on the silky-smooth skin high on her thigh. She's stunned I am aware of the tiny dot generally hidden from view.

She shouldn't be. I watched Cleo for months before I made contact, and although I have no intentions of playing the same game with this unnamed brunette, I need her to finish the one I started years ago, so I'll monitor her just as closely. She may only be a pawn on my chessboard, but every piece has its place when it comes to the king's entertainment.

The little skitzo's eyes expand when Lee kneels in front of her. The longer his narrowed gaze takes in my stroking finger, the tighter his jaw becomes.

Confident I've got him where I want, I remove my hand from the silent little mouse's thigh. Her disappointing whine is barely a whimper, but it doesn't need to shatter my eardrums for me to know of its arrival. I can smell her arousal lingering in the air.

She wants my touch as much as Lee wants to cut my fingers off for touching her.

Incapable of harnessing his jealousy for a second longer, Lee asks, "Is that right, Claudia? Did you give *Dexter* permission to touch you? Do you like *his* touch?" He sneers my name the same way I do Marcus's anytime I reference him.

Claudia remains quiet. She doesn't need to answer Lee's question for my unasked ones to be resolved, though. Lee's reaction answered them on her behalf. He's a rook who was just shadowed by a king. One wrong move, and he'll be taken down.

Realizing we're only at the beginning of our game, I jest, "I'm kidding, Lee. I didn't ask permission. I just touched her. I couldn't help it. I'm toey, and even fuckers like you who get to go home to a warm bed every night know what it's like being locked up here for hours on end. Everyone gets a little edgy."

Lee's eyes drift to mine. They're icy and lifeless, an exact replica of mine. "Then how do you know about the freckle on Claudia's thigh?" His words sizzle out of his mouth, his anger both volatile and impish. He should never play poker. He's too easy to read. He'd be flat broke before the second round, if not dead.

I lean in close to his side to ensure my words aren't overheard. "I learned of its origin the same way you did." I muster up a grin that warns his days are numbered. "We can look all we like... as long as we don't touch. Am I right?"

My eyes lower to the gold band circling his finger to emphasize the words I can't say. *I'm watching you as much as I am her, mother-fucker. I've seen you eye every female patient as if they're selections on a menu. I've watched you lick the evidence from your fingers when you move from the female ward to the male's. I know what you're doing, how you are doing it, and when you're fucking doing it, so maybe your focus should switch to something other than skirt-chasing before your fucked-up ideas on 'helping the needy' lose you more than your job. Your days are already numbered, Lee, but they diminish even more for every second you spend mocking me.*

As if he heard my thoughts, Lee stands to his feet. He slides his hand into his trouser pocket to hide the wedding band that's been on his finger so long, the skin beneath the gold is as white as his cheeks. He heard the threats I couldn't vocalize. He feels the danger surrounding him. He's just unsure if it's one of my *supposed* multiple personalities speaking on my behalf or me.

One wrong move, and he'll soon find out.

"As I said, Mr. Elias. We don't touch without permission." His calm and neutral voice impresses me. With how hard his thighs are shaking, I was anticipating an equally nervous reply. "Do it again and your privileges will be revoked."

I hold my hands in the air, acting scared by his threat. The fucker should be grateful I'm playing nice today. If I weren't in game mode, he'd be licking his blood off my boots.

Stupidly believing he has me backing away like a coward, Lee shifts his focus to Claudia. "Come on, Claudia. You've got a meeting with Mrs. Whitlock this afternoon, remember?" He nudges his head to one of the many exit doors of the rec room. It isn't one that leads to the counselors' offices. It is the female sleeping quarters.

Although I can feel Claudia's wide eyes peering at me beneath a screen of dark hair, begging for me to intervene, she stands before shakily moving to the door Lee gestured to. Her steps are as cagey as the look she gave me when I touched her. I doubt Lee has the balls to put moves on her now that I've marked my territory. He merely wants her away from me.

He should. I'm dangerous. Not just to Claudia, but to him as well.

This afternoon's foray went exactly as I anticipated, but Lee's machoism is sparking a side of me I haven't seen in years. I want the guards eating out of Claudia's hand, which, in turn, will have them eating out of mine, but if they succumb to temptation too quickly, my entire plan will go to shit.

I need Claudia eating out of my hand before she consumes Lee's dick. To do that, I need her to trust me, to believe I'll place her safety above my own.

I won't, but if she thinks she's my equal, the less time she'll glance over her shoulder, waiting for the inevitable stab in the back.

I played the same game with Cleo, the whole keep-your-friends-close-but-your-enemies-closer tactic. I'm still strategizing my next move in our drawn-out game, but there won't be a game to finalize if I don't get Claudia on my side.

Realizing what I must do, I stand from my chair and shout, "Hey, Lee!" My voice is loud enough to wake half the continent.

When he turns his massively dilated eyes to me, I scan the room, seeking something to use as a distraction. Upon spotting a set of exercise balls at my side, I secure one in my hand, then ask, "Wanna play catch?"

Not giving him the chance to respond, I peg the ball at his head. My years on the pitcher's mound come in handy when the ball grazes his left ear before hitting the wall behind him with a loud thud.

I didn't miss. I want to distract him, not knock him the fuck out.

"You missed. Here, try again."

I continue hurling balls across the room until my ruckus disturbs the other patients. Half join my game of patients versus guards dodgeball, whereas the other half scream in hysterics.

The only one not hollering like a maniac locked in a psych ward is Claudia. She slips out through the door unnoticed, her exit as quiet as the silent thanks streaming from her eyes.

She shouldn't be thanking me. Very soon, she'll be sucking Lee's cock—just not until I tell her to.

3

DEXTER

Three days later, I enter the rec room on Bryce's heels. He overturned the two-week ban Lee instilled in retaliation for our one-sided game of dodgeball after he 'accidentally' entered my room while I was dressing.

It wasn't an accident, but since a peek at my cock was required for me to regain access to Claudia, an impromptu strip was in order.

Bryce is hoping his leniency will increase his chance of us becoming friendly.

He is sorely mistaken.

Sneaking a peek at my flaccid cock is one thing. Touching it is another. I've toyed several times with the idea of killing him just for wanting to look. It's mainly in fantasy, for the most part. I want to see if he squirms the same way when his veins are drained of blood. I doubt his thighs would still press together after I nicked the vital artery pumping through them for my experiment.

After pushing aside the joy I get from imagining the life fade from his eyes, I return my focus to the task at hand. It takes me scanning the loon-filled space three times before I spot Claudia sitting in the corner of the room. She's wearing her favorite attire —a floral print dress and ankle boots. Her hair that looks recently washed is pulled back with a fancy clip, and her face is void of any marks.

Lucky or the silent threat I issued Lee three days ago would have become a reality. I don't give a fuck if the carcass is riddled with maggots. If I've claimed it, you don't touch it—ever!

My steps to Claudia slow when a high-pitched voice squeaks, "You won't get anything out of her. She's a cookie that's been dumped into a coffee mug too many times... all soggy and crumbling."

An emo-looking female with heavy eyeliner, stark black hair with a purple stripe down one side, and a face as white as a ghost steps out of an alcove. As she heads my way, she tugs down her sleeves to hide the fresh cuts on her arms. She tries to act tough like she hasn't detected the evil leaching from my pores, but her wobbly knees give away her genuine response.

She's petrified. Justly so. The guards are wary about approaching me, and they're armed with skull-cracking batons and mace, and don't get me started on their mind-fucking candies.

Hoping to divert my attention from her, the unnamed female nudges her head toward Claudia. "She doesn't talk. Not that she doesn't want to. She just doesn't. From what I've heard, she hasn't spoken a word in over five years."

Although I've never been one to believe rumors, this goth-lover has an honest edge not unusual for the disturbed. She doesn't cut herself for attention. She does it for the solace. An immense amount of silence comes when people don't understand you. That's why I'm shocked she's reaching out to me. I don't give off friendly vibes because I'm not a welcoming guy.

A vein in the unnamed girl's neck twitches when I hover over to her. "If she's mute, who's your source?"

My back molars grind when she swings her eyes to the right. Lee is standing at the side of the rec room. He wears his uniform cap down low, hoping it will hide the direction of his gaze.

It doesn't.

Even if I couldn't feel the heat of his stare, the rapid bounce of his head as he strives to keep Claudia and me on his radar is a surefire indication that I've secured his attention, much less his hand floating over the undone clip of his baton case.

My eyes drift back to Ms. Sun-hater. "Are you *friendly* with the guards?" The way I express 'friendly' ensures she can't mistake my question.

She quirks her black-painted lips before pulling a face. "No. I'm not their type." Her voice is more pleased than dissatisfied. After scanning the room to ensure we don't have any extra eyes focused on us, she murmurs, "But I am roommates with Claudia, so I've got my ears close to the ground."

I arch a brow. I was under the assumption Claudia's pasty white skin meant she was a patient on my side of the ward—the one for the real loonies. I had no clue she walked the halls with the lesser evil crazies. This is an interesting development I never anticipated, one I hope to exploit to my advantage. I ignored the voices in my head for years to get transferred to a facility like Meadow Fields, as the freedom was worth the boredom. But Claudia and this freaky-Friday contestant don't have to walk the same line I'm walking. They can occasionally step over it.

That's an advantage—a fucking massive one.

"Have the guards ever paid Claudia a late-night visit?" I clench my jaw, annoyed at the protectiveness in my voice. Claudia isn't a little doll for me to play with. She is a pawn. Nothing more.

Don't get me wrong, I like my women broken, but Claudia is

an entirely different type of cracked. I crave women with disheartened spirits, not ones with destroyed heads. Claudia has both.

She is all types of fucked-up.

The sun-hater shakes her head. "They're too scared I'll scream on her behalf."

"Are you looking out for her?" I ask, pretending I didn't hear the hostility in her voice.

Her shake turns into somewhat of a nod. "Yeah. I guess. She's got that vibe, you know? The one where you can't help but protect her. She reminds me a lot of my little sister." Her voice tapers to a whisper before her last sentence.

Her confession is surprising, considering she doesn't look a day over twenty-one. Claudia would be at least mid-twenties if not close to her thirties, so why the fuck would this emo believe she is younger than her?

The blue-eyed girl shifts her eyes from Claudia to me. "Is that why you're looking out for her too? Does she remind you of family?"

Her inaccurate assumption makes me smile. It isn't a happy smirk. It's one of a man who's hurt more women than he's loved. Usually, the only women I pursue are the ones who remind me of my mother, but that isn't the case with Claudia. She's my ticket out of this place, a free pass back to the life I had before *he* fucked it up. I have no intention of playing her as I did Cleo, so you can be assured that means I won't be fucking her either.

I watched Cleo for years before Marcus entered the picture. My game plan was long, but the secrecy behind it was addictive. I loved knowing that most of Cleo's struggles were influenced by me. Her prolonged stint in the hub often referred to as the 'dungeon' at Global Ten Media, the constant misplacement of her security ID tag, and the lack of funds in her bank account. That was all me.

I kept my sneaky transfers on the down-low, ensuring no one would discover her wages were thirty percent less than the rest of the staff. It worked for nearly three years. My scheme was only unraveled when Mr. Carson returned to the helm of his ship. He didn't just snoop. He found a way to increase her wages as well. That altered my game in a way I never thought possible. It made it more challenging, which was both a welcomed and unwanted change.

Although I didn't need to work at Global Ten Media to fund my campaign for revenge, I did so I'd have access to Cleo twenty-four hours a day. She was furious when she discovered Marcus had been spying on her for months. I wonder how she'd handle learning I had been watching her for years longer. Just the thought of her tears hardens my cock.

Not wanting the emo-lover to get the wrong idea about my extended crotch, I end our conversation. "No. She doesn't remind me of my family. And I'm not looking out for her either." Since both replies are honest, they're delivered that way.

I step away from the goth, only to be stopped three strides later. If I weren't conscious of the four sets of eyes on me, dying for the chance to intervene, I'd pass on my dislike of being manhandled in a non-verbal way. But since I'm skating on thin ice, I shelve my retaliation and return my eyes to my new best friend.

"For a couple of benzos, I could give you an in with Claudia." She keeps her tone low, ensuring the guards won't hear her.

My chest rumbles with silent mocking. "Are you not getting enough brain-fucking medication during your *pleasant* stay at Meadow Fields?"

I don't know why I ask my question. I don't give a fuck if she pops sedatives until she dies. I'm just stunned by her request. Her eyes are so lucid I'm beginning to wonder if anyone here is taking their meds.

"They're not for me. They are just—"

I stop her midsentence by slicing my hand through the air. She flinches like all good women do. "I don't give a fuck who they're for. I just need to know how many you need."

Although I'm not interested in developing a relationship with this vampire groupie, some of the best contacts I've developed are ones who have come to me. For all I know, she could be holding a swipe key to Claudia's room in her hand, so the least I can do is play along with her ruse by feigning interest.

The stranger licks her dry lips before murmuring, "I need enough to take down a grown man."

Her reply piques my suspicion, but not enough for me to act on it. "Alright. I've got the funds. I'll get you what you need." She stops peering at me like I'm a god when I add on, "But first, you need to give me something in good faith. Prove you've got the goods to deliver your side of the deal."

I expect her to balk at the insinuation in my tone, but she does no such thing. She just hands me a slip of glossy paper like one document is the answer to her prayers.

The manic tick of my jaw increases when my eyes drop to the folded-up magazine article. I am thrust into a spiraling tunnel. It's a dark and lonely place that immediately derails my train from its track.

When I pin the unnamed emo to the wall by her throat, the guards shout my name in the same manner the bailiff did during my trial. Her airway is cut in an instant, her eyes bulging just as fast. "Who gave you this! Was it the guards? Was it Lee?"

She doesn't speak. She can't. I'm clutching her throat so firmly she's seconds from collapse.

Ignoring the pleasurable sting of her fingernails shredding my hand and the whacks of batons on my back, I assess the article more diligently, seeking clues to its origin.

The more I read, the hotter the blood in my veins become.

Marcus is in multiple photos in a two-page feature. He's smiling like he has the world at his feet. He somewhat does, considering Cleo is at his side, wearing a white wedding dress and a bright smile.

Her happiness angers me more, and my clutch on the sun-hater's throat tightens. I'm still suffering the consequences of Cleo's betrayal, so shouldn't she still be mourning the death of her unborn child?

The reason for her lack of bereavement comes to light when a pair of bright hazel eyes capture my attention. The little girl in the picture, who would only be a few months old, has the eyes of both her mother and father—Cleo's dirty chocolate eyes mixed with Marcus's barren green ones.

They have a child.

A daughter.

A bastard who was born before they wed.

I pledged to save Cleo's future children from turning out like him. Her master—*her taunter*—the man who stole her away from me. Even if it kills me, I will keep my promise. I just need to work through the drugs numbing my arms and legs and push through the pain of the guards' batons battering my skull hard enough to crack it, and the blackness attempting to swallow me whole. I need to remember that no one is higher than the king. I am a god, and everyone else is merely a pawn on the board I call life.

They are cowards.

When the sting of a needle hits my neck for the second time, my knees collapse beneath me. My limbs suddenly become heavy, and the guards' shouts are nothing but a buzz of noise.

The unnamed emo's bones stop crunching when I drop my hand from her throat to yank the sedative dangling from mine. I slot the lengthy needle between my fingers before swinging my hand wildly through the air. If they try to sedate me again, they won't do it without injury.

As the world spins around me, the magazine article on a Rise Up's band member's latest wedding slips from my grasp. It floats across the stark white floor, only stopping when it reaches a pair of ankle boots.

Impassive of the ruckus occurring around her, Claudia bobs down to collect the thin slip of glossy paper. When her eyes lock on the article, they widen like mine did when I speed-read the document. She looks both angry and aroused, which is an odd combination, but it matches mine to a T.

Seeing Cleo for the first time in years thickened my cock, but the event behind the featured spread not only pissed me off, it also resurrected a devil years of counseling couldn't control.

Feeding off a surge of inhuman strength, I stand with a roar. After knocking off three guards as if they're weightless, I head in Claudia's direction. She's to blame for the hate thickening my veins, so shouldn't she pay the penance for it?

My steps halt mid-stride when Claudia's eyes lift to mine. They're carrying as much violence as mine, and her quest for revenge is just as palpable. I take a step back, stunned by the sheer hate in her slitted gaze. I didn't think a demure mouse could pull off such a horrendous look.

Before I can work out the cause of her repulsed expression, the third prick of a needle drops my legs out from beneath me and has me seeing black.

4

CLAUDIA

My breaths come out in ragged pants when the latch on the door gives way without too much protest. Usually, I'm breaking out of rooms, not entering them. After storing a hair clip and rusty nail in the hidden pocket of my dress, I stand from my crouched position and cautiously enter the room I'm breaking into.

I don't know why I am here. I've deferred the attention of both the staff and patients for longer than I can remember, but there's something about this man that draws me to him. I thought it was the magazine article he gifted me, but that was weeks ago, and he's still in my thoughts every day.

He isn't like normal men. His hair is as black as the devil's heart, his eyes just as lifeless. He doesn't look like my Nick in the slightest. My one true love is pure and innocent. This man is wicked and immoral. The ruckus he's made in my life the past six weeks has been anything but pleasant, but his attention reminds me that I have a heart pumping in my chest. Its beat is weak and pitiful, but it is still beating all the same.

Perhaps that's why I'm drawn to him? I'm not allowed to talk about Nick, much less have an opinion on any aspect of my life. Even the slightest utter about my love in a breathless whisper has me subjected to scrutiny by unpleasant doctors with bushy brows and malevolent faces.

That's why I no longer talk. I'd rather be mute than controlled. The doctors say I have erotomanic delusional beliefs about relationships and that nothing I am feeling about Nick is true. They say being rejected makes me lash out and do violent things.

I think they're the crazy ones.

Dexter has been a part of my life for a little over six weeks now, and this is the first time I've broken into his room. I didn't even make it a week before I snuck into Nick's home to watch him sleep.

My sneaky steps into the room slow when a deep, raspy voice snarls, "Ouch. Don't bite. I'm trying to be nice, and you're biting me. What the fuck is wrong with you?" He has the same clipped voice my daddy used when angered by something I did.

"I said regular Kool-Aid, this one is sugar-free."

"Why do my trousers have pleats down the front? Do I look like I sit sideways?"

"You should go live with your mother. I bet the worms would make good use of your hollow head."

So many criticisms for a man who preached godliness. My father was a horrible man. He was nothing like Nick. He didn't love me with every fiber of his being, nor did he cherish the ground I walked on. He spat at my feet and called me names when I told him I had found The One.

He paid for his sins as I am now for mine.

I tried to hurt Nick's baby, and in return for my error, he sent me here. One day he'll return to collect me. I just need to be patient. I'm confident he hears my pleas for forgiveness and feels my sorrow. He won't keep me waiting much longer. A love like ours can't be undone. It's a lifetime commitment that only ends one way.

I stop listening to the voices in my head blaming *her* for keeping him away from me when an angry roar vibrates my eardrums. "I swear to god, Bryce, if that is you, you won't leave this room with your heart still functioning. I don't care how much shit you pump into my veins, nothing will alter your ugly face enough for me to suck your dick." The man snarls, baring teeth. "I'll rip off your little pecker with my teeth if it gets within an inch of my mouth."

He rolls his head in my direction, his movements so slow it is as if his head is the weight of ten bowling balls. When he spots me standing frozen inside his once-locked door, he startles. He seems as shocked by my presence as I am to be standing before him.

This wasn't my plan. I didn't keep my head down and mouth shut for the past five years to have a stranger unravel my wish for freedom, but since this man confuses me as much as he excites me, I couldn't harness my curiosity for a moment longer.

I need to know why he's nice to me. No one is nice to me, not even Nick, once *she* became a part of his life. *She* hates that Nick loves me and that he only sees me when he looks at her. But more than anything, *she* hates that she'll never own his heart because he gave it to me years ago.

Even via a photo in the glossy magazine Dexter gifted me, I could feel her evil eyes glaring at me. *She* knows it is only a matter of time before Nick returns to collect me.

He will be angry when he hears I've spent time with another man, but it won't stop him from coming. *Will it?*

I freeze, disturbed by my inner monologue.

Oh no, what have I done? I must leave this instant.

"No, wait!" Dexter shouts when I spin on my heels and head for the door.

The plea in his voice stops my flat-soled shoes from pounding the white tiles, but his slur keeps my back facing him. I feel his eyes scanning the room, mindful the sedatives may have him mistaking my presence.

I should leave and let him believe I am an illusion, but the sheer confusion radiating from him has me spinning on my heels instead. As my daddy always said, 'I made my bed. Now I must lie in it.'

"Claudia?" Dexter asks, clearly confused. "Is that you?"

Nodding, I step out of the shadows. Dexter gasps in a sharp breath as if excited to see me. The thought both pleases and dissatisfies me. I'm sure when I explain to Nick the reason for my visit to Dexter's room tonight, he won't be overcome with too much jealousy.

Although this is the first time I've been in another man's room that wasn't Nick's or my father's, so it may still be a bitter pill for him to swallow.

I'm snapped from my thoughts when Dexter asks, "What are you doing in my room?" His words are remarkedly strong for how dilated his eyes are. They're glassier than usual, making my motive for entering his room more plausible.

Before I can respond, Dexter's tongue darts out to clear away the sweat beading on his top lip as effectively as it's drenched his hair. His body's response to the chemicals seeping into his brain isn't surprising. If he discards his morning and afternoon prescriptions as often as I've seen him reject his lunchtime dosage the past six weeks, the sedative the guards hit him with when he refused to move to his side of the rec room this afternoon must be turning his brain to mush.

I don't know why he wanted to sit with me, but I don't blame him for not wanting to take his medication. They make my mind fuzzy as well. But with every refusal comes an increase in dosage. I learned the error of my way very quickly my first year. If Dexter doesn't conform to the rules soon, he'll be a zombie by next month.

I guess that's why I am here, to stop him from getting hurt. He and my roommate, Ashlee, have saved me from Lee's grabby hands multiple times the past two months, so the least I can do is ensure he understands the rules.

When Dexter's wintry blue eyes glare into mine, demanding I explain why I am disturbing him, my lips twitch, but I remain as quiet as a church mouse. I can feel the words I want to express on the tip of my tongue, but no matter how hard I try to fire them out of my mouth, they refuse to budge.

Although he protects me, I don't know him well enough to trust him just yet. The devil is known for wearing many masks, so I must remain wary.

The deep ridges of Dexter's chiseled cheeks indent when he struggles to stifle a grin. "You're worried about me?"

I shouldn't nod, but I do. He wouldn't have gotten in nowhere near as much trouble the past six weeks if he wasn't always protecting me. By sheltering me under his umbrella, he placed himself in direct sight of the law—the law being the men and women in this facility who are more deranged than the patients they're guarding.

My agreeing nod pleases Dexter.

I'm glad.

Men are less evil when they're happy.

"Can you untie me?"

The demand in his voice turns my nod into a shake.

"Oh, come on, Claudia. If you're truly worried about me, how can you not help me?" His deep snarl warns me to remain cautious, but the way he purrs my name makes my insides gooey.

"I won't hurt you. I just want to make sure no one else does. Especially not the person you saw in the article last month."

I peer at him in shock.

He knows about Nick's fiancée and the horrible things she did to me?

Upon spotting my scrunched brows, Dexter pledges, "I can stop the injustice, Claudia. I just need you to untie me first."

Hesitantly, I pace closer to him, wanting to verify if his twinkling eyes belong to a devious man or an honest one.

My short trek is a woeful waste of time.

An in-depth glance at his massively dilated gaze doesn't ease my curiosity in the slightest. He has beautiful oceanic eyes that promise to immensely reward obedience, but they're also full of hate and deceit.

I want to trust him, but when you've been hurt time and time again by those you love, it's not an easy thing to do. It is the equivalent of reaching into a beehive and hoping not to get stung. I might live in a mental hospital, but I'm not stupid.

Well, I wasn't before the doctors made my brain gooey.

"Please, Claudia." Dexter jangles the leather cuffs pinching his wrists and ankles, amplifying his plea. "I won't hurt you. You can trust me."

After a short stint of deliberation, I set to work on freeing him. It's the least I can do after all the help he has given me.

It is also a reminder as to why I can't trust anyone.

The instant the final cuff is removed from Dexter's ankle, he snatches my wrist, drags me onto his bed, then flattens me like a pancake with his fit, sweat-slicked body.

A torrent of horrible thoughts bombard me when his hand creeps up to clamp my shrieking mouth. They include images of my daddy's hands testing the strength of my lungs when his meal wasn't served at precisely six o'clock, followed by the putrid stench of his breath hitting my face when I did the same thing to him years later, but for several minutes longer.

Then, finally, the visual a thousand days hasn't stripped from my mind. The big, masculine hand of a man my love sent in his place because he was too angry to look at me. He placed me in psychiatric care, locking me away until I pay for my sins. He said it wasn't my fault and that he was sorry for what he had done. I accepted his apology because I could see the remorse in his eyes. He wasn't hurting me because he hated me like my daddy did. He was being forced against his wishes, as I am now.

I won't go down without a fight this time, though. It's been years since I last saw Nick, but I'm confident our love is still strong. He hears my whispered promises floating through the air, the pledges of celibacy and atonement. He is waiting for me. He just hasn't worked through his anger just yet. That is why he stood next to *her* in the magazine article, smiling and acting happy. It was a façade to hide his pain. I hurt him, but one day, I'll make it up to him.

One day soon, I hope.

My wailing softens when Dexter whispers, "Shh, Claudia. I won't hurt you. I just need you to be quiet." The angry snarl of his voice doesn't match the sincerity of his words. "Once the guards leave, I'll remove my hand from your mouth, but you need to be quiet, okay? If you yell, we'll both be in trouble. You don't want us to get in trouble, do you?"

It's stupid for me to do, but I shake my head. If his eyes weren't locked on mine, I wouldn't have, but something in his eyes makes me reckless, and I'm not going to mention the funny sensation zapping through my body from being squashed by him. Although his weight is kept off me by his elbows, the lower regions of our bodies are touching.

"Good girl," Dexter praises when he notices my attempts to remain quiet.

When he slings his eyes to the door, I mimic his movements. My heart rate I've just settled breaks into a canter when the shadows of two guards darken the frosted glass of Dexter's door. Their presence is shocking, not because they're doing their job but because they altered their routine.

The guards at Meadow Fields follow procedures to the T. They *never* vary from the routine. That's why I'm visiting Dexter's room under the cloak of darkness because I knew the hallways would be empty since the staff is in the process of bringing on a new shift.

For them to be outside Dexter's room, something must be wrong—*horribly wrong.*

Since Dexter's pulse is roaring through both our bodies, I am unable to hear what the guards are whispering. Whatever it is, it must be unpleasant, as the longer they talk, the faster Dexter's heart pulses.

It also lessens the heavy rod nestled between my legs.

Dexter's crazy heart rate only slows when the shadows disappear from his door a few minutes later. Mine remains high. That's expected since Dexter's focus has returned to me. He is an extremely handsome man, but no amount of charm can hide black insides. I've tried to conceal mine for years. I've never been successful.

"I'm going to remove my hand. Don't scream."

His raspy voice makes the lack of oxygen in my body more noticeable. Because his request is more a demand than a question, he doesn't wait for me to respond. He slowly drops his hand from my mouth, bringing it to within an inch of my breast.

The frantic thrust of my lungs brings our bodies closer with every gulp I take, but the harder I struggle to control my breathing, the more worked up my lungs become. Within seconds, my erect nipples are scraping Dexter's firm chest.

The sensation is odd. It's a feeling I've never experienced. It's as if electricity is surging through my body before it does a weird thing to the ungodly womanhood between my legs. It feels nice but naughty at the same time.

I sink into the mattress, conscious my love wouldn't like me being this close to another man, much less having the wicked thoughts I am.

A little voice inside me whines when Dexter rolls off me a few seconds later.

It's the naughty one I'm not allowed to listen to.

Although Dexter appears as confused as me, his focus remains clear. "How did you get in my room?"

His words are as wobbly as his legs. They expose that his earlier sedative isn't the only thing his body is combatting. I've never heard his voice so low and brittle. Normally, it is stern and dominant and demands the attention of everyone in the room.

When I remain quiet, Dexter's wide eyes scan my face, neck, and chest before they drop to take in the rest of my body. That earlier unknown commotion between my legs triples when his eyes linger on me longer than I'm usually perused. I've never been given a look like this before. I'm a one-quick-glance-without-a-second-look type of girl. The only time I've been appraised for longer than twenty seconds is when I'm in a room with a handful of people wearing white coats.

"Is there a *reason* you're in my room?"

I slant my head to the side and raise a brow. Why did his voice hitch like that? It had a weird twang to it like when Daddy was thirsty, but I hadn't fetched water from the well yet. It was throaty and deep and, in all honesty, a little scary.

Hoping if I alleviate his curiosity, he will ease mine, I join him bedside while taking my hair clip and rusty nail from my pocket. Dexter's eyes light up like a Christmas tree when he spots what I'm clasping. "You broke into my room!" I don't know why he sounds delighted, but I'm certain that's the emotion he is displaying.

After preparing my face for the sting of his hit, I nod.

Dexter's slap never comes. He continues peering at me with joy on his handsome face like I am the answer to his prayers. It's the same look Nick gave me when I offered him a ride all those years ago. He was so pleased for my assistance, love and admiration poured from every orifice in his body.

Dexter returns my focus to him by tucking a strand of my hair behind my ear. I like that. That's a nice thing for him to do. It makes me feel cherished—loved even. "Can you pick any locks, Claudia, or just the ones on patients' doors?"

The awe radiating from him inspires a competitive edge I haven't felt in years. I've been picking locks since middle school. It started more as a hobby before it grew into a need.

I needed to see Nick, but the locks on his door kept us apart.

I soon took care of them.

My eyes stray to the itty-bitty lock on the window in Dexter's room. It will be an easy latch to showcase my talents. It won't even take a second.

My steps toward the grill-covered window stop when Dexter says, "Not that one. That's too easy for someone as talented as you. How about we find a harder one?"

His velvety tone secures my attention, but his index finger pressed against his lips holds it. His lips are incredibly plump, similar to how Nick's looked after he kissed me for the first time. We only kissed twice, but I've never forgotten them. Our kisses were sweet and full of mutual admiration.

Dexter waits for me to agree to his request to be quiet before he tiptoes to his bedroom door. He cracks it open then checks if the coast is clear. Happy the hallway is empty as it should have been five minutes ago, he gestures for me to follow him. I do, although warily.

"What about that one? Can you work your magic on that one?" Dexter asks a short stroll later.

He hooks his thumb to a door the guards stomp in and out of every morning and afternoon. The lock is more intricate than your standard household locks, but it's no more difficult than the dead-lock Nick's dad placed on his front door after Nick rudely kicked me out of his house.

Nick had no right to be angry that day. I wasn't the one who constantly visited a whore the instant the love of my life left town.

Argh! The things they did together made my blood boil. It is too disgusting for words. My daddy said there's only one time a man should touch me where Nick touched *her* that is when he wants to put a baby in my belly.

Nick placed a baby in *her* belly not long after they met, so he had no reason to do what they did again.

And again.

And again.

Fueled by annoyance about what Nick and his whore could be doing right now, I storm to the door to assess the lock more diligently. I've been toeing the line for years with the hope good behavior would get me back to my love sooner rather than later. It didn't work, so it's time to step outside the box.

The lock is a multiple-teeth combination that will require more than two instruments. I'm honestly unsure if my woozy head is up to it. Dexter's constant bickering with the staff didn't just affect his dosage of medication. My increments increased as well.

"What is it?" Dexter asks a short time later, confused by the delay.

His response is expected. I did bolt over here like my backside was on fire, only to wilt like a sunflower stuck in a shadow. That happens a lot when the doctors alter my medication. I have soaring highs and devastating lows.

With my head a twisted mess of confusion, I scan the corridor, seeking additional equipment I can use to jimmy the lock. Dexter's mischievous afternoon awarded him an additional visit from grumpy guards, meaning a tray of medical equipment stands a few paces up from his bedroom door.

I point to the cart, wordlessly demanding Dexter bring it to me. He follows suit without a single qualm. That's more shocking than the excitement radiating from him in invisible waves. And I'm not going to mention the crazy things it does to my muddled heart.

With a hair clip, syringe, and my trusty old nail, the security office door pops open thirty seconds later. My mouth hangs as low as Dexter's. I didn't think I had it in me, but this proves nothing can stand in the way of greatness.

Maybe I still have a chance?

Perhaps I'm not too late to prove to Nick how much I love him?

I just need to get him away from *her* long enough he'll remember the connection we share.

The esteem raising my chest high deflates when Dexter slaps his hand over my mouth before dragging me inside the security office. I nearly wail and scream. The only reason I don't is because my eyes lock on the clock clanging noisily in the corner of the room. The staff's change of guard is over. We're seconds away from being busted.

Oh no.

As tears roll down my cheeks unchecked, my jumbled mind strives for a solution. It took me hours to build up the courage to enter Dexter's room, but instead of being awarded for my valor, for the umpteenth time in my life, my inability to follow the rules will unfairly strip away my will to live.

I can't go back to the hospital I transferred from two months ago. The staff members were mean. They didn't understand me. They hurt, poked, and prodded me twenty-four hours a day.

I can't do that again.

I *won't* do that again.

With my hands clamped over my ears, I curl into a ball and rock.

I want the pain to end.

I want the mean voices in my head to stop yelling at me.

But more than anything, I want to be free.

I shift my wide gaze to Claudia, expecting hers to hold the same amount of excitement as mine. I'm not sure if anything happening is real or a figment of my imagination, but I do know one thing—I haven't experienced anything this thrilling in years.

Just the thought of getting caught has my cock pressed against my zipper and my heart leaping in my chest. I miss the adrenaline that comes from doing what I like when I like. Conformity has never been a part of my life. I like things messy and complicated. I like my world completely fucked-up.

The thrill scorching my veins fades when my eyes lock on Claudia. Hers aren't carrying the same eagerness as mine. I can't even see them since she's cowered in the corner, rocking like she is seconds from a meltdown.

I glare at her like she's an illusion. My response is the same I gave when she entered my room nearly thirty minutes ago. I thought she was a mirage, a byproduct of the trillion sedatives the staff pumped me with when our tussle earlier today turned violent.

I am so out of my fucking mind, I spent half my night talking to the dragon tattoo on my shoulder, unhappy at its attempt to bite me. It was only when Claudia's fruity shampoo lingered into my nostrils did I realize I wasn't delusional.

She was hesitant to release me from the restraints Lee and his minions used to contain me. Rightfully so. Even though my brain felt seconds away from exploding in my skull when I pinned her to my bed, my body didn't respond with anywhere near as much disdain. My cock was hard as a rock, and my relief in the shower this morning was a forgotten memory.

Although pissed at my body's response to Claudia's nearness, it can be easily excused. The longer I stalked her, the more intriguing she became. Usually, I read women like open books, the joy of discovering their every secret revealed in under an hour.

That hasn't happened with Claudia. Even watching her like a hawk the prior six weeks hasn't unraveled the woman behind the muted stance.

She isn't just an onion.

She is many layers of fucked-up.

There's only one thing I've unearthed. Claudia isn't mute because she can't speak. A million thoughts streamed from her eyes when she glanced at the magazine article last month. She just prefers expressing herself without words.

For the most part, I find her quirks amusing. But right now, I don't have time for humor.

I always knew Claudia was my ticket out of here. I just had no fucking clue she was also the key. I shouldn't be surprised. There was something in her eyes last month that warned she was a game-changer. That doesn't necessarily mean starting a new game. It could merely mean she is initiating an old one—

one I've been waiting years to finalize—one I can't wait to get back to.

After pinning her to the wall by her throat, Ashlee was hesitant to interact with me, but once I supplied her enough benzos to take down three grown men, she miraculously became less reluctant. She filled in the gaps Claudia's eyes failed to reveal.

Just like me, Claudia isn't here because she is psychotic. From what we can gather, she merely obsessed over the wrong man. That's why she reacted the way she did when she saw the magazine article last month. The man she wants had his arm wrapped around another woman—a petite blonde the report stated is his wife and the mother of his two children. His name is Nicholas Holt. He is the lead guitarist of Rise Up—the same band Marcus is a member of.

Although shocked about our bizarre connection, I have no intention of aiding Claudia with her dilemma. I'm merely continuing the game I initiated weeks ago. Tonight's development is the last piece of the puzzle. I didn't bite Lee because I wanted my brain drained. I did it because I knew Claudia was watching.

She can't articulate it, but I know she's grown fond of me the past few weeks.

I can't blame her. When I bring out the charm, the ladies don't stand a chance. Her arrival at my room in the middle of the night confirms my assumption that she's right where I want her.

I had hoped she'd save me tonight, which, in turn, would expose the locksmith capabilities Ashlee informed me about earlier this month. I just had no clue Lee would take my maiming so harshly. He's grown severely agitated the past four weeks. I also can't blame him. Every time he gets within sniffing distance of Claudia, either Ashlee or I stop his fantasies from becoming a reality.

He's nervous, which is dangerous.

You can't get an edgier man than one who's been deprived of touch.

I know this firsthand.

Ignoring my heaving stomach's demand to dispel the slug sitting in the bottom of it, I get back to the task at hand. The little vein in Claudia's neck flutters when I scoot closer to her. "One more lock, Claudia, then we're out of here." I purposely include her in my statement, hoping my false promise will have her agreeing to my suggestion more quickly. We don't have time to dawdle.

Claudia shakes her head as rapidly as her body trembles. Well, I think she's shaking. With how twitchy my body is as it struggles not to overdose on the lethal mix of sedatives Lee gave me, I can't be sure. I feel like my brain has been replaced with dark, moody clouds. I'm equally spaced out on drugs and adrenaline.

After a quick head shake, I return my eyes to Claudia. When she feels my stare, she sheepishly peers at me through a sheet of mousy hair. The submissiveness in her eyes is the equivalent of seeing flashing lights when I'm driving drunk. It sobers me up in an instant.

It also makes me hard as fuck. If I weren't conscious this is my *only* chance to escape, I'd fuck the goodness straight from her marrow, only stopping once every inch of her body is covered with my cum.

I freeze, disturbed by my thoughts. *What drugs did they feed me?* My brain is sliding out of my ears, yet all I'm worried about is being served my last rites. I didn't play nice for years to let little Ms. Psycho's fruity shampoo and big, innocent eyes unravel me. I've got revenge to exact. Little bastards to save. I don't have time for this shit.

"If you don't do this, Claudia, we'll get in trouble. Is that what you want? Do you want to make the guards mad? I might not be able to save you from Lee this time. He's growing impatient." My words are more angry than sincere. I'm not angry at Claudia. I'm pissed at myself. I'll never forfeit a game, but the drop of her pouty lip as she stares at me in fear makes me want to call time out.

I suck in a deep breath, the distress in her hooded gaze thickening both my blood and cock. Her big doe eyes would inspire a saint to sin to save her virtue, but I see a patch of darkness beneath her wholesomeness that reveals the saint's plight would be made in vain.

She's already danced with the devil, and she came out the other end smiling.

When Claudia shakes her head, advising she doesn't want to get in trouble, I clasp her hands in mine. Her body responds the same way it did when her nipples brushed my chest. She blossoms under my touch—whether intentional or not.

Given the situation we find ourselves in, her body is extremely responsive, so imagine how receptive it would be outside of these circumstances?

I grit my teeth, warning my mouth it better articulate the right set of words before muttering, "Just one more lock, then we can go home. You want to go home, don't you, Claudia? Back to the man who's waiting for you?"

I doubt Nick is waiting for Claudia. If it is the standard groupie/bandmate stalker case regularly seen on *TMZ*, he's probably already forgotten who she is. But if it gets me closer to escaping, I'm not above using her 'condition' to my advantage.

I hit a bullseye when the color on Claudia's cheeks doubles as her chest swells high. Her response shouldn't piss me off, but it does. I'm a competitive man—even when it's against a man I have no right to compete against. Nick might be friends with the bane of my existence, but I have no qualms with him. If he doesn't get in the way of me keeping my promise, we'll have no issues.

Claudia's eyes bounce between mine for the next several seconds as she contemplates a response. I'd shake her to hurry her up, but the last thing I want is her hollering at the top of her lungs before she's unlocked the gun case we're crouched next to. If it were an electronic lock, I would be in within seconds, but this is an old-school lock that would take me over thirty minutes to crack.

I don't have thirty minutes.

I don't even have thirty seconds.

"You can trust me, Claudia. I'll never hurt you."

Fuck! The drugs messing with my head are so potent, even I'm on the verge of believing my slurred promise. Claudia glances up at me like I am a god. Although it's a look I've been given many times before, it feels different coming from her.

Hopeful the drugs fucking with my head aren't causing me to misinterpret the silent questions streaming from her eyes, I confirm, "Just this one last lock, then you'll be free. You can go home."

Her lips twitch like she wants to speak, but not a syllable escapes her mouth. She doesn't need to talk for me to understand her, though. Her scoot to the gun cabinet I've been eyeing as intensely as her shapely frame expresses more than her words ever could.

"Good girl," I praise when the tall black locker pops open only a few seconds later.

I'm so spaced out on personality-altering drugs, I slap my hands on her cheeks and plant a sloppy kiss on her lips.

Meds must be at play, or why would I continue praising her like she's a queen?

"You did it, Claudia. I'm so fucking proud of you."

Ignoring the sensation buzzing through my mouth, I shift my focus to the gun cabinet. It's full of weapons every psycho loves—

shotguns, standard black pistols, and enough tear gas to recreate the river that flowed from Cleo's eyes when my knife pierced the meaty flesh in the lower half of her stomach.

The image of her tear-stained face that night is one I'll never forget. It was beautiful. Beyond perfect. One I'd give anything to witness time and time again.

My attention diverts from my cock-thickening daydream when the heavy thud of boots bellows into my ears. The stomping stops a few hundred feet from our location. At the door we left unlocked.

He's standing outside my vacant room.

"Code 44," screams a tormented voice only seconds later.

I recognize the snarl in an instant. It belongs to the same man who taunted me relentlessly only hours earlier.

"Let the drugs do the job, Dexter. You'll need your energy when the sun goes down."

"Do you prefer being topped or taken from the bottom? I guess it doesn't matter as long as your ass is being invaded."

"Only a few more hours until your nightmares come true."

"I can't wait to watch Bryce ride you like you're a float in the Thanksgiving Day Parade."

"Once Bryce is finished with you, I'm going to do the same thing to your girlfriend."

With the growl of a psychotic man, I snatch a black pistol from a stash of many, curl my arm around Claudia's frantically heaving chest, then stand. Claudia's heart thuds against my arm when the barrel of my pistol pinches the skin on her temple. Although I'd rather point the gun at the man rushing our way, this will do for now. Once my senses are no longer suffocated by locked doors and vented air, I'll exact my revenge on the insolent man who believes he runs the show.

"Stay calm, Claudia, and you won't get hurt. I promise you that."

Although my promises are as worthless as the breaths that deliver them, this one I intend to keep. I've been seeking a way out of my predicament for years, so her assistance tonight ensures she'll never be a discarded pawn on my chessboard.

The manic beat of Claudia's pulse kicks out a new tune when Lee stops outside the security office door. Her fear is felt from the strands of her hair to the tips of her toes.

I shouldn't relish her paralysis, but I do. It adds to the vigor thickening the air, giving it an edge my fried brain feeds off.

With one hand bracing the baton on his hip and the other clasping his two-way radio, Lee casually steps inside the security room. His pompous attitude doesn't surprise me, but he'd be wise not to underestimate me. Even being doped up on a dangerous dose of hallucinogenic drugs hasn't weakened my resolve in the slightest. If anything, they've made me more manic.

"Dexter—"

"Call in a false alarm. Tell them you were mistaken." I nudge my head to his radio to amplify my request.

Lee smiles, loving the harsh slur of my voice. "I can't do that..."

His words trail off when I dig my gun into Claudia's temple, causing her to squeak. I don't mean to hurt her. I'm just using her temple to hide how badly my hands are shaking. My body is tremoring as it fights not to shut down.

Stupidly believing my shaking is in fear, Lee drops his focus to Claudia. "It's okay, Claudia. You're safe. I won't let anything happen to you."

After issuing the rest of his false promise with his eyes, Lee raises them to mine. He thinks his slick grin and boyish looks have Claudia fooled. He's an idiot. I didn't need to feel the response Claudia's body gave when he glanced at her to know she hates him. I can smell it in the air, taste it on my tongue. She's calculating his demise as readily as I am, just like all good little psychos do.

"Let Claudia go, Dexter. She's not a part of this—"

"She isn't a part of this?" I interrupt, my voice sterner than I anticipated. "Oh. Then what did you mean earlier when you said you're going to fuck her the instant Bryce finished having his way with me? What did you say again? 'You couldn't wait to tear her up.'"

Claudia freezes for the quickest second. She isn't shocked by my revelation that Lee wants her beneath him—he's made it more than obvious. It's discovering pussy-footed Bryce is more fucked in the head than she is that has her balking.

He played the part of devoted warden slash want-to-be-counselor the first two weeks, but it all went downhill after that. He isn't merely sadistic. He's on the wrong side of the fence altogether. He and Lee should be patients at Meadow Fields, not staff.

Lee doesn't attempt to hide the deceit in his eyes while replying, "You must have misunderstood what I said. I'm a married man. I have a daughter not much older than Claudia. I'd never hurt her."

His lies fill me with a violent rage, and I'm not the only one fuming. Claudia's body temperature rises as rapidly as my anger. Her teeth gnash together, their hearty grinds so compelling, the sweet scent of blood swamps my senses seconds later.

After a final whiff of the intoxicating smell, I return my focus to the task at hand. The slick grin on Lee's face triples my agitation. He thinks he has all his ducks in a row, that I'm too spaced out on drugs to stay upright, much less act on his insolence.

I guess I better teach him a lesson.

With a grin of a man who has nothing to lose, I drag my pistol away from Claudia's temple and point it at the pinched skin between Lee's brows. For how hazy my vision is, my aim is scarily precise. One wrong move, and he'll be toast, and he knows it.

The distress oozing from his pores is nearly as enticing as the smell of Claudia's blood. If his earlier distress call didn't leave me short of time, I'd relish his fear a little longer. Instead, I say, "Call in a false alarm. Tell them you were mistaken, then I might let you live." This demand is more violent than my first. I don't like being treated like an idiot, but even more than that, I loathe authority with every fiber of my being, so you can be assured scum like Lee are at the very bottom of my totem pole when it comes to leniency.

Annoyed that he failed to jump at my command, I cock the trigger back to the halfway point. It may even be three-quarters compressed.

"Okay, okay, don't shoot." With one hand raised in the air, Lee squeezes the button on his radio as firmly as I am squeezing the trigger. "Stand down, patient was found hiding in the restroom. I repeat, stand down from Code 44. Patient was located safe and without injury."

The crackling of a radio sounds through my ears, closely followed by a breathless, "Jesus, Lee! How many times have you been told to check their hidey-holes before sounding the alarm?" Bryce sucks in three ragged breaths before adding, "You scared the living shit out of me. We don't want any crazies running wild with the turkeys this weekend."

Lee laughs as if Bryce is funny—like he wasn't standing outside my door thirty minutes ago discussing an appropriate time for Bryce to return unnoticed. A wireless receiver crackles before Lee says, "Yeah, sorry about that. It won't happen again."

His promise is more for me than Bryce. He knows I heard their plans to return to my room before daylight. He knows what they were going to do to me.

Just like he knows what I plan to do to him for his stupidity.

"Shall we do this in here or out there?" I drift my eyes to the single glass door separating the criminally insane from the general public. "There'll be less mess for Bryce to clean up outside."

Lee's Adam's apple bobs up and down before he follows the direction of my gaze. "D-D-Do what exactly?"

I grin. It's the smile of an insane man. This will only get better when the tangy smell of Lee's piss filters through my nostrils. I love how cowards lose the ability to control their bodily functions when they're scared. They piss and shit their pants like babies, which only encourages my campaign to free them from the madness. Stephen cried like a baby when our game reached the final two hours. Lee should be grateful time isn't on my side.

"Outside it is," I answer on Lee's behalf when he continues staring at me like a fish out of water, hopeful he's misreading the silent warnings streaming from me.

He isn't, but you can't blame a guy for being optimistic?

"Hurry up, Lee. We haven't got all night." My voice comes out crackly. The surge in Claudia's heart rate complements my raspy tone. If I didn't know any better, I'd swear she was scared.

It's a pity I know better.

Just like me, she's feeding off the adrenaline thickening the air.

Lee is all thumbs when he secures an overloaded keyring from his trouser pocket and an employee ID from his jacket. His hands tremble uncontrollably when he scans his credentials into a wall-mounted scanner before twisting his key into the lock.

"Walk through before us to ensure there aren't any snipers hiding in wait," I demand.

Lee glares at me like I'm clinically insane. I don't know why he's shocked. My paranoia reached fever pitch the instant he became a part of my life. I'm a plotter. I methodically plan out each stage of my life in precise detail. Men like Lee ruin my game plan with their rules and expectations.

When Lee remains bullet-free after crossing the threshold between the clinically insane and normality, I cautiously inch Claudia and me outside.

"Come on, Claudia. No one will hurt you. We're just going home," I whisper in her ear when her reluctant steps slow me down. Her hesitance is surprising. I thought the first whiff of fresh air in years would have had her legs pumping as fast as her heart.

Taking my pledge as gospel, Claudia lightens her steps.

She trusts me.

She shouldn't. I'm not a trustworthy man.

Getting her out of here alive is the most honorable thing I've ever done. I could leave her, but the fewer witnesses to my escape, the better. She wouldn't talk—she's fucking mute, for crying out loud—but there's an edge of danger associated with her that warns me to remain vigilant. No one expects a killer with an angelic face and dazzling eyes. That's how I flew under the radar so long.

I'd still be free if it weren't for *him*.

The thrusts of my lungs turn frantic. Not because Marcus entered my thoughts but because freedom is so close I can taste it on the tip of my tongue. The crispness of a late fall breeze floats across my skin as the crunch of grass underfoot sounds through my ears. Even the brutal clap of thunder above my head can't detract from the brilliance. It's been years since I've heard such an intoxicating sound. I'll be fucked if I let anything take it away from me again. I'd rather die than return to being caged like an animal.

After directing my gun back to Lee's head, I drop my lips to Claudia's temple. "On the count of three, you're going to run, okay? Don't look back. No matter what you hear, you are never to look back. Do you understand?"

The wooziness in my head amplifies when her hazel eyes glance up into mine before she weakly nods. Her trust is addictive, headier than any drug I've been given, but her dazzling eyes in a low-hanging moon are even more hypnotizing. They're remarkably clear for a patient at a hospital for the criminally insane.

"Alright, it's time for you to go home. Are you ready?"

Ignoring Lee's warning that state troopers will find her within minutes of fleeing, Claudia nods again. Her determination inspires me. It also has me thinking recklessly. I'm precariously dangling between borderline insane and a mere man. I don't know which one I'd rather be right now.

As birds begin their early morning chirping, I commence my countdown. When my tongue flattens against my front teeth to pronounce the 'th' in three, Claudia pushes off her feet. She charges for the tree line barely visible in the dark conditions, her strides as chaotic as my pulse.

I wait for her to join one of the many stars dancing in front of my eyes before returning my focus to Lee. He holds his hands out in front of his body when he spots the murderous demon hiding behind my sparkling baby blues. "Hey, come on, Dexter. You said you'd let me live if I called off the warning."

"No." I shake my head so rapidly my brain rattles. Although the hammering of my brain against my skull is painful, I'm grateful to learn it isn't all sludge. "I said 'I *might* let you live.'" My ear touches my shoulder when I shrug. "I lied."

He stupidly smiles, believing a friendly approach will reduce the severity of his punishment. It does—somewhat. I gun him down in cold blood instead of removing his stomach via his throat as I threatened earlier tonight. That's more due to lack of time than respect.

He wears a bullet hole well. It does wonders to the deep crinkle in the middle of his brows.

Just as Lee's lifeless body slumps to my feet, a commotion inside Meadow Fields gains my attention. I was so caught up watching the life fade from Lee's eyes, I neglected to notice we have company.

The guard's pudgy midsection slows his steps as he races toward me. He is decked out in full riot gear—three-sizes-too-small helmet and all.

I laugh. With my mind still gooey from the substances Lee forced down my throat, I either laugh or go on a rampage.

Revenge will always exceed my need to be entertained.

After firing off four shots, my aim dismal, I push off my feet and head in the direction Claudia fled. If my mind wasn't hazed by drugs, I would have taken more than one gun. Alas, I'm not close to being smart when my brain is on fire.

Wet grass coats my bare feet as I charge across the soaked ground. The heavens have opened up, one God happy to assist another with his escape.

That's not surprising. Gods stick together when it is for the greater good.

I'm halfway to the edge of the woods when the burn inside my skull drops a few inches. Something shreds through my body, and the downpour of rain is unable to cool its unexpected arrival.

I make it another few feet before the agony scorching my lower back buckles my knees. The pain is intense, but it is nothing compared to the fury coursing through my veins from my body not responding to the prompts of my brain.

I don't give up when I am down. I thrive under pressure.

With the strength of ten men, I stand to my feet then spin around to face the person responsible for the seeping hole in my back. The man chasing me startles, as surprised by my presence as I am by his. He balks so rigidly his helmet falls off his head.

"Not who you were expecting?" I ask, my usually deep voice huffy and breathless.

Bryce shakes his head, certain the sedatives Lee gave me would have taken down an elephant.

It's a pity he underestimated me.

It is also a shame I'm five seconds away from passing out from substantial blood loss. The wound in my back is gushing. It is soaking my shirt more swiftly than the thunderous sky above my head.

Noticing I am injured, Bryce steps closer. "Drop the weapon, Dexter, and we'll pretend tonight never happened."

My manic laughter smears my teeth with blood. "Your partner's last meal was lead, so there's no way we can pretend this never happened."

I don't know if it's a lack of oxygen to my brain or the sedatives, but Bryce doesn't seem the least bit concerned about the death of his colleague. If anything, he looks pleased.

"Lee got what was coming to him."

Shockingly, Bryce nods in agreement.

"Now you're going to get the same."

With my body in the process of shutting down, it takes a mammoth effort to lift my gun, and even when I do, I'm too late. Bryce is pointing an assault rifle at my heart. His finger is already on the trigger. I won't fire off a single round before I'm gunned down, but at least I won't die a coward.

Just as my finger yanks back the trigger, Bryce's gun falls from his hands. He stumbles forward while clutching the back of his head. The tiniest sliver of silver behind his left shoulder is my only clue to the cause of his wobbling steps.

As blood oozes from his mouth like a tap, Claudia rears back her weapon of choice for the second time. This time around, the impact of her shovel to the back of his head is so firm, the life in his eyes vacates before he hits the drenched grass like a bag of shit.

I stare at Claudia in awe and in all honesty, turned on as fuck. She just took down a man three times her weight and double her width wearing a floral dress and a smile.

You can't get more cock-thickening than that.

6

CLAUDIA

"*C*laudia... what the fuck? I told you to run."

Dexter's words are slurred, and his face is as white as Bryce's. When he stumbles forward, I barely catch him before he hits the dirt as rapidly as Bryce did.

With him being a good foot taller than me and at least thirty pounds heavier, it takes all my strength to keep him upright so we can continue into the woods. I wasn't sure if the bangs ricocheting off the dense tree line were from the thunder clapping above my head or gunshots. Now I know without a doubt.

I shouldn't have turned around. I should have kept running until my legs gave out from exhaustion, but after hearing the things Lee and Bryce planned to do tonight, I would never truly be free if Dexter didn't also escape.

I've been seeking a way out of this hellhole for years, but with the front doors secured with a pick-proof lock, I could never hatch a suitable escape plan. That's why I toed the line like a good, obedient girl.

When my mother died, I wanted to fall to my knees and weep.

My father would have none of it. She was not to be mourned. She was forgotten, pushed to the back of my mind. I had to act like she never existed, and that's precisely what I've done the past five years. I acted as if I am a ghost.

And what did I get for my efforts?

Another man who wanted to use and abuse me.

The gleam in Lee's eyes when he told me I was safe was one I had seen many times before. It was the same glimmer my daddy's eyes got before he punished me. Even his slimy grin was identical. If it weren't for Dexter, he would have hurt me—possibly in a way I've never been touched. The notion alone had me spinning on my feet to ensure Dexter escaped the fiery depths of hell with me.

A few minutes later, a harrowing moan grumbles from Dexter's mouth. With nearly all his body weight on my shoulders, I assumed he had passed out.

"Right." He grunts his one word as if it is an entire sentence, and the nudge of his head strengthens his demand.

I take a sharp right, which veers away from the streetlights peeking over the horizon and the sirens howling in the distance. I drop my eyes to Dexter's, seeking further instructions. Pain fetters his face, but only for a short time. It is in and out in under a second. He doesn't want to add to the panic misting my skin more effectively than the big drops of moisture falling from the sky.

"In approximately two miles, there's a cabin. There are clues in the grass to help you find it. It's hidden by shrubs." His deep voice is garbled with pain. "They won't find us there. We can bunker down for a few days."

We?

I like the sound of that.

I was scared to death about entering the bush alone. It wasn't the men chasing me causing my throat-pounding response. It was the bats hovering above my head and the occasional scrape across my ankles not caused by fallen tree limbs.

"Can you see the marks? They look like bear prints," Dexter asks, his words barely audible. My feet skid to a stop as I scan the area. Upon hearing my thrashing heart raging in the silence of the night, Dexter chuckles, "They aren't real bear prints. Just made-up ones. My father leaves them as clues so he can find his way home."

I'm glad he can find humor in our situation. I can't. When I drop my eyes to my shoes, nothing but sludge and mud reflect back at me. I can barely see the ground, much less old marks that have most likely faded with time.

"Trust m-me, Claudia," Dexter stammers after reading my thoughts with an edge a stranger shouldn't have. "There's a cabin here somewhere. You've just got to follow the clues."

Panic rises to my chest when his head flops forward. Within a mere second, his arm clamped around my shoulders triples in weight. I scream his name on repeat inside my head, but he doesn't wake up. He's passed out, quite possibly dead, but it's too dangerous for us to wait here until he regains consciousness, and if he's wrong about the bear prints being fake, we're a sitting target.

We have to keep moving, I just don't know how.

While recalling my daily routine of scaling the stairs of my family home with my drunk dad on my back, I tighten Dexter's grip around my shoulders before hoisting him off the ground. My knees wobble under the excessive weight, but with my lower back bearing most of the pain, I take a laborious step forward.

Because Dexter is taller than me, his feet drag across the mud with every painstaking step I take. In a way, it's a godsend. It hides my footprints from anyone seeking them, and any evidence he fails to remove, I'm sure the rain will take care of.

APPROXIMATELY TWO HOURS LATER, my slug-like steps come to a stop. A cabin is standing roughly twelve feet in front of me. It is canopied by creeping weeds and overgrown grass as Dexter said.

I'm wary to approach. It appears empty, but three shingles on the rickety awning have been newly repaired, announcing someone was here more recently than the unkempt appearance alludes.

"*Ugh.*" I nudge Dexter with my shoulder, hoping my grunt and bump routine will wake him.

It doesn't. He continues drooling on my neck, and the flutters of his breath in the blood pooled in the corner of his mouth are the only indication that he's alive.

"*Oomph,*" I try again.

He remains as quiet as I've been the past five years.

Confident my trembling legs are two seconds away from collapsing, I trudge toward the dark cabin. My steps are soundless. Only the crunch of dried leaves is audible.

The closer I approach the wooden cabin, the wider my eyes grow. It's one of those properties you'd expect in a horror flick. It is dingy and dark and reminds me of my childhood home.

My family estate wasn't always derelict and rundown. Before my mother passed, it was a beautiful country manor. I tried to keep the property to her level of cleanliness after her death, but no amount of scrubbing could mask the scent of her corpse. I tried. It just wasn't possible.

When I take the first stair on the warped patio, it creaks under our combined weight. My eyes rocket to the door, hopeful the massive screech hasn't announced our arrival. The last thing I want to do is startle a man with a gun. We had unexpected visitors arrive on our property all the time when my mom disappeared.

They had big books filled with tiny little words and pointy, screwed-up noses.

They stopped coming after my dad greeted them with a shotgun slung over his shoulder.

We never had any visitors after that.

When the creak fails to result in any lights coming on, I make my way to the only door on the entire property. It's not surprising there is only one exit and entry point. The space is so small, it's only half the size of the living room in my family home.

I hiss and moan as we enter the dark room. I sound like an alley cat in the midst of a brawl, but if it saves me from being shot, I'm all for it.

The room is very basic. There's a box under a dusty window on my right, a double mattress to my left, and a stack of old pallets being used as a pantry. I think there may be a bathroom hidden behind the back wall, but with half-casted moonlight my only source of light, I'm not willing to advance any closer.

Confident the only living thing inside the cabin is mold and mildew, I head for the double bed shoved in the far left-hand corner of the poorly lit space. Dexter releases a long, simpering moan when I place him on the bed.

The reason for his pained groan comes to light when he rolls onto his stomach. The back of his shirt is bright red. The blood seeping from a circular wound is flowing at a frantic rate. I must act quickly, or he will bleed out.

Although Dexter's eyes are snapped shut, I wordlessly advise him I'll be back in a minute. I know he can hear me. We've communicated like this many times the past six weeks. Brief glances, furled lips, and the occasional note slip not only kept me out of harm's way, but they also piqued my curiosity.

That's why I arrived at Dexter's room tonight. My inquisitiveness got the better of me. Although I would have preferred our night not be filled with violence, my heart has never raced so fast. The adrenaline rush you get from rule-breaking is addictive— almost as enticing as the moan that left Bryce's lips when I struck him with the shovel.

I gag, scream, and nearly give up on my endeavor three times before I gather all the instruments needed to fix Dexter's wound. I don't know who owns this cabin, but they should be ashamed of themselves. The moldy sandwich in the sink is swarming with bugs, and the mirror above the vanity is smeared with so much dust, I thought I was a ghost. There's only one time a home should be this messy—when you're hiding the scent of a decaying corpse.

With half a bottle of whiskey, a sewing kit, and a sturdy length of thread I plucked from the hem of Dexter's shirt, I exhale a deep breath then sit on a tiny stool next to the bed. I'm not a doctor, but I had ample experience mending broken bones and cracked faces during my childhood.

When I patched her up, my mom was as brave as Dexter is being now. Not once did she cry when crippled with pain. Some days, her legs didn't work, yet she still packed my school lunch every single day.

I really miss her.

More than I should.

Daddy said she is the reason I am sick, that the bug in her head transferred to mine when I grew in her stomach. I thought she was perfect. Her moods fluctuated a lot, but that's what made her so much fun. There were days when she sang songs at the top of her lungs while painting my room with bright yellow sunflowers. Then other days she'd make the bathwater so hot, my skin bubbled with blisters.

She was different, but she was my mom, so I loved her all the same.

Apology after apology rolls through my head when I pry

Dexter's shirt away from his wound. The drenched material comes away without too much force but discovering the cause for the frantic flow of blood makes me gasp. Dexter has been shot, but there is no exit wound.

That can only mean one thing.

The bullet is still lodged in his back.

I smack my forehead four times, shutting up the stupid thoughts streaming through my mind. I can't dig the bullet out. I just can't. I don't like blood. It is pretty and bright, but it generally accompanies death.

I don't want Dexter to die. That's why I carried him on my back for over two hours.

If you don't remove the bullet, he will die!

My palm bangs my forehead until it's raw. I hate listening to the voices in my head, but this time, I don't have a choice. She is right. If I don't remove the bullet, Dexter will bleed out. It isn't a matter of if. It is a matter of when. It could be an hour. It could be minutes. I haven't watched enough crime shows to gauge a better timeframe.

Before I lose the courage, I plunge two fingers into Dexter's wound. I freeze in surprise when my body doesn't respond how I was anticipating. I thought I'd gag or, at the very least, squeal in disgust, but the stark coolness of his blood is too shocking.

Is this normal?

Should he be this cold?

Ignoring Dexter's groans from my fingers digging around in his wound, I continue to hunt for the bullet. I pretend I am seeking the shards of glass my mom hid in my dad's porridge. It's like a treasure hunt, just gorier and tainted with the smell of death.

The gagging I expected earlier comes full force when my fingers curl around something cooler than Dexter's blood. Its smooth surface leaves no doubt of its identity. It is a soul-stealing bullet.

My hands are tiny, but there's no way I can remove them along with the bullet and not rip Dexter's wound. I have to hurt him to save him—just like my dad did for my mom

I grunt in apology when Dexter's painful moan coincides with his eyes rolling into the back of his head. The wound didn't tear too much. He'll only need a few more stitches, but his groan speaks to the torrent of pain raining down on him.

After dumping the blood-smeared bullet onto the bedside table, I secure the bottle of whiskey in my hands. It's supposed to remove germs from the wound before I sew the hole shut, but my hands are shaking so badly, I take three giant swigs before pouring the remnants over the singed hole.

Dexter roars as violently as my throat burns from the amber liquid sliding into my gut. He thrashes against the mattress, his battle cries the loudest I've heard. Panicked his screams will alert people to our whereabouts, I muffle his mouth with my hand. I am shaking so profoundly, the tremble of my hand shudders up my arm, but my shakes have nothing on the frenetic quivers wreaking havoc with Dexter's body. He's shuddering as if he is surrounded by six inches of snow.

Once Dexter's groans simmer to a purr, I remove my hand from his mouth. I don't want to get back to the next stage of my operation, but I don't have a choice.

Last part, then you're done, I say in my head while working up the courage to pierce a threaded needle through Dexter's angry, red skin.

Mercifully, he handles the needle's sting much better than the burn of alcohol. He lies perfectly still as I stitch his wound in the same pattern my daddy taught me when we sealed my mother's eyes shut. He is so motionless I worry I clamped his mouth too long. If it weren't for the goosebumps prickling his skin, I'd check for a pulse. Your skin doesn't show signs of being cold when you're dead. It goes blue and smelly. Sometimes it even slides away from the bones it's covering.

My shoulders straighten when I finalize the last stitch. My medical skills are rusty, but the thick, white thread that contrasts with Dexter's olive skin has successfully closed his wound.

Now you need to work on his plummeting body temperature.

After warning my head to be quiet, I sling my eyes to the right before shifting them to the left. The owner of this cabin must be a daytime-only visitor because there aren't any blankets or clothing in sight.

When I stand to inspect the cabin more thoroughly, my dress clings to my skin. Dexter isn't the only one saturated head to toe. My hair is stuck to my shivering back, and my dress is so drenched even my panties are soaked through.

While rubbing the goosebumps on my arms, I circle the old wooden floor. The creak of the warped material matches the squeaks of the mattress springs from Dexter's violent shudders as he works through the pain. My thorough search of the tiny cabin comes up empty-handed. I am no closer to discovering a way to increase Dexter's body temperature.

You could...

"*No!*" I shout at the voice inside my head.

My daddy said getting into a bed with a man without my clothes on would send me to hell. I don't want to go to hell because my father will most likely be there waiting for me. I was only freed from his madness because my love for Nick triumphed over the love I had for him. If it didn't, I'd still be walking amongst the flames.

I didn't want to kill my father, but I had no choice. He told me I had to choose between Nick and him.

I picked Nick.

I've never regretted my decision.

No! I internally warn again, hating the whiny voice in my head cautioning me that Dexter will die if I don't do what she's suggesting. I don't want him to die, but there must be another way I can save him that doesn't involve removing my clothes.

Ignoring the other voices in my head calling me names, I pace to the window box on the opposite side of the room. Perhaps if I put some distance between Dexter and me, the crazy thoughts will stop, and clarity will form in its place.

I should let him die. Dexter isn't like Nick. He's evil. *He's bad.* He doesn't love me with every fiber of his being. He was just using me as a means to escape. *Wasn't he?*

You're so stupid!

"*No, I'm not!*" I pound my head, teaching the snarky voice a lesson about what happens when you're mean to me.

The rattle of my brain against my skull shuts them up right away.

I'm not stupid. I am merely confused by Dexter's attention. He brings out my reckless side, the side not worried about the wicked thoughts in my head. The evil in his eyes encourages my evil to flourish. We are similar, yet different, if that makes any sense?

Although my life would be less complicated without him in it, I can't help but be drawn to him. It isn't just his wild spirit. It's something much deeper than that. For years, I thought my heart was broken. It still ticked, but its beat was slow and out of time.

Dexter reset it.

Imagine you're looking at a heart monitor. See the flat, bland line? That was my heart two months ago. Now imagine a massive surge of electricity jolting through my chest. The flat line spikes up high on the graph before it returns to a standard, rhythmic beat.

Dexter is the surge.

Nick is the normality.

I return my eyes to Dexter, grateful for the surge but frightened by what it means. He's still shuddering. The purple bruise around his wound is barely distinguishable since his olive skin is pale and blue.

"Stop it!" I shout at the voices in my head, my demand accompanied by ripping out several chunks of my hair. I'm sick to death of the stupid things they say every single day.

Do this.

Do that.

That puppy would look better without its tail.

Nick will never forgive me if I sleep with another man. For that alone, I can't listen to them.

Wanting to silence their snarky comments, I slide a pill bottle out of the pocket in my dress. These tablets are the ones the doctors prescribed after I informed my teacher that my father had killed my mother. He told everyone I was sick. That what I saw wasn't true. I thought it was, but within a few months of taking these pills, I began to wonder if I was mistaken.

Maybe my dad didn't stab my mom twelve times until her pale blue dress turned into a sea of red. Maybe he didn't leave her sleeping in their bed for six months until the smell of her decaying body became so unbearable he had no choice but to bury her. I was certain he hid her in our barn because he didn't want anyone to know he had killed her, but maybe I was wrong. These tablets do make me confused. They make me doubt everything and everyone, but at least they numb the pain.

I tap three tablets into my palm. The voices in my head will never be fully silenced, but my prescription calms me down so much, I barely hear them. It is a double-edged sword. If I don't take them, the pain in my heart won't stop. If I do take them, my daddy was right. I am a Grade-A lunatic.

I should take them. The memories surfacing in my head are more violent than usual. I'm not surprised. The blood streaming from Dexter's wound matches the stain I scrubbed from my parents' mattress the day after my mother was buried. His painful screams when I poured the whiskey over his wound were as vocal as my mom's before my dad silenced her cries with his blade.

I hate feeling confused, but the pain in my chest is too intense to ignore. I have no choice. I can either be medicated or believe my father murdered my mother as callously as I killed Bryce.

Preferring to pretend neither of those events transpired, I raise my hand to my mouth. Here it comes—a blackness so dense, it doesn't just numb my thoughts, it freezes my heart as well.

7

CLAUDIA

*J*ust before my tongue laps up the personality-disorienting tablets, a long growl rumbles through the cabin. Dexter is awake, and his hand is creeping toward the stitches in his back. Although his low growl makes my heart flutter, it also kickstarts my legs.

"*Uh. Uh!*" I grunt, warning him to stay away.

My tablets skid across the floor with a clatter when I sprint across the dark space. My steps are so fast I reach Dexter in two heart-thrashing seconds. I swat his hand three times before he grips my wrists in a painful hold. He tosses me over his body, his lack of effort making it seem as if I am weightless.

I hit the wall opposite the bed with a thud before landing on the smelly mattress face first. I want to say that is the end of the horror. Unfortunately, it isn't. Dexter is on my back two seconds later. With his blood-scented breaths quivering against my neck, the raging beat of my heart drops several inches lower. It aligns with a stiff region of Dexter's body digging into my backside.

"What the fuck did you do to me?" he hisses, his snarl brimming with violence.

My excitement shifts to fear. I try to grunt. I try to move. But I don't do either of those things. His body pinning mine to the mattress is too heavy. I can barely breathe, let alone respond.

The fear depriving my lungs of oxygen diminishes when Dexter murmurs, "Claudia?"

He burrows his nose into my hair before inhaling an enormous whiff.

I shouldn't like that he can identify me by my scent, but I do.

"Claudia." This grumble is a confirmation, not a question.

When he rolls off me, my nostrils flare. I pretend I'm refilling my lungs with air. In reality, I'm trying to calm the heat roaring through my body. The snarky voices inside my head were right. Together, Dexter and I have enough heat to keep half the continent comfortable this winter. Blankets would be an unnecessary requirement.

After his eyes float around the cabin, Dexter returns them to me. "You found it."

Warmth spreads from my toes to my scalp. I love the praise in his tone, but I wish it was missing the slur he delivered it with. He has the same garbled voice my daddy used in the minutes leading to him crashing onto the floorboards of our living room. I didn't think it was possible to get drunk from pouring whiskey on open wounds. Now I'm not so sure.

Dexter's teeth grit when he twists his torso to face me. Although his eyes are pained, his face remains deadpan. "We'll rest here for a few hours before moving on to the next stage."

I smile, pleased he's including me in his plans. The way he sent me into the forest hours ago had me worried I was going it alone. I was truly terrified. I've been seeking freedom for years, but every step I took toward the exit door of Meadow Fields was extremely frightening. Just the idea of conquering this giant, scary world alone daunts the living shit out of me. I don't know what state we're in, much less which direction I need to travel to find Nick.

My eyes snap to Dexter when he gripes, "It's fucking freezing. Did you start the fire?"

When his eyes shift to the side, I follow the direction of his gaze. There's an open fireplace on the back wall. The ash in the bottom shows it has been used recently, but it isn't dispersing any heat. With the only light from the occasional flash of lightning, I could use poor visibility as an excuse for my ignorance, but then how would I explain Dexter's perfectly crafted stitches?

After a quick swallow, I return my eyes to Dexter. He growls when I shake my head, but the faint tug of his lips gives away his true response. He thinks I'm funny. I don't know why. Nothing happening is humorous.

"There's wood outside. It's under a tarp." When he attempts to stand, a painful groan emits from his lips. "Argh! What the fuck?"

He bends awkwardly in his quest to identify the source of his pain. With no way of showing him his wound without breaking his neck, I gesture for him to sit before scampering to the door he was heading for.

"Bring in enough to get us through the night." The roughness of his voice prickles my skin with excitement.

My body shakes more with every step I take. It isn't from fear. It's from losing the heat of Dexter's gaze as he gawks at my drenched body.

Is that why he smiled? Is he laughing at me?

No one has ever seen me this disheveled. I learned vanity from my mother—nice clothes, pretty hair, and just a touch of makeup so I don't look like a whore. That's the motto I practice daily.

Right now, I'm a mess. My hair hangs in tangled chaos halfway down my back. The torrential rain washed away my makeup, and my clothes are stuck to my body so profoundly, I might as well not be wearing any.

I stop, frozen for a beat. That's the second time tonight the voices in my head were right. They said I was practically naked, so why not use my body heat to warm Dexter?

Pretending it's perfectly sane to talk about myself in third person, I return to my mission of gathering firewood.

I find the pile of wood Dexter mentioned approximately three minutes later. The tarp that used to cover the wood pile no longer exists.

"Goddammit!" Dexter roars when I enter the cabin with two chunks of drenched wood in my hands. He's sitting up, but the dangerous slump of his shoulders reveals he is feeling the pain he refuses to acknowledge. "They won't light without a gallon of gasoline."

With a shrug of agreement, I dump the wood into the fireplace before cleaning the gunk off my hands with my dress. It won't help anyone now, but if I keep the wood out of the rain for a few hours, we can use it later.

I stop dragging my hands down my stomach when a strange sensation zooms through the middle of my legs. It's a hard feeling to describe, but it's similar to when I'm busting to use the bathroom, but my bladder is empty. It's a nice tingle but very much foreign.

When my eyes survey the area the sensation is coming from, I discover the cause for the pleasing zap. Dexter is staring at me. His eyes are hooded, and he looks extremely hungry.

Did he not eat supper before calling it a night?

After licking his dry lips, he says, "There's a way we can keep warm until the wood dries..." His words trail off when I take a step back, then he smiles as if pleased by the challenge. "You're soaking wet, Claudia. If you sleep like that, you'll get sick." His tone doesn't relay worry and neither does his wolfish grin.

I shrug like it's no big deal. It isn't. I've grown accustomed to the cold. I wear summer dresses rain, hail, or shine. They were the only items hanging in my mother's wardrobe when she died. Since I outgrew my childhood clothes within three years of her death, I either walked around naked or wore her dresses. I chose the latter.

The blue tinge my toes get in winter reminds me of her. Her eyes weren't blue, but her lips were for a very long time.

"Claudia..." Dexter's growl has my heart rate picking up. Not once the past six weeks has he spoken to me in such a way. His words were gentle purrs and nurturing rumbles. He never raised his voice. I'm not saying I don't like his rough tone. I just need to get used to it.

I point to the window seat, advising Dexter I plan to sleep there.

"Whatever. Freeze. See if I care." His grumbled comment proves he understands me even without any verbalization.

This is only the second time in my life I've communicated without words.

First Nick. Now Dexter.

I like that.

We do too.

Air whizzes through Dexter's teeth when he rolls over. I don't know whether his huff was because of my denial or the pain no doubt rocketing through his body from his stitches tugging. I'm no one special, so I suspect it is my last assumption.

I realize I'm way off the mark when he tugs his wet pants down his naked backside two seconds later. He isn't grunting because he's in pain. He's struggling to remove the stiff material from his body.

My eyes drop to a loose stitch in my dress when he tosses the rigid material onto the ground. It lands with a thud on the grimy floor halfway between us before he snickers, "Night. Sleep tight. Don't let the bed bugs bite."

Although his tone is brimming with sarcasm, I scan the room, petrified about what bugs he is referring to... and perhaps to catch the occasional glimpse of his naked backside.

ROUGHLY TWENTY MINUTES LATER, the chatter of my teeth becomes too annoying for Dexter to ignore. I'm shivering uncontrollably, equally cold and terrified. It isn't the bugs scaring me. It's how many times I've ogled Dexter's ass the past twenty minutes. I'm eyeing the ridges of his muscular back and backside without constraint, not the least bit worried about what Nick's reaction will be at discovering I've eyed another man.

If I hadn't spent the last five years in a psychiatric hospital, I'd admit myself for my ludicrousness. I'm stunned at the thoughts streaming through my head tonight. I only ever killed for one man. Tonight, I killed for another.

What's wrong with me?

After jackknifing into a half-seated position, Dexter throws his legs over the bed and heads my way. I'm tempted to scream for him to stop, but the image of his... *penis*... swinging with every step he takes is too mesmerizing. I've only seen two penises in my life. One was my father's, so it doesn't count, and the other was Nick's. But even then, it was never up close and personal like this.

My dad's was when he'd forget to close the bathroom door when showering. Nick's was anytime he was with *her*.

He must have *really* enjoyed the heinous things they did together because they did them a lot.

By a lot, I mean a minimum of two to three times a day.

My body got the same thrilling sensation back then as it has tonight, but tonight's is more powerful and missing the red-blooded fury that kept my thoughts far from sane while I plotted ways to destroy their relationship.

Air leaves my lungs in a grunt when Dexter snags my wrist, yanks me to my feet, then shreds my dress straight off my body. You'd think the drenched material would give him a little trouble. It doesn't. It's like tissue paper in his big, manly hands. It floats to the floor like a feather, the brutal grunts emitting from my mouth helping it soar.

It takes me a few moments to realize what's happening. When I do, I grunt, demanding the focus of Dexter's eyes.

He doesn't give it to me.

"If you want me to stop, Claudia, just say the word." He keeps his eyes on the down-low, ensuring he won't spot my unspoken denial.

Since he refuses to hear the words I can't speak, I slap his hands, chest, and face, forcing him to feel them instead.

My fight only encourages his campaign. The harder I hit him, the more violently he tugs at my dress. Before I know it, I'm standing before him in nothing but a bra and a pair of modest panties.

Well, they were modest before torrential rain had its way with them.

After taking three steps back, Dexter's eyes slowly rise to meet mine. They take their time, absorbing my pressed thighs, quivering stomach, and erratically panting chest on the way. When they finally reach my face, that tingling sensation I mentioned earlier doubles. The hunger in his eyes is even more noticeable than it was twenty minutes ago, and his penis is more than three times its original size. It is seeping with want and throbbing with need.

"If you remove your bra, I'll let you keep your panties." The voice he uses this time is one I've never heard. It's husky and raw, and in all honesty, pulse-quickening.

When I shake my head, wordlessly denying his demand, he takes a step closer to me. The fire in his eyes warns me he'll remove my bra as viciously as he did my dress, but that isn't my greatest concern. It is his rapidly thickening penis. It is growing at a rate my hazy mind can't comprehend.

Is that normal? Should it grow so fast that angry, pulsating veins throb all over it?

Nick's penis only grew like that just before he...

I can't say it.

I won't say it.

We hate her.

My eyes lift from Dexter's penis when he warns, "This is your last chance, Claudia. Remove your bra, or I'll do it for you." When his tone reveals his demand isn't a suggestion, my eyes drift to the only window in the cabin. A spark of lightning breaks through the dark clouds, adding to the eerie sensation bristling between Dexter and me. The air in the cabin is roasting, making me confused as to why Dexter's campaign is so vehement. The energy teeming between us makes a furnace unnecessary, much less the heat of his massively dilated eyes raking over my scarcely covered body.

Not wanting to weather a storm in panties and a bra—and interested in exploring a set of emotions I've never felt—I return my eyes to Dexter. The tick in his jaw lessens when I start to unhook my bra.

As one arm lowers the dowdy scrap of material to the floor, the other maintains my modesty.

I don't know why I bothered. The instant my bra hits the dusty floorboards, Dexter curls his arms around my back and drags me toward his thick, bumpy body. His steps to the bed seem long and drawn out as if he wants to keep me in his arms forever.

Disturbed by my inaccurate assessment of the situation, my eyes stray to the pill bottle on the floor. I really should take my medication as the thoughts streaming through my head don't belong to a sane woman.

I love Nick.

My heart belongs to him.

So why am I hoping Dexter will keep me forever?

8

DEXTER

*W*hen my hand darts up to switch off the drill pounding my skull into the next century, a soft moan makes me freeze midair. Against better judgment, I snap my eyes open. Mousy brown hair is fanned across my chest, and a cushiony ass is nestling my stiffened shaft.

Pain flies through my body when I scoot backward, lost and confused as fuck.

Where the hell am I? And how the fuck did I get here?

It takes me several minutes of scanning the dingy space to gather my bearings. I'm in a cabin my dad uses for hunting.

Not the hunting you're thinking, but that's a story for another day.

You're probably also thinking, *How convenient you happen to own a cabin a few miles from the psych hospital where you were admitted.*

Once again, it's not what you're thinking.

My father owns many cabins, more than four in each state. When you hunt as regularly as he does, you take advantage of any location you can get. The closer, the better. That means his arsenal of properties is well into the thousands. Not all of them are as rundown as this cabin, but he doesn't need comfort for what he is doing. He needs seclusion.

Ignoring the throb shooting through my back, demanding I remain still, I slowly rise to my feet. The world spins around me as the contents in my stomach threaten to spill at any moment.

While tugging on a pair of discarded pants dumped near the bed, my eyes drift to my sleeping companion. The scent of her hair already gives away who she is, but the impish thoughts drifting through my mind triple its guarantee. Even with my brain back to standard working order, my cock still wants to sink into Claudia's heat.

Or should I say, "Wants to sink into Claudia's heat *again*?"

Did we fuck? Is that why I'm so sore?

To say my mind is hazy would be an understatement. I have no clue what happened last night. I assume since I'm sleeping in my dad's cabin that Claudia and I escaped Meadow Fields, but how we got here and why we're naked are complete blanks. The last thing I recall is biting Lee. I assume that's why my mouth tastes like garbage?

My confusion deepens when my eyes stop tracing Claudia's curves at the lower half of her body. She's wearing panties. If we had fucked, they'd be shredded on the floor like her dress. I don't like panties. They represent the very essence of why I hunted with my father.

I love the smell of a woman's cunt. It is as enticing to me as the scent of her blood. Even now, though doubtful her near-unconscious state is from me fucking her brains out, I can smell Claudia's seductive scent. It's as alluring as the aroma of fresh blood filtering through the air.

When I cast my gaze down, I discover the cause for the cock-thickening scent. A t-shirt is crumpled at the side of the bed. It's the same style all the male patients at Meadow Fields wear, it just has an added accessory. A large circular hole in the bottom left-hand corner surrounded by a ring of blood.

What the fuck?

I take off for the attached bathroom, my body screaming in pain with every step I take. After clearing away the gunk from the mirror with my hand, I twist around to face the cracked shower stall at the back of the dingy space.

Fuck it. I'm too short to see the area throbbing in pain.

After throwing down the filthy toilet lid with my foot, I balance on the seat's rim. This is no easy feat with how woozy my head is, but it gives me enough leeway to view a line of stitches in the lower quadrant of my back. If I had to guess, I'd say fifteen to twenty butterfly knots are holding together a recent bullet wound.

I jump down from the toilet, hoping a few minutes of silence will ease my confusion.

All it gives me is a truckload of pain.

I'm the most lost I've ever been, and I am also in the most pain.

Did Claudia shoot me? If so, why stitch me up? I couldn't have been shot by a guard. Otherwise, how did I get to my cabin? It's miles away from Meadow Fields. Claudia is a little firecracker with more gusto than her demure mousy composure displays, but she struggled carrying two logs of wood last night. She'd never manage a man of my height and frame.

I freeze, stunned. That was a memory. It was as worthless as a stripper who doesn't give extra services when you hand her a hundred, but a memory all the same.

Realizing only one person can give me answers, I charge back to the main area of the cabin. My steps aren't as thunderous as my earlier ones, weighed down with both confusion and pain.

Claudia rouses when the mattress dips under my frame, but

she remains asleep. Even with her back facing me, I can tell her chest is rising and falling in rhythm with mine. I'd even go as far as saying her breaths are just as regular. Her hair is tousled from a restless night, and her face is void of makeup. She looks peaceful. So much so, I almost feel bad sneaking a peek at her breasts.

For a lady with a fucked-up head, she has a nice rack. Her rosy-pink nipples sit high on her chest, as puckered and inviting as her ruddy lips. She's more attractive out of her clothes than she is in them. I'm not surprised. Lee didn't have her on his radar for no reason. Her tempting body was the second thing I noticed after her virtuous eyes and face. Her fantastic tits were most likely the first thing Lee noticed.

I remain rooted in place for the second time when another memory breaks through the fog in my head. It's of Lee and his soulless eyes. Not the lifeless ones he generally carries.

Soulless—*soulless.*

As in dead.

I killed him.

He's dead because of me.

Damn—my morning just got ten times better.

Desperate to feed off a surge of adrenaline and eagerness to get back to the game I started years ago, I snag a set of keys from a canister in the makeshift kitchen then exit the cabin.

I like Claudia—my fingers itch to corrupt her curvy frame—but she's all types of fucked-up, and I've got business to take care of.

Business that doesn't include bedding a psychotic woman.

THE GLEAMING grin I've been wearing since my Pontiac GTO kicked over at the first turn of the keys thirty minutes ago turns blinding when the radio switches to a news broadcast. I'm not just grinning at the report that two long-serving guards at a penitentiary for the criminally insane were killed last night. It's knowing my dad is still at the top of his game.

I've been locked up so long, my GTO's battery should have died years ago. The fact it started on the first try proves he's still playing the game he taught me the day of my sixth birthday.

I didn't get a toy truck or any other gift you'd expect a normal child to receive. I was given an invitation to an exclusive club, a club so secretive only the founder knows each member's name— my father.

I'm not going to lie. I pissed my pants when I spotted their target for the day. The girl was young, around my mom's age when she had me—approximately sixteen. The welts on her body and face were so disfiguring, the only thing I can recall about her now is the scent of her blood.

Although I did the occasional hunt with my dad in my teens, my interests did a one-eighty when Shelley entered the equation. My dad was disappointed, but he understood. He didn't have much choice. He had done the same thing with my mother. She was supposed to be his victim, not occupy his bed.

I don't know if my father altered the rules because my mother's stomach was swollen with me or because he had an instant connection with her like I had with both Shelley and Cleo. But whatever it was, I'm certain it was fate.

He raised me as if I were his own flesh and blood. His parenting methods were unheard of by the many doctors my mother had probe my head in my early teens, but I wouldn't be the man I am today if it weren't for my father.

For that alone, I'll be forever in his debt.

My mind drifts from fond memories when the radio crackles, announcing a news bulletin. "Police are on the lookout for three patients who escaped Meadow Fields Penitentiary for the Criminally Insane last night. Dexter Elias, Claudia Sanchez, and Ashlee Vought are considered armed and dangerous. Extreme discretion is advised before approaching the assailants."

"Three?" The rest of my curiosity comes out in a groan.

Claudia's escape makes sense. I played the game right. But Ashlee? I'm at a loss.

From the pieces of my memory I've stitched together the past thirty minutes, I'm confident Claudia was with me during my escape, but Ashlee hasn't come up once in my endeavor to clear the fog from my mind.

We interacted a few times when I strategized a way to put my game plan into play, but I never clued her in on my plans to escape. As far as she was aware, my interest in Claudia was purely to bed her. Hearing Ashlee escaped with me is more shocking than waking up with a sleeping Claudia in my arms.

Snickering at my stupidity of being lumped with two loons, I continue my trip. I make it another forty miles before I have to pull over to pump gas. My father's staff kept my battery charged, but they weren't as courteous with the gas tank.

With police two counties over seeking Dexter Elias, I secure one of three wallets in my glove compartment before clambering out of my car. The gas stations have drastically improved from what they once were. I can watch the news broadcast of my escape on a small television in the pump while my gas guzzler's tank is replenished.

Every image of Lee and Bryce flashing across the screen spikes my pulse. I don't feel remorse when the broadcast shows their blubbering families. They should thank me. I saved them from a life of misery by taking out their trash. Once the dust settles, I'm sure they'll understand that.

After filling the tank to the brim, I head to the restroom inside the gas station. All their money must have been spent on the fancy gas pumps as their washrooms aren't up to standards. They're dingy and old, nearly as rundown as the cabin I left over an hour ago.

While taking a leak, my mind wanders to Claudia. Not because she bores the piss out of me, but because I can smell her on my cock. My mind is still hazy, but it's clear enough for me to remember what happened last night. We didn't fuck. We snuggled.

Just the thought has my cock wilting in my hand.

I don't spoon. Come to think of it, I've never slept in the same bed as a girl. I hurt her, fuck her, then leave. I don't do sleepovers. I didn't even break the rules with Shelley and Cleo. Don't get me wrong. I watched them sleep. I just never slept over. That's entirely different.

Claudia is still on my mind when I stomp past an ancient computer advertising a minute of internet usage for a quarter. Although I want to pretend I'm feeding coins into the meter as a means to track down Cleo, the article Ashlee gave me last month ensures I know which direction to head.

Marcus didn't just upend my chessboard when he joined my four-year game with Cleo. He upended Cleo's entire life. She's no longer a resident of Montclair, New Jersey. She is a shiny new citizen of Ravenshoe.

I wonder if the mayor of that nondescript town knows the vile man it raised in its carcass.

As I wait for the wired connection to find a match on Claudia Sanchez nee Brown, I slouch in my chair. I'm not tracking down Claudia's info to finish what we didn't start last night. I'm merely curing weeks of confusion.

I hate that I can't read Claudia, but secretly, I also love it. It kept things interesting the past two months, which is a task in itself when you're locked in a mental asylum. Easing my curiosity will make the transition to the next phase of my game plan a lot easier. It has nothing to do with Claudia's fruity smell on my skin.

Nothing.

At.

All.

Ignoring the recurring denial echoing between my ears, I lean in close to the monitor. It's blank. I'm not talking I'm-a-seventy-year-old-geriatric-who-doesn't-know-his-way-around-a-computer blank. It is blank, Claudia-isn't-who-she-says-she-is blank.

I take a few moments to ponder my next move. If I were half the man I was before being locked in a mental asylum, I'd leave this gas station and continue my quest for revenge. But since I am as inquisitive as I am determined, I search a different subject.

Nicholas Holt brings up more information than a standard Google search. Thousands of paparazzi pictures of him and his bandmates, an extensive list of musical accomplishments, and one lonely request for a restraining order against a woman named Megan Shroud is presented before me.

"Megan Shroud? Who the fuck are you?"

My fingers fly wildly over the keyboard when I replace Nick's name with Megan's. It brings up the standard stuff you'd expect to find. A driver's license, a dated Myspace page, and a handful of old photos every school nerd uploads when preparing for a class reunion. But it's the stuff behind the search I'm the most interested in, the stuff I'm certain is the cause for Claudia's mute state.

Claudia Sanchez is Megan Shroud. If her dazzling hazel eyes and heart-shaped face weren't already telltale signs, the hairline crack in Claudia's front tooth when she smiles is a surefire indication. Megan's photos display she had a cracked front tooth. It is in the exact spot Claudia's tooth has been patched. They are the same person. I'm certain of it.

The only thing I can't fathom is why Megan's family admitted her to psychiatric care under an alias? My family ties must remain obscure since my father's last name is infamous, but that can't be the reason Megan's family hid her identity. She is from some bum-hick town in the middle of nowhere, so what secrets could she be possibly hiding?

Deciding there's only one way to satisfy my curiosity, I sign out of the general public search forum and log into a more secure one. This one isn't accessible to the general public. I have to perform numerous magic tricks just to ensure my search will be unde-tectable, and I'm a genius at this shit.

This search is a lot more interesting. Megan Shroud is twenty-eight. She's been missing for over five years—presumed dead. My lips twist in surprise when I discover a man is currently serving life for her murder in a state penitentiary not too far from here. Her mother's name and identification are not listed on any records, and her father has been deceased longer than Megan's been missing.

"Are you fucking kidding me?"

I scoot in closer to the screen, certain what I am reading is wrong.

Megan Shroud killed her father.

The coroner's report states he was poisoned over a twelve-month period. That wasn't the cause of his demise, though. He was strangled to death before being hung from a beam in his barn. By the time local authorities were alerted to his death, his body was well on the way to decomposition.

During preliminary investigations, police discovered a second body. This person was also murdered, albeit years earlier. She was a female—believed to be in her late twenties and a mother.

As my brain struggles to sort through the facts, I slump into my chair. I don't know what detail to work through first. The fact

Claudia... *or should I call her Megan?*... is an orphan, or that she is a murderer?

No matter how many ways I look at it, the facts never alter. The arrest warrant must be wrong. Claudia has seductive curves, but she is tiny. There's no way she could have hung her father. She wouldn't have been able to lift him when he was alive, much less dead. Trust me, people are heaviest when they're lifeless.

The image of Claudia lugging a man up rickety stairs makes my tenth memory of the day smack into me. This one is so vivid it launches me onto my feet.

Claudia carried me! She fucking carried me on her back for over two miles.

I fall back into my chair with a thump as memories of last night steamroll into me. I didn't kill Bryce. Claudia did. She hit him with a shovel, her smile brightening before her second hit. Then she dug the bullet out of my back and stitched me up before protesting about my proposal for us to sleep naked to keep warm.

She kicked and screamed for several minutes when my stiffened shaft pressed against her ass. When I told her to stay still or I'll fuck her to death, she took my warning literally.

It was for the best because I wasn't joking.

The more I read Megan's police record, the faster my heart gallops. How did I not see this earlier? Claudia's not psychotic. She isn't even fucked in the head. She's a female version of me.

She is inhumane.

Determined.

Un-fucking-scrupulous.

She wasn't just my ticket out of Meadow Fields. She is the bullet, and I am the gun.

Together—we *will* be unstoppable.

Don't misunderstand, though. Claudia is still a woman, which means she'll always be below me, but she doesn't need me as a reward. She needs *him*.

I lower my eyes to the monitor displaying pictures of Megan's childhood bedroom. Every inch of the pale white walls is covered with photos of one man, proving Claudia isn't obsessed with Nicholas Holt. She wants to own him.

I'm going to give him to her, and in the process of doing that, I'll distract Marcus from my true endeavor. It's a win-win for all involved. Claudia gets her man. I get revenge... *and Marcus gets what's coming to him.*

Slowly, very, *very* slowly, I type a string of text into the Google search bar. It's the exact set of words every FBI agent from here to Ravenshoe will be searching for. But instead of directing them at Marcus as I have in the past, I direct them to Jenni—Nick Holt's wife.

By dangling a carrot to their right, they'll fail to notice me sneaking up on the left.

What did I tell you?

I'm fucking brilliant.

9

CLAUDIA... OR IS IT MEGAN?

*W*hen a door's creak sounds through my ears, I stop raking my fingers through my hair. My spine snaps straight as a hiss rolls up my chest in warning to my intruder. I really hope my guest isn't one of the many rodents I've heard scuttling in the bushes the past six hours.

After being forced to sleep with Dexter, I never expected to wake up alone. I was so taken aback I searched the cabin top to bottom. There wasn't much floor space to explore, but my examination was thorough enough to gobble up an hour of my time.

Not a shred of evidence was found to corroborate my claims I escaped Meadow Fields with Dexter. Even the blood-soaked shirt I left on the floor last night was gone. The vacant cabin left me with nothing but confusion and a mismatched set of lingerie.

I also have my pill bottle, but with the water from the bathroom tap as sludgy as my heart, I skipped my third dose in a row.

Perhaps that's the reason I don't feel guilty for sleeping with Dexter? I can't be expected to apologize for something I was forced to do.

But in all honesty, even if I weren't coerced, I still don't believe Nick deserves an apology. He slept in Jenni's bed multiple times during our relationship, yet I still found it in my heart to forgive him, so why can't he do the same thing for me?

Additionally, I like what Dexter and I did last night. He didn't hurt me. His big, protective body curled around mine made me feel safe and protected like he'd never let anything happen to me.

It's been an incredibly long time since I've felt safe. It was around the age of six or seven. With every year in a mental hospital the equivalent of five in the real world, it's also been an extremely long time since I've slept like a baby. I doubt I slept like one even when I was one.

Gratitude for a restful night's sleep flies out the window when I discover the cause of the creak. Dexter is entering the cabin. His sneer is as muddy as his sludge-covered boots. I don't know why he's glowering at me. I'm not as presentable as I was yesterday, but for what I lack in glam, his cabin certainly makes up for.

Despite my moodiness, I've spent the past five hours cleaning. On the outside, the cabin is still rundown and dated, but its insides are sparkling like the shiners my dad inflicted on my cheeks monthly. It's not as pretty as the country estate where I grew up, but it is a hell of a lot better than it was.

I wouldn't say I'm anal about cleanliness. It just saves my sanity. It was a tedious task to get this cabin presentable, but it was a great distraction from my depraved thoughts. Not all my deliberations centered around my dad and Nick. Many included Dexter as well.

When Dexter stalks across the room, I watch him through a sheet of hair that has fallen in my face. He isn't wearing the same clothes he had on last night. His blood-stained shirt has been swapped for a light gray undershirt and a black leather jacket. A pair of dark jeans hides the enticing visual I spent half my night striving to ignore. With his nearly black hair combed away from his face, his defined cheekbones are mesmerizing, and his blue eyes pop right off his face. He looks appealing in a sleek, bad-boy type of way.

Actually, come to think of it, he reminds me a lot of Noah, the lead singer of Nick's band.

After dumping a handful of bags onto the now glistening two-seater dinette table, he pivots around to face me. The panicked skitter my heart got when he arrived breaks into a sprint when his eyes land on mine. They're carrying the same hunger they held last night, but something in them has changed. They are less murky like he's pleased to see me.

I shouldn't be tickled pink by the idea, but I am.

"*Ugh!*" I grunt when he seizes my wrist in a firm grip to yank me to my feet. I'm not angry at him. I am more confused than anything.

When I woke alone, I was fuming mad, but the bags he arrived with reveal his time away was well spent. I just wish he had left a note, or better yet, taken me with him. I guess that would have been hard to do since he shredded my dress to beyond an inch of recognition.

A dusting of dark hair falls into Dexter's bright blue eye when he slants his head to the side. "Miss me?" he asks, his tone facetious.

I shouldn't nod, but I do. I did miss him. I don't know why but lying won't alter the facts.

Dexter blinks two times as if stunned by my reply.

Was he expecting me to say no?

With the smile of an evil man, he replies, "Then how about I fix the injustice?"

Not giving me the chance to seek clarification, his hands drop to the elastic of my panties. A daring gleam in his eyes makes me slap his chest before witnessing the consequence of my resistance. I get in three good whacks before a flash of silver stops me. Dexter has flipped open a switchblade razor. Even without it touching any part of my body, I know from experience how sharp it is, and the remembrance ensures my compliance.

Dexter protects my skin from being nicked by the razor before dragging the blade down the cotton maintaining my modesty. The material falls away from my body even more freely than my dress did last night. My bra is removed just as swiftly.

Both items puddle at my feet, giving me more freedom than I expected. I thought I'd be fuming with anger, but all I am feeling is euphoria. That probably has something to do with the look Dexter is giving me. I've never been awarded a look like this before. It's an odd stare like he equally detests and loves me.

He's most likely mirroring the image I am giving him because right now, I'm torn between wanting to slap him and kiss him.

What?

My eyes stray to Dexter's bags of goodies, hoping he purchased water during his visit to the store. If I don't take my medication soon, I'll start believing the ideas in my head are logical and that I should act on them. I like that my mind isn't as woozy as it's been the past decade, but the thoughts I am having can't be sane.

I've only ever cared for two people in my life. Both betrayed me. I can't open myself up to the carnage a third time. I've barely survived the past five years. I doubt my heart can sustain more injuries.

Dexter's eyes stop absorbing my body when they land on my sandal-covered feet. My shoes are modest—thank God. After my effort last night, the blisters on my feet are the size of a small country, so imagine the massacre if I had worn fancy heels?

With a mocking roll of his eyes, Dexter returns his narrowed gaze to mine. "You need to shower. You smell."

His comment knocks the wind from my lungs. From the pleasant glint in his eyes, I was anticipating a compliment, not a scolding.

When he pushes off his feet, I gather my undergarments in my hand, drop them into the trash can, then follow him. By the time I stop at his side, he has removed two pairs of panties—if you can call these mere scraps of material panties—a plain white shirt and a three-pack of socks from a Nordstrom bag.

I lift my eyes from the clothing to him, wordlessly asking if they're mine. When he nods, I snatch them up and hold them to my chest, hoping to maintain a semblance of modesty.

"I don't know if this is the right stuff, but it smelled like you, so I figured it would do." He dumps my favorite duo of hair products onto the stack of clothes I'm balancing.

Even naked and unsure what the hell is happening, I can't stop my smile from stretching across my face. He's pretending he is mad, but it's all an act. The fact he sniffed shampoo to match it with my scent reveals his cranky demeanor is a ploy.

He likes me. He is just confused as to why.

He isn't the only one who is confused. The instant he handed me bottles of fruity shampoo, my desire to kiss him overtook my wish to slap him.

I'm drawn from my wicked thoughts when Dexter says my name. I'm not talking about the standard name every doctor in the state has called me for the past five years. I'm talking about my Christian name—the one I was given at birth. He called me Megan.

"It is Megan, isn't it?" Dexter confirms, unsure if my gapped mouth stems from confusion or shock.

Tears blur my vision as I nod. I argued with the doctors for months that my name wasn't Claudia, but no matter how many times I told them Megan wasn't 'a figment of my imagination' or 'one of my multiple personalities,' they never believed me.

I stare into Dexter's eyes, praying he will see the words I can't express. *My name is Megan Shroud. I am twenty-eight years old. Before I was put to sleep by a scary man with large hands, I resided in a small, rural town over four hundred miles from my true love. I didn't do the things the doctors said I did. I've done other things*—many terrible things—*but I'm a good person.*

Well, I was. Now I'm not so sure.

The thoughts I've had about Dexter the past few weeks can't be healthy, but it's better than not having any feelings at all.

In an uncharacteristic way, Dexter curls his hand around my quivering jaw to clear away the moisture slipping down my face. My cheeks burn in shame when I stupidly nuzzle into his embrace. Something flares brightly in his eyes. I don't know him well enough to identify what it is.

"Would you like me to call you Megan?"

To ensure I don't lose his touch, I faintly nod.

"Okay. I can do that for you." His voice is higher than normal, kind of husky.

The unidentifiable spark in his eyes gains intensity when he drags his thumb along my lower lip. The look on his face is foreign, but it rips a fire through my mind, burning up everything I thought was true and leaving nothing but ash in its place.

"Do you want me to kiss you, Megan?"

His velvety tone seduces me so well, I nod without thinking.

My heart skids to a stop when his soft and inviting mouth inches toward mine. I should pull away. I should grunt for him to stop. But all I do is remain frozen, in a trance, somewhat excited and somewhat scared.

My last thought is appropriate when our kiss ends up nothing like I expected. Dexter doesn't devour my mouth in slow, tantalizing licks and sucks. He sinks his teeth into my lower lip, biting it so painfully, blood tingles my taste buds.

Before I can register the shock of being bitten—not just the callousness behind it but the flooding of warmth it caused between my legs—Dexter swipes his purchases off the table, arches me over the wobbly material, spreads my feet to the width of my shoulders with a tap of his boots, then places a firm whack on my ungodly region.

Now I understand why my daddy said vaginas are the reason women turn into whores. Dexter's slap is painful but in an erotic I-can't-help-but-meow-like-a-kitty way.

"Don't ever look at me like you did, Megan. Do you understand? If you ever look at me like that again, I'll do more than punish you with my hands. I'm the monster hiding in the shadows. The bad man waiting for you in the alley. The reason fathers lock away their daughters. I am not a man you glance at with adoration!"

He slaps the aching slit between my legs another four times, his strikes gaining intensity with each blow. "This is just a taste of what you'll get if you *ever* look at me like that again. I am not your savior, Megan. I'm your worst nightmare."

After a final whack, he returns me to a standing position, which is virtually impossible with how hard my legs are shaking. Sweat mists my nape when my wide-with-excitement eyes lock with his. That shouldn't have been enjoyable, but it was. Very much so.

Dexter's eyes narrow when he spots the thrill in mine. When a furious growl rumbles up his chest, I wipe the animated expression from my face in less than a nanosecond. Nothing can eradicate my inflamed cheeks, though. I've never been touched like that. I don't mean the roughness of his caress. I mean where he touched me. Only one person has had their hands *down there*. It was a doctor who wanted to confirm I was pregnant with Nick's baby.

My mood shifts from happy to anguished faster than I can snap my fingers. I don't know what that doctor did, but my baby with Nick was never born.

I stop tiptoeing into a dark and lonely place when Dexter says, "While you're in the shower, take care of that." His eyes drop to a patch of curly hairs spread across my genital region.

Confusion slashes my features when he shoves a canister of shaving cream into my chest. It is closely followed by the blade he used to undress me.

He can't be serious, can he? Why would I shave my pubic hair? It wouldn't grow there if it wasn't meant to be there.

"Hurry up, Megan. We haven't got all day," Dexter barks when I remain standing at his side, silenced by stupidity. "The quicker you do this, the sooner you'll see Nick."

That's all it takes to get my legs moving.

I race into the bathroom, my steps as spirited as my hope. It's been years since I've seen Nick, but I'm confident the moment I lay my eyes on him, the stupid, irrational thoughts I've had about Dexter the past six weeks will vanish in an instant.

I hope.

Maybe.

10

MEGAN

A raspy groan rolls up my chest. I've washed my hair and pampered my skin with the luxury body wash Dexter handed me when he entered the bathroom to 'supervise' my progress, but no matter how hard I've fought to control the hazardous conditions between my legs, the situation has worsened.

On Dexter's advice, I went for a smooth edge, grassy inland cut. Instead of my pubic region replicating an island in the middle of paradise, it resembled an out-of-control jungle in the Bermuda Triangle.

Believing I could make it better, Dexter suggested I trim it into an even strip.

That only made matters ten times worse.

I know what the issue is. I'm so afraid of cutting myself, I'm mowing the edges instead of removing the weeds altogether.

With a shrug, I exit the bathroom. I can't be expected to perform miracles when I have no clue what I'm doing. My lazy strides come to a stop when the heat of a gaze freezes me in place.

Dexter is sitting on the edge of his bed. His jaw is ticking, and his icy blue eyes are arrested on my bare legs. Since the shirt he purchased is two sizes too big, I've twisted it into a knot in the middle of my stomach. Match that with knee-high socks and a pair of scant panties, and I've got what Ashlee likes to call the naughty- schoolgirl look down pat.

She warned me against it, said men are more violent when they think you're innocent, but with my sexual experience made up of two kisses and a heavy penis braced on my backside for ten hours straight, I can't help but display virtue.

Dexter's eyes come up to mine. "Come here," he demands with a jerk of his chin.

I go without a thought crossing my mind. I wouldn't if he were the one clutching a razor blade in his hand. Since the shoe is on the other foot, I want to find out if he sees me as an enemy or an ally. Threat is a great way to discover whose team someone is on, so how about we find out?

Dexter sweats—just not in the way I anticipated. Beads of moisture mottle his dark brows, but I'm certain the sweat is not from fear. Even though he was a stranger weeks ago, I'm confident in my assumption. His eyes divulge many secrets, let alone the rapid rise of a sinfully wicked region of his body.

"Let me see." Just like he didn't seek permission before entering the bathroom, he doesn't wait for approval before slipping my panties to the side. "Hmm." His throaty purr rumbles through the area he is inspecting. "It's still not right. We're not in the seventies. Bush went out long before your mother died."

I freeze as horror shreds through me.

I still can't think about her without tears looming in my eyes.

Dexter takes advantage of my frozen state to snatch the razor from my grip and flop me onto the bed. With my emotions fixated on the last time I saw my mother, I don't protest him sliding my panties down my thighs. His closeness enabled me to sleep an entire night without a nightmare, so who's to say his touch won't be just as effective at dispelling negative thoughts?

I'm so busy calming my spiking pulse, I fail to notice Dexter exiting and re-entering the room until the slickness of shaving cream smothers the heated region between my legs. I prop myself on my elbows, equally mortified and in awe. His touch is gentle, but the spasms it sends rocketing up my spine are as violent as the devil.

"I knew I wouldn't need water," Dexter murmurs under his breath.

He dips his head to press a toothy kiss to my thigh before scooting closer to the area suddenly throbbing in agony.

"Keep those thoughts in your head, Megan," he warns. "Or your mouth won't be the only section of your body feeling my bite today."

I peer down at him, wondering how he heard my thoughts when he wasn't looking at me.

Upon feeling the heat of my gawk, he raises his eyes to mine. "You're wet," he informs me like it should answer all my questions.

It doesn't.

Not in the slightest.

But he continues chipping away at my confusion. "And your clit is pulsating with need."

I'd press my thighs together to ease the ache his raspy tone caused if his thick body wasn't lodged between them.

A knot low in my belly tightens when he growls, "Once we've dealt with this mess, I won't need to see your cunt to know it's dripping."

After snickering at my hanging jaw, he gets back to work. The strokes of his fingers are more probing than his earlier ones. Once my vagina is covered with a generous helping of cream, he flicks open the razor and commences shaving me. He glides the blade over the patch of hair at the top of my pubic region before tracing it down the edge.

"Stay still," he warns when my legs wobble from the heat of his breath fanning the slippery surface. "I don't want to nick you... *yet*."

Now I'm shaking in fear. The razor-sharp blade is butted against an extremely delicate area of my body. Only the clinically insane wouldn't panic.

I freeze as morbid fear makes itself known. I was diagnosed as mentally unstable at the age of twelve, so the last emotion I should be sensitive to is panic.

When Dexter feels my balk, he raises his eyes from my hack job to my face. They're as dark as death, his pupils so wide they're swamping his entrancing baby blues with pits of black. "Did I cut you?"

I glare at him, shocked by the hope in his voice.

Does he want to cut me?

When he raises a brow, demanding I answer him, I briskly shake my head.

"Hmm... pity. I would have lapped up the blood if I did. It is, after all, the right thing to do." His deep timbre vibrates through the area he is shaving, adding to the wetness.

Dexter continues shaving me for the next several minutes. Sometimes he gets right up close to ensure he doesn't miss any areas hidden by tiny folds and crevices. Other times, he leans so far back, the long rod in his jeans becomes exposed.

His attention amplifies the pleasing zap shooting up my spine, and his occasional glances into my eyes make my stomach knot tighter, but not once does he nick me.

After a few more minutes, he pats the silky-smooth surface three times with a washcloth, then rises to a half-seated position.

"Done." His eyes stray to mine. They're more effervescent than ever. "Want to take a look?"

I nod a little overeagerly. If the visual is as wondrous as his eyes are portraying, I don't want to miss out. Anyone would swear he was gawking at a rare eclipse for how dilated his pupils are.

"Wait," Dexter demands when I attempt to scoot off the bed. "I'll bring the mirror to you, then you can view it how I see it."

He rolls off the bed before heading to the bathroom. My pulse pounds in my ears when the shattering of glass bellows into the room not even two seconds later. I would check on him, but he told me to wait, so I must wait.

When he re-enters the room, he is clutching a shard of glass in his blood-soaked hand. The hunger in his eyes is as notable as earlier, but there is a dangerous edge to it now. I should be wary. I should be scared, but all I am is turned on.

Dexter is a big, moody man, carrying a dangerous weapon and an even more hazardous smile, and I am without medication. My response is highly accurate.

My thighs spread wider when Dexter pierces the shard of glass into the mattress a mere inch in front of my aching vagina. I shoot my eyes up to him before dropping them back to the thought-provoking visual.

Is that what it's supposed to look like?

It's bald, void of a single hair.

"Do you like what you see, Megan?" Dexter's long drawl of my name returns my focus to him.

My lips twist as I pause for thought. It looks okay, but it's *very* exposing. There's nothing to hide the wetness. The folds of skin rippled down the middle glisten like Dexter's eyes when he takes in the same visual.

After a few moments of silent deliberation, I give a half-hearted shrug, truly unsure.

"It will grow on you," he assures me before removing the mirror wedged between my legs and tossing it into the fireplace.

I sit up with the hope of finding my panties. I've barely risen to a half-seated position when a click sounds through my ears. I glare at Dexter, certain he is where the noise originated from.

A jeering smile spreads across his face as he glances down at the sleek black cell phone in his hand. "What do you think? Too risqué? Or tastefully seductive?" He spins the device around to show me. A picture of me is on the screen. Although the area he shaved is on display, it's partially hidden by my clamped thighs. "I think it'll work. Let's send it, shall we?"

I dive for his state-of-the-art phone when a swoosh ricochets through the dead-silent cabin. I don't want my photo on the internet for the world to see, especially not a partially naked one. If I still had my pubic hair, it wouldn't be as demoralizing, but if they zoom in, they'll see every inch of my ungodly region.

"Whoa, hey, settle the fuck down!" Dexter roars when my frantic lunge knocks his phone out of his hand.

While pinning me to the bed by my throat with one hand, his other darts down to grab his phone from the floor. I'm afraid he'll squeeze my neck until I pass out when I spot the hairline cracks my violence caused his screen. It was as smooth as my vagina ten seconds ago.

When Dexter's furious eyes snap to mine, I swallow harshly. "Why did you do that? I'm trying to fuckin' help you!"

I want to respond, but even if I weren't mute, I wouldn't be able to. His clutch on my throat is too firm. So instead, I use my eyes and a windless grunt. *I don't want anyone to see that.*

"If I don't send Nick proof of your existence, he won't know you're alive. If he doesn't know you're alive, he won't expect you. You want him to be prepared, don't you, Megan? You want him to welcome you home with open arms."

The vicious growl of his last sentence freezes my lungs as effectively as his clutch on my throat. I stop prying at his fingers so I can answer his question by asking one of my own. *You sent the photo to Nick?*

"Yeah, I did," Dexter answers, proving he can read me like no other. "But now I wish I didn't. Maybe I should have upped the ante? Sent him one with my hand wrapped around your throat... or perhaps my tongue in your mouth." He leans in closer, bringing his lips to within an inch of mine. I lick them, still feeling the sting of our last foray. "Or maybe I should send him one of your greedy little cunt swallowing my cock. Would you prefer that, Megan? Do you want him to see how wet I make you?" He sucks in an exaggerated breath that makes my airless lungs envious. "I can smell how aroused you are, and I barely laid a finger on you."

A groan rolls up my chest when he loosens his grip on my neck. I'm not grunting in anticipation. I read the warning in his eyes. I know what is coming. He isn't going to violate me like Nick did to Jenni. He's releasing me from his hold, freeing me from the torment.

Leaving me hanging.

I'm snapped from my thoughts when Dexter's feet slap the floorboards. After securing a pair of tiny jeans from a discarded bag, he throws them at my head. "Put these one, then get in the car. We have a long trip ahead of us."

Gone is the man who devoured me whole using only his eyes, replaced by a man who looks like he wants to carve out my liver and eat it for dinner.

Remaining quiet, I yank on the skintight jeans. I hate his silence, but I have no way of ending it. I haven't uttered a syllable in such a long time, I'm beginning to wonder if I know how.

When Dexter spins around to gather the bags left on the floor, I sneakily close the razor and slide it into my jeans pocket. "You'll need more than a two-inch blade to take me down," he warns, startling me. After pivoting to face me head-on, he continues, "But I'll give you half a point for attempting to fight."

I run my thumb over the razor's blade. It's so sharp, I'm certain one nick to the artery pulsating in Dexter's throat would drop him to his knees. But for some reason unbeknownst to me, I didn't secure the razor to hurt him. I took it to protect him.

"There you go with that look again, Megan," Dexter half-growls, half-moans. "A little angel with a heart as black as death rushing in to save me." He helps me to my feet, his movements not as abrupt as earlier. "You already killed a man for me. You don't need to prove your devotion any more than that." He taps my bottom in the same manner my father did to my mother before things went sour, then exits the cabin. "If you're not in the car before me, find your own way to Ravenshoe."

Trusting his threat, I snag my medication off the floor and skirt past him before he's even halfway out the door.

11

DEXTER

*M*egan sits in silence the first four hundred miles. That isn't surprising considering she's mute, but she's not communicating in a non-verbal way either. She's mad at me. I can't fathom why? I'm traveling over twelve hundred miles to take her to the man she is obsessed with. I even made her presentable for him with fruity shampoo and a glistening snatch. She should be thanking me.

Megan is an attractive woman, but it's obvious she was raised by a man. She doesn't have a clue about seduction or how to make herself sexually appealing to the male eye. I guess that's why she is so naïve? No one has ever paid her any attention.

She wouldn't have an issue if she removed the psycho from her eyes and switched up her wardrobe occasionally.

Outside of her clothes... *fuck*. I don't have any words. I rarely use the term beautiful, but I would for Megan's body. I can still smell her seductive scent on my fingers. That's why I've been scrubbing my stubble so rampantly the past several hours. I want her scent embedded in my skin so deeply it will have no chance of being removed.

I grip my steering wheel tightly, annoyed at my train of thought. This isn't the first fucked-up one I've had today. It's not even the second.

I shouldn't be so hard on myself. It's been years since I've had a cunt presented before me like that, but even then, none smelled as amazing as Megan's. It was a little musky with a hint of spice. I'm certain it will taste as good as it looks and smells.

The restraint it took not to carve my name into her bare snatch was one of the biggest battles I've undertaken. I didn't just want to warn other men to back the fuck away. I was aspiring to discover if her blood smelled as erotic as her cunt. I should have done it. I should scare her to within an inch of her life, then maybe she'll stop peering at me from beneath lowered lashes.

Although, being denied her sneaky glances may agitate me more. I like her eyes on me and the way her teeth rake her lip when she peers at me like I'm a god. I can see she is confused, but for the most part, she's eager to submit.

I think.

I honestly don't know. This chick is messing with my head, fucking me over better than any medication I've swallowed. I'm getting edgy, which is bad. Bad shit happens when I let my brain run wild. That's how I got in this situation to begin with. I was so mesmerized watching the life in Cleo's eyes drain when I took care of her bastard child, I let my game plan get away from me.

First, Richard fucked everything up by choosing Cleo's life over his own. Then the undercover agent guarding Cleo's house was a tank who refused to go down. You'd think six bullets would have stopped him sounding the alarm, but no, that fucker didn't stay down even while carrying multiple bullet wounds. Next time

I'll aim for the wrinkled skin between his brow instead of watching his blood ooze from his stomach and spleen.

Megan's eyes dart to mine when I abruptly yank my GTO down a dusty driveway. The hotel parking lot I'm pulling into is the standard two-star joint you find on every highway between New York and Florida. It's dingy and cheap, making it the perfect location for me to realign the pieces of my chessboard.

If I don't center myself, I'll do something I will regret.

Revenge should be on the forefront of my mind, not wondering how loud Megan screams in ecstasy. The only good thing that has come from Megan's attention is how occupied she's keeping my mind. I can even say Marcus's name without my blood boiling. It still simmers, but it's nothing compared to the usual fury I feel.

What the fuck is this woman doing to me?

Maybe it is the drugs Lee gave me? He did hit me with a three-month supply in one night. Maybe I'm still tripping? It's unlikely, but I'm open to any possibilities, no matter how fucking whacked they are.

I need to get my dick sucked. That will clear up my confusion.

The stitches in my back niggle when I clamber out of my car in front of the motel's twenty-four-seven lobby. Megan remains seated, following the routine I enforced each time I stopped to pump gas or take a leak. The only time her ass lifted from its spot was when she used the bathroom one hundred miles into our trip. I made her pee in the bush. Not just because I'm an ass who was pissed she cracked my new phone, but because she has a highly recognizable face. It has occupied my dreams numerous times the past six weeks, and I've only ever seen her as a pawn to be used and discarded, so who's to say some random won't recall it? It has been flashing across news bulletins every hour on the dot for the past twelve hours.

Before throwing open the warped door, I lower a cap over my eyes. I can alter my face with a few days of stubble and a change in glare, but nothing can modify the scar above my left brow. I got it when my mother tried to drown me in the tub within hours of my birth. When my father wrenched me out of her arms to resuscitate me, my head smacked into the vanity.

The scar bothered me when I was a kid—more how I got it than its lightning strike design—but as I got older, my opinion of it changed. It reminds me why I am the man I am. It stops me from being weak and makes me strong. It is a constant reminder of how gods prosper and cowards cower.

That's why I'm still breathing, and my mother isn't.

Old gospel music crackles over a radio in sync with my wingtip boots when I cross the lobby's tiled floor. For how rundown this motel is outside, its insides are on the opposite end of the spectrum. The white tiles are so gleaming I see my lips move when I throw two Benjamin Franklins onto the counter and say, "Twin for the night."

My tone alone reveals I have no intention of signing the guest register, but in case it doesn't, I add an additional two one-hundred-dollar bills to the stack.

"Are you sure you want a twin? She's mighty fine-looking," replies a voice with a deep southern twang. "If you don't want her warming your sheets, perhaps you should send her my way. I won't even wash the sheets when she bleeds out. The scent of her blood will give me many peaceful nights."

I raise my eyes, bringing them level with the man standing behind the counter. He presents as a typical hotel clerk—rounded stomach and all—but the evil in his eyes exposes his true self. He is the vicar to the devil, a founding member of my father's club.

"Joseph." I lower my tone, playing the game as I've been taught.

Joseph, a man in his mid-sixties with a crooked smile and greasy hair, doesn't return my greeting. He's too busy drinking in every visible inch of Megan to formally invite me onto his playground.

He isn't called The Vicar for no reason. He was a priest before his love of hunting altered his perspective on good and evil. A lesser man would assume his oily hair is because he isn't taking care of himself. I know better. It isn't grease. It is sweat from ogling Megan. She is *exactly* his type—shy, demure, on the verge of pure.

"She's still in training." I take a step to my left, blocking Megan from Joseph's hopeful eyes. "You should have seen her when I caught her... so malnourished and weak. In a few weeks, she'll be good game. Perhaps then we can exchange digits?"

Joseph's lips purse before he nods. He is what the others like to call a capture-and-release hunter. He doesn't release his victims once the game is finalized, though. He takes them back to his dungeon, repairs their injuries, and releases them before once again capturing them.

His variation in rules means his kill count is paltry compared to my father's. At last calculation, he was only sitting at a measly fourteen victims.

Annoyed I've removed Megan from his radar, Joseph lifts his deadly black eyes to mine. "Bring her in. Give her something to eat. That will get her energy levels up."

I nod at his suggestion. I don't have any other choice. It's either accept his invitation or blow my cover that Megan isn't my target. If I announce she isn't mine, Joseph will claim her as his in less than a nanosecond. I don't know why, but that bothers the fuck out of me. Megan isn't mine, which I don't mind, but she isn't Joseph's either, which I find greatly pleasing.

"She will eat with us, but she will not thank you for the meal." Joseph's eyes snap to mine, the violence in them picking up. "She is not doing it to be rude. She's been summoned to silence as penance for an earlier wrongdoing." Because not all my reply is a lie, it presents as honest.

Joseph quivers, news of Megan's muteness enticing an unusual response from his body. "Come, bring her in. We will have Scarlett serve us." He slides a hotel key across the counter. "She is also in training. Perhaps you can take her for a spin after we eat?" His eyes expose a question his mouth failed to produce. *Then perhaps you'll consider sharing your new toy?*

His unspoken words have more impact than his spoken ones. It frees the chaos from my mind, finally allowing me to see things clearly. Megan isn't my pawn. She is a toy, a new plaything for me to explore. She isn't like the dolls I usually play with. She's more feisty—*more real.* She challenges me. Just the way she snuck the blade into her pocket earlier today proves this. She will be a fun way to occupy my mind until the *real* game begins.

"Yes?" Joseph verifies, interrupting me from my delicious thoughts.

Smiling to hide my sneer, I confirm, "Yes."

Mistaking my validation as agreement with his unspoken question, Joseph's eyes light up.

It is a foolish move on his behalf, one I plan to exploit.

───────

UNKNOWINGLY, Megan plays the part of a captive well. She bows her head when Joseph's slave serves her food and waits to eat until she is instructed. If I didn't know any better, I'd swear she has been enslaved before. She is nearly a spitting image of Scarlett—same light brown hair, bright hazel eyes, and sultry figure. The only difference is she sits at Joseph's side instead of at his feet as Joseph commands Scarlett.

Scarlett must be a few years into Joseph's game because she doesn't flinch at his sharp tone or cower when he raises his hand in anger. Megan is on the other end of the spectrum. She spends more time silently begging to be excused than she does consuming nutrients. She looks uncomfortable as if the razor in her pocket is weighing down her morals.

I really wish she would express herself freely. Joseph may be an acquaintance of my father's, but I don't owe him anything. If Megan wants to slit his throat because he inappropriately grabs her every time he thinks I'm not looking, she can. I won't hold it against her.

Joseph, on the other hand, needs to be reminded of the rules. Whether it is true or not, as far as anyone is concerned, Megan is mine, so Joseph has no right to touch her. Especially not directly in front of me.

I don't know if he is aware of my recent incarceration or he has forgotten who raised me, but his insolence cannot go unnoticed for a second longer.

After placing an empty glass of red wine on the cozy four-seater dining table Scarlett set up for our impromptu get-together, I tap a napkin at the Bolognese sauce in the corner of my mouth. The instant the stained napkin lands on my half-consumed meal, announcing I'm finished, Megan's eyes lift to mine. Her plea is more apparent than ever.

I suck in a deep breath, relishing the panic rising off her before asking, "Are you ready to call it a night?"

She nods before half the words leave my mouth. I'd scold her impatience if I didn't find it endearing. Her eyes have never been so wide, her scent more provocative. Precum has seeped into my jeans many times tonight from the frightened-lamb look she's given me. There's just one difference between her scared expression and the dolls I generally play with. She doesn't want Prince

Charming to ride in on a white horse and save her. She wants an imp on a stallion, a monster who will slay the dragon before drinking its blood. She wants a massacre, and that is precisely what I will give her.

"Go with Scarlett and grab your coat." My voice is husky with need and raw with desire.

Megan peers up at me, wordlessly announcing she didn't arrive with a jacket. I shouldn't love how easily I can read her, but I do.

"Go grab *my* coat then—"

"Scarlett, get the man his things!" Joseph roars, scaring the living hell out of Megan. She snaps to her feet in an instant, her body responding to his command before her brain can register it wasn't directed at her.

When Megan locks her wide eyes with mine, I nudge my head to the only exit, advising her to go with Scarlett. She is so eager to leave, she barges past Scarlett before sprinting down the dark corridor.

I wait for her pounding heart to stop ringing in my ears before swiveling my torso to face Joseph head-on. His eyes are planted in the direction Megan and Scarlett just went. If they held the same disdain they did every time Scarlett was in his presence, I could pretend he was eagerly awaiting her return. Unfortunately for all involved, I know what caused the crinkle to his top lip and the pungent aroma in the air. His eyes were locked on Megan's ass.

"You like her." I'm not asking a question. I am stating a fact. "Even though she is *mine,* you still want her beneath you." The violent roar of my words secures Joseph's utmost attention. His pupils widen as they dart between my wildly possessive eyes and the steak knife I am clutching so firmly the spiky blade digs into my palm. "Were you aware I could see what you were doing? Or did you not care you were disrespecting me?" Although my tone alludes to a question, Joseph doesn't answer me.

That agitates me more than anything.

"Answer me! Were you aware I could see your filthy hands touching her?"

"Yes," Joseph answers, his head bobbing up and down sardonically. "I knew you were watching."

My jaw clenches so firmly, my back molars grind together. "Yet you still did it? You must have a death wish."

He smiles a slick grin, proving he's remembering me as the six-year-old who peed his pants during his first hunt instead of the man who would hang his own flesh and blood with their intestines if they dared to disobey me.

His smile sags when my steak knife plucks his Adam's apple out of his throat. My stab, twist, and extract technique is precise and done without hesitation. Blood squirts from his inch-wide wound, spraying the four-course meal Scarlett prepared for us. Its coloring is a cross between the Bolognese sauce and the aromatic red wine we consumed. It is a beautiful mess—almost as intoxicating as the scent of Megan's skin when she is scared.

Mindful Scarlett might not be as welcoming to the carnage as Megan, I hand Joseph a napkin. His wheezing breaths when he removes his hand from his blood-smeared neck to accept my gesture is liquid gold to my ears. They are whispered apologies—penances for his sins, not just for me but for Megan as well.

He garbles out some words, but the gurgling of his blood in his esophagus drowns them out. I pat him on the back three times, advising him I don't need to hear his words to know what he is saying.

I'm sorry for disrespecting you. It will never happen again.

"It won't, will it? Not really your choice, though."

After standing from my chair, I lower my cap over my eyes. I'm not hiding my face from surveillance devices. Joseph would have taken care of them the instant he took over the rights of this property. I'm concealing Joseph's blood from my face. If Megan discovers I killed for her, it will even our playing field. It might possibly end our game before it truly begins. Considering my heart has never beaten in the rhythm it has tonight, that's the last thing I want to encourage.

Scarlett's hurried steps slow when she crosses the bridge between the dinette and the kitchen. My jacket falls from her hand when her eyes lock on Joseph's slumped frame. He's not dead—only halfway there. He will be soon enough. I simply didn't want to keep all the fun to myself.

After snatching my jacket from the floor, I stop to stand in front of Scarlett. Her massively dilated eyes bounce between mine when I remove her hand clamped over her mouth, then her breathing shallows when I place my bloody steak knife into her palm.

"Do with it as you wish." Her throat works hard to swallow as her bright eyes dim with blackness. "No matter what, he'll die in approximately two minutes anyway. Maybe thirty seconds with how hard he is wheezing."

Ignoring her dropped jaw and thankful eyes, I clamber onto the sidewalk in search of Megan.

12

MEGAN

"*I*s that why you killed your father? Because he touched you like Joseph did?"

I stop seeking a way to ease the sting of Joseph's chubby fingers on my thigh by shifting my focus to Dexter. He has been as quiet as me the past twenty minutes. I'm not giving him the cold shoulder. I was merely giving him time to calm the manic tick in his jaw.

He's mad. Rightfully so. His friend was kind enough to invite us for dinner, but instead of thanking him for the meal, I spent the two hours planning his demise. It is lucky Dexter announced I could leave when he did, or I may have done something very bad.

Joseph is not a nice man. He taunts his daughter, Scarlett, as badly as my father criticized me. No matter what she said or did, he treated her like scum. He even made her sit on the floor instead of joining us at the table. Seeing her degraded like that filled me with horrible memories.

Unfortunately, not all of them revolve around my father.

Perhaps if I hadn't skipped my medication, I may have responded differently to Joseph's overfriendliness, but with my mind the clearest it's ever been, all I felt was dirty when he continually touched me. The looks he gave me when his pinkie grazed my vagina through my jeans mimicked the ones Dexter used while shaving me, but not once did I get an enjoyable tingle. They made me feel like I am in desperate need of a shower and had me thinking recklessly.

That's why I bolted when Dexter gave me permission to leave.

It was either leave or stab my fork in Joseph's eye.

The crimp of my lips is pushed aside for a frown when Dexter growls, "Megan..." The vicious snarl of my name reminds me I failed to answer him.

I shake my head without pause for deliberation. My dad was a terrible man, but overzealous hands weren't the reason I killed him. He hurt my mom. If that wasn't bad enough, he was a giant obstacle when it came to my relationship with Nick. He said there was only one way I could return to Nick—over his dead body. I took his threat as literal.

Once it was done, I thought I would be free.

I had no clue there would be multiple challenges for me to face. Nick didn't want me. No matter what I said or did, he continually pushed me away. I thought he'd look at me with pride when I told him I had taken care of everything so we could be together. All he did was glare at me in disgust. He yelled at me and called me a liar before suggesting I 'take care' of our baby.

Although confused earlier, with my veins being weaned off medication, I remember what occurred to the baby I was having with Nick. I never had an abortion. The doctors said I was never pregnant, that I had a neurological psychosis that made me believe I was carrying Nick's baby when I wasn't.

I mourned our baby even though it never existed. It was the only part of Nick I truly owned, and it wasn't even real.

Bad memories stop playing havoc with my mind when Dexter asks, "Was it in retaliation for what happened to your mom?"

I peer up at him, surprised by his tone. He seems genuinely interested in discovering why I killed my father like it is more important than his next breath.

Is he shocked I'm a killer? Or worried I'm going to hurt him?

If he's worried, he doesn't need to be. I don't regret what happened to my father. I did what needed to be done, but murder isn't something I regularly attempt.

Well, it wasn't.

I didn't have a choice with Bryce. I either killed him, or he killed Dexter. Dexter is nice to me. Bryce wasn't. It made my decision so much easier.

When Dexter glares at me, frustrated by my lack of conversation, I half-shrug. His death can be attributed to both my mom and Nick, and if I am being honest, me also. As I said, my father was not a kind man.

"Hmm..." Dexter murmurs in a long drawl. "That's understandable. I had considered doing the same thing to my father when he killed my mother." He returns his eyes to the pitch-black sky, his face deadpan. "He loved her. She just wouldn't conform. First, she took me to a local shrink without his permission, then she poisoned our food with medication. At one stage, it felt like I was losing them both, so I guess it is better to lose one parent than be an orphan like you."

A grunt simpers through my mouth before I can stop it. I love that he's being open and honest with me, but I wish he could do it without the insults. Dexter has a hard, seemingly impenetrable shell, but deep down in a tiny crevice in the bottom of his heart is a spot just for me.

Dexter's snickered amusement at my cranky response furls my lips. "Don't get me wrong, I like orphans. *I like them a lot.*" His brows waggle during his last statement, his mood drastically improved from what it was. "It just makes you vulnerable to people like me."

My brow arches, wordlessly demanding further explanation. I understand orphans don't have their parents' guidance, but how does it make them easy prey? If anything, it should make them harder nuts to crack as they grow up fast.

Well, I assume that is the case.

I've matured more in the last twenty-four hours than I have the past decade. I'm unsure if Dexter's presence is the source of my newfound wisdom or if it's because my veins are being weaned off the medication they've been pumping through me the past sixteen years. Whatever it is, I'm the most wired I've ever been.

My absentminded hunt for my prescription ends when Dexter says, "Orphans feel unloved, so they seek love in unhealthy ways. Take your relationship with Nick as an example. He could do whatever the fuck he wanted, and you were always there waiting for him. Am I right?"

I want to shake my head. I want to call him an idiot and tell him to leave me alone, but since his comment is the most honest thing I've heard him say, I nod instead.

"See? Vulnerable. Nick is a douche. He fucked anything that walked before he got a random girl pregnant, then he married her to save face, most likely at the request of his publicist. Stupid. No other words." His eyes stray from the road to me. "You should be glad you didn't get lumped with his kid. You would have been tied to him for life."

My brain struggles to absorb the enormity of his reply. He's not making any sense. Isn't he taking me back to Nick so I can be with him for eternity? If not, why are we traveling to Ravenshoe in the darkness of the night?

Only yesterday morning, the idea of seeing Nick again filled my stomach with butterflies. Tonight has the same effect, but these butterflies have nasty stingers in their backsides and yellow and black stripes.

I love Nick—I always will—but as my mind clears, I'm realizing he's given me nothing but years of pain.

Maybe Dexter is right? Perhaps I was vulnerable because I was an orphan? My father was alive when I met Nick, but he may as well have been dead. He never left his favorite recliner which sat in front of the television—not even to use the bathroom. I practically raised myself after my mother died.

It was an extremely lonely and dark time.

Before Nick came into my life, I tried to end it many times. That's how we met. I was on my way home from a short stay at a facility similar to Meadow Fields. Dr. Marc said it would only take one person to revive my will to live. He was right. It was Nick.

'Was' being the operative word.

My transfer to Meadow Fields was a result of my sixth failed attempt at suicide in the past year. It was a more secure facility that could handle patients 'like me.' I didn't want to die. I just wanted to end the misery, to stop the intense pain that shreds through my heart every second of every day.

Already hating the blubbering idiot I'm about to become, I slip my prescription from my pocket and tap three pills into my palm.

My movements are soundless, but Dexter must have supersonic hearing. "What's that?"

His question is delivered so sternly, I jump, which, in turn, knocks the tablets from my hand. After gathering the discarded pills from the dark-fiber carpet, I toss the half-full bottle to Dexter. He veers back onto the right side of the road before dropping his eyes to the tattered label.

I'm so distracted by the massive hole burrowing in my chest, I swallow the pills whole. It's no easy feat with how dry my throat is, but I'll suffer the injustice if it stops stupid emotions from bombarding me. I don't like feeling like this—dirty and disturbed. I'd rather be emotionless than miserable.

"Fuck!"

Dexter's tug on the steering wheel is so violent, my temple smacks the frosty glass. While I cradle my throbbing skull, he throws off his seat belt, tosses open his door, then stomps to my side of his car. The hinges squeal in protest when he violently flings open my door.

"*Ugh!*" I grunt when he drags me from my seat. He's in such a hurry, he doesn't bother removing my belt. It's lucky I'm barely over five feet four in height, or I'd be a tangled mess.

"Do you have any idea what's in those pills?" he growls under his breath, his angry snarl quickening my pulse more rapidly than the medication seeping into my veins. "How many did you swallow?"

If he wants me to answer him, he needs to remove his fingers from my throat.

"This is their way of mind-fucking you, Megan! By making you stupid, you won't fight back. Is that what you want? Do you want them to win?" He shoves his fingers to the very back of my throat, making me gag. "You were born this way, Megan. This is who you are. Don't let a bunch of pricks in white coats tell you any different. Every sunrise creates a shadow for bad people to hide in. Every dream unlocked invites thieves to steal it so you're forced to create more. Just like every person has a little bit of black in their heart. Greed. Incest. Adultery. People act on their desires every single day, so why should we hide ours just because they're a little darker than average?"

He continues ramming his fingers down my throat until the three pills are discharged on the roadside—along with my dinner.

It's probably for the best. I wasn't feeling too good after guzzling down the red drink Joseph kept serving me.

"How many did you take?" Dexter asks while bobbing down to count the number of pills in my vomit. "One... two..." He pushes a large chunk of meatball to the side. It is so substantial in size it looks like I didn't chew before swallowing. "... three. Did you only take three?"

He raises his eyes to mine, knowing no words will escape my lips. A spark of relief fires through his squinted gaze when I nod. "Good." He licks his dry lips before continuing, "Do you have any more prescriptions besides what's in this bottle?"

My headshake is pushed aside for a squeal when he throws my medication into the dense tree line curving around the roadside. I'd go in search of them, but his throw is so impressive, I know I have no chance of finding them.

Returning my eyes to Dexter, I silently ask, *Why did you do that?*

"Because I'm saving this." He taps his index finger on my temple. "Those pills are vile, Megan. They make you into a robot who says and does exactly what it is told to do. They aren't medication. They're sedatives prescribed to control every aspect of your life." He locks his eyes with mine, the possessiveness in them making me hot. "I can sure as hell tell you, if anyone is going to control your life, it won't be a fucking tablet. It will be *me!*"

He throws his head back before scrubbing his hand down his face violently. He appears as stunned by his declaration as I am. I knew he cared for me, but what he just did, and hearing him say what he just said, I don't have any words. I am utterly speechless.

It's probably for the best when Dexter's eyes snap back to mine. They're not as stern as they were when he entered his car over an hour ago. They are more worried than agitated. "How long have you been taking that prescription? From your lack of maturity and sexual awareness, I'm guessing it was before you turned sixteen?"

Although my ego sports a bruise from his underhanded criticism, I still nod. Second only to obeying his every command, honesty was my dad's number one policy.

Dexter bites out a string of profanities. "How old exactly? Sixteen? Fifteen? Fourteen?"

He stops counting when he reaches twelve. Not because he's given up but because of the dip of my chin.

My heart stops beating when he shouts, "Twelve! You're fucking twelve. Great!"

I shake my head before stomping my foot. *I am not twelve!*

My immature display doesn't help plead my cause, but it does gain me Dexter's attention. "I don't mean literally. I mean in here." He taps my temple once more. "If you've been taking those tablets since you were twelve, your brain is stuck in a time warp. It still thinks you're twelve..." He stops talking as his face screws up. I can't tell if it is a good grimace or a bad one. "If you think you're twelve... does that mean... are you... has anyone popped your cherry?"

I balk at the crudeness of his tone.

When I attempt to shut down his interrogation by returning to his car, he grips my elbow firmly, stopping my fast exit. "Answer the question, Megan. Has anyone popped your cherry?"

His deep voice sends heat rushing to my cheeks. Once again, I don't know if it is a good bloom or a bad one. Considering it coincides with a warm slickness forming between my legs, I am going to assume it is good.

Incapable of a more suitable response, I pull a face as if he is being ridiculous. It's all a ploy. I'm not exactly sure what 'popping my cherry' means, so I'm fairly certain I haven't done it.

"Has a man ever put his cock in you? In your mouth? Your

hand? Your *pussy*?" There he goes with the dipping tone again, and I'm not going to mention his mind-reading capabilities.

Although mortified at the direction of our conversation, I shake my head. It is fast but instantly affects Dexter's sanity. His second string of curse words vibrates in my chest, alerting me and half of America's population to his anger.

I don't know why he's angry. Shouldn't he be pleased?

"Of course, you're a virgin. That's why Lee was itching to have you beneath him. Every man loves the smear of virginal blood on his cock."

If my stomach weren't empty, I might have vomited at his comment.

You're a pig.

When he snickers at my soundless remark, I roll my eyes before heading toward his car. This time, he lets me go. *Regrettably.*

While latching my seat belt, I run our conversation through my head. Some of what he said makes sense. I don't feel like I've aged a day since I began taking the pills he disposed of. But the part about virginal blood was disgusting—a*nd it makes my insides tingle*—but we're going to ignore that. I've got enough confusion to wade through. I can't add bizarre sensations into the mix.

13

MEGAN

After a prolonged conversation with himself, Dexter slides into the driver's seat of his car. He remains quiet for the next ten miles, only speaking when obtaining my approval on a roadside motel.

This is a first. Usually, he tells me what we're doing, and I follow along. He's never sought my permission before.

He pulls to the very end of a dusty parking lot before his eyes drift to me. "Can you pass me my wallet from the glove box?"

Nodding, I throw down the leather-stitched compartment with care. My heart leaps into my chest when a news article is the first thing my eyes land on. It's a clip of a recent tour Nick did with his band. He's smiling at the camera with his guitar slung over one shoulder, and a strawberry blonde is draped under the other. He looks happy.

I'm glad. One miserable soul is always better than two.

I push aside the article to find Dexter's wallet underneath, shut the glove box, then hand it to him. He eyes me curiously for several minutes. His stare is so prolonged, I run my finger across my lips, worried I have a vomit stain there.

After a grumble too quiet for me to hear, Dexter exits the car, secures a cash-only room, then gestures for me to join him under the weather-damaged patio. With every step I take, worry leaks from him like the air from a stabbed tire. I hate this, the way he is looking at me. It is one of the reasons I've never *consorted* with a man before. My daddy said they'd look at me differently. He was right. Dexter is already giving me weird vibes, and all we did was sleep in the same bed.

My pace slows. *Is that what popping a cherry means?* If so, mine was popped years ago. I slept in Nick's bed once. He was passed out from the excessive amount of alcohol he drank and fully clothed, but he did kiss me the next morning. It wasn't as passionate as Dexter's kiss slash bite, but it was still a kiss, none-theless.

I guess it is kind of different. Dexter and I didn't have any clothes on. My sleepover with Nick was also missing the weird buzzing sensation Dexter's attention gives me. Nick makes my heart flutter, but Dexter still has it scaling that surging upshot I mentioned earlier. The dip hasn't arrived yet.

I hope it never comes.

This is bad for me to admit, but I like the power Dexter's atten-tion awards me. He looks at me like I could have stabbed Joseph in the eye with my fork, and he wouldn't have gotten mad.

Nick would have been mad. He would have been very, very mad. I only gave his fiancée a special medication to deliver his son early, and he was considerably angry. *Imagine if you had done one of the many other things the voices told you to do?*

Nodding in agreement to the kind voice in my head, I enter the door Dexter is holding open for me. Further deliberation will have to wait. It is a little after two in the morning. I am beyond exhausted.

"Shower first," Dexter demands, stopping my beeline to the only bed in the room.

I shadow him into the bathroom. This one is more adequately outfitted than the one at his cabin. A large freestanding shower is at our right and a triangular spa bath is in the opposite corner. It's a funky orange color but still a cool accessory to have access to. I haven't had a bath in years, not since I discovered not all birds can swim. My mom said it was a science experiment, but my father was still angry. At times, I swear he loved his birds more than us.

"It's too late for a bath now. You can have one tomorrow before we leave," Dexter murmurs upon noticing my appreciative gawk.

He removes his cap, places it on the cracked sink, then spins around to face me. My heart rate skyrockets when I notice splatters of blood on his face. A normal person may mistake the vibrant streaks of red as lipstick or paint. Alas, I am anything but normal. I know the color so well it is embedded in my retinas.

I dart across the bathroom, my panic roaring with every step I take. A guttural moan rolls up my chest when I reach Dexter, my way of asking what happened.

He removes my hands from his face, his expression half-peeved, half-thankful. He doesn't like me fussing over him, but he prefers it over my silence.

"It isn't my blood," he assures me, his tone gruff. His eyes drop to my massively dilated ones. "Even though I doubt you'll care who it belongs to, I won't share."

Pretending he hasn't spotted the stream of questions pumping from my eyes, he heads for the shower to turn on the faucet. Once he's happy the water is at a nice temperature, he pivots to face me. Although his composure is a little askew, my hands still move to the hem of my shirt. I don't need to hear his demands to know of their arrival. I can see them in his eyes, read them from his mind.

Dexter watches me undress with the same set of eagle eyes he had when he entered the bathroom yesterday afternoon. But instead of taking in only the private regions of my body, he devours every inch of me. His hungry eyes skim over my breasts that are aching with need before weaving down my stomach like a snake making its way through a desert, then they stop for a long, voracious glare at the bare mound between my legs.

When his eyes return to my face, I take a step back. His look is hungry, but this time, I'm not stupidly confusing it with a hunger for food. He is famished. Thirsty. Overwhelming every sense I own.

"Put them in the trash. I have new ones for you in the car," he commands when I start to place my folded clothes onto the lowered toilet lid.

It seems like a waste, but I do as I'm told. My father taught me obedience and what occurs when I don't follow the rules.

"Do you not want your razor..." Dexter's words trap in his throat when I twist my wrist to hold out my hand palm side up. The smile he releases when he spots the silver instrument nestled in my palm sends goosebumps scuttling across my skin.

He returns his eyes to my face. There is something in them I haven't seen before.

Is it pride?

"Did you want to use that on Joseph tonight, Megan?" I nearly lie until he cuts off the shake of my head with a stern warning. "If you lie to me, I'll cut out the little freckle on your thigh and send it to Lee's family as a parting gift."

Trusting his threat, my shake switches to a nod. I'm not stupid. He was being honest.

He steps closer to me, crowding me with his impressive frame. "What did you want to do to him?"

I flick open the switch then slice an X pattern in the air half an inch from Dexter's neck. My movements are so rushed, cool air rustles between us.

I'm fully anticipating for Dexter to check if I've maimed him, so you can imagine my surprise when he doesn't. He merely sucks in a prolonged breath through his flaring nostrils before dropping his eyes to the bald spot between my legs.

"You are like me, aren't you, Megan." Although he appears to be asking a question, his tone doesn't allude to that. It was a confirmation.

When his eyes slowly stray back to mine, demanding a reply, I can neither agree with nor deny his statement. His hand is gripping my locks too firmly for me to do anything but glance up at him. The threat of him tearing my hair from my scalp isn't the sole cause of my silence, though. It is the confusion bombarding me.

His hold should be frightening, but for some reason, it isn't. It increases my pulse, which surges in an area stripped as bare as my heart right now. I love Nick—I gave him my heart for eternity— but as I stare into Dexter's fiery eyes, I can't recall if Nick's eyes are darker than Dexter's or paler. Does he have more lashes or less? Are his eyes even blue? I only saw his photo mere minutes ago, but I truly can't remember what he looks like.

My response shouldn't be shocking. A ravenous wolf has me in his sights, and the only thought I can muster is, *"Yes, please."*

I am the most mentally unstable I've ever been.

"Don't tempt me." Dexter's warning is more a growl than an actual threat. "You couldn't be so lucky to have someone like me pop your cherry, but every woman must drudge through the minor leagues before stepping up to the big hitters. It is a rite of passage."

His grip on my hair doesn't stop my eyes rolling skyward. His reply should have me immediately shutting down our conversation. I should demand he release me this instant from his barbaric grip. Or better yet, use the razor to force his relinquishment, but with my veins free of mind-numbing medication, the thoughts streaming through my head don't belong to a rational woman.

I don't want to dodge Dexter's attention.

I'm encouraging it.

When I return my eyes to Dexter, my determination obvious, his lips curl into a heart-fluttering smirk. "But you're not like normal women, are you, Megan?" The agitation that generally arrives with his questions is nipped in the bud when he quickly adds, "You're special. Unique. Completely fucking fucked-up."

A thrill jolts down my spine when he yanks my head back. He drags his nose down my neck, sucking in my scent with a long, undignified whiff. Goosebumps follow the trek his tongue makes when it travels the same path, just in the opposite direction. It glides along the throb in my throat, only stopping when he reaches the base of my ear. "As sweet as heaven but as sour as Satan," he growls into my ear. "Tell me to stop before I drag you to the depths of hell alongside me."

I shake my head, deepening his breaths.

Conscious of what is about to transpire, his bite doesn't hold half the sting it did yesterday. His teeth sinking into my earlobe spikes my heart rate and causes the slippery situation between my legs to become more apparent.

I grow wetter when he growls at the taste of my blood on his tongue. "I can make your cunt bleed just as readily. Do you want that, Megan?"

My mind scrambles for a reply when he seeks a response in a non-verbal way. If I went off my first thought, I'd scream yes, but with my mind as knotted as my lower stomach, I settle on a half-hearted shake.

I don't want you to hurt me.

"Oh, trust me, it's going to hurt. Whether me or a man with half a cock, you will bleed."

I don't understand the origin of his slurred words. He drank more glasses of the fruity drink Joseph topped off all evening than me, but his eyes aren't carrying the same drunken edge my father's always did.

"But I can show you how you can achieve pleasure from pain. Would you prefer that?"

I nod without thinking, the promise in his eyes deserving a decisive response.

My scalp stops screaming in pain when Dexter releases it from his grip to shove me backward. I land on the wall with a thud, the pain barely noticeable since my focus is locked on his looming frame. The veins weaving through his thick biceps pulsate as his glassy eyes scan my body. His watchful glance sends a fiery sensation shooting through me. This one is welcomed since it is minus the truckload of confusion it generally arrives with.

Only now am I realizing why I had an instant connection with him. We're one in the same—two misunderstood people shrouded by darkness. He doesn't care about the immorality in my eyes because he has no intention of dousing it. He wants to nurture it, to see it reach its full fruition.

The thought is both terrifying and exciting. For years, I was told to ignore the voices in my head. I won't have to do that with Dexter. I can explore why it feels good to stand a little jagged and separate from the crowd. I'm not different. I am unique. Those are two entirely different things.

"When was the last time you were medicated, Megan?" Dexter

raises his eyes to mine before counting down. He starts at mere minutes before extending to hours, then days.

"Three days?" he confirms when I nod.

I nod again.

His lips twist as he contemplates. I don't know what he's pondering, but he reaches his deliberation quickly. It isn't just the fire in his eyes bringing me to this conclusion. It is the growth between his legs that even a sturdy pair of jeans can't hide.

"Fifteen is old enough to bleed." My pupils widen to saucers when he adds, "I'm not going to cut you today. We'll work up to that, but I will lick your greedy pussy. Tease your clit. Maybe bite it a little. Then once you shatter like glass, I'll teach you how to please me."

I shudder at the thought. It isn't a scared tremor. The confidence in his tone assures me this will be a lot of fun.

"Then you'll stroke me with your hand, your mouth, and your pussy." He tugs my hands away from my erratically panting chest to expose my breasts to his hungry gaze. "I might even fuck these."

My nipples stiffen into hardened buds.

"Then, once you've mastered my lessons, you can test them out on Nick, be one of the many hoes he fucks while on tour. Is that what you want, Megan? Do you want me to show you how to please *him*?"

Just the mention of Nick's name has my feet scampering backward. Not because I'm filled with remorse at how horny Dexter's words make me feel, but because of the hate in Dexter's eyes. He isn't looking at me with love and admiration. He's glaring at me like he despises me. Like he wants to use and abuse me like every other man in my life.

I thought he was above the manipulation and underhanded tactics men like my father used.

Clearly, I was wrong.

"*Ugh!*" I grunt when the back of Dexter's hand grazes my erect nipple. He chews on his lower lip, loving how it buds even more firmly under his touch but blinded to my growing anger.

I slap his hand two more times before ducking low and skirting past him. It is virtually impossible with how imposing his body is, but I manage—barely!

My feet nearly slip out from underneath me when I enter the slimy shower stall at the speed of a rocket. With a grunt, I close the soap-scum-covered door before raising my eyes to Dexter. He's watching me as fervently as he was earlier, except this time, his eyes aren't blazing with lust. He is fuming mad.

He isn't the only one. My fists are balled so firmly, the razor in my hand sends droplets of blood dripping down my palm. The ghastly scent is even more rampant because of the steamy conditions, but it has nothing on the undisclosed scent lingering in the air. If I weren't stuck in mind-debilitating confusion, I would say it was angry lust, but since I can't contend with more confusion, I'll say it's unexplainable.

Dexter steps closer to me, his strides as wobbly as the sneer on his face. "He told the world you were scum, yet you still want to be with him?"

I shake my head, but even with him staring straight at me, he doesn't see my reply. He's too deep into his psychosis to see or hear anything.

The harsh lines between his brows deepen when I adjust my grip on the razor so it sits between us. Dexter smiles as if amused by my attempts to protect myself. He shouldn't be so quick to judge. If I didn't know how to defend myself, Bryce's death would be the only one on my scoreboard.

"You wanted to play, Cleo, so let's play."

I don't know who Cleo is, but I don't have time to ask questions. Dexter is storming for me. His eyes are as dark as death, his lips hard and straight.

When he throws open the shower door, I slice my blade through the air twice. The first sliver of the blade misses its target —intentionally. The second hits exactly where I intend. The thin trail of red from Dexter's ear to his Adam's apple is barely a scratch but more than adequate as a warning.

If you come any closer, I'll slice you ear to ear.

My plans go to shit when Dexter knocks the razor from my hand before his other hand shoots up to my throat. He pins me to the slimy tiles, his hold so firm, my feet dangle midair.

His disgust at my attempt to maim him floods his face as he glares into my bulging eyes.

As my body panics over the lack of oxygen in my veins, I dig my nails into his hand. I was so surprised by his attack my lungs didn't have a chance to increase their capacity. I'm on the verge of collapse within seconds. My throat is burning as fiercely as my eyes teem with moisture.

When my nails pierce the skin on Dexter's hand, he draws me forward before slamming me back. My brain rattles in my skull from the brutal impact, and my vision blurs. The coppery taste in my mouth is vastly different than the fruity scent in the air. It is an odd balance of sweet and sour.

As the first signs of a migraine creep up on me, I lessen the severity of my thrusts. I'm too tired to fight, and perhaps this is for the best? I've wanted to die for a very long time. Now Dexter can finally grant my wish.

The groove between Dexter's brows fades when I stop thrashing against him. It smooths even more when I drop my hands to my side, giving up without so much as a single tear.

I'm done fighting. Kill me. Please, I silently request, staring down at him. *It may be the most humane thing anyone has ever done for me.*

Dexter's nostrils flare, seemingly annoyed that I'm accepting my fate.

He wants me to fight.

He wants me to maim.

He shouldn't be shocked by my cowardly ways. I've done nothing but disappoint my entire life.

"Fuck!" he roars when my pulse fades under his fingertips. His word is delivered so violently it colors my face with the hue his grip stole. "Fuck! Fuck! Fuck!"

After a final squeeze of my throat, announcing he isn't happy about his decision, he releases me from his grip. My backside hits the floor with a thump. My mind is so shut down it doesn't register the pain. My body starts to revive my lungs without waiting for permission from my head. It wants to live so it can discover why it thrums every time Dexter is in its presence.

Even while being hurt by him, it bloomed under his touch.

The hair slumped in front of my face clears away when Dexter crouches down in front of me. He tucks it behind my ear before raising my eyes to his via my chin. His pupils have returned to their normal size, his psychosis over as quickly as it arrived.

The water pelting out of the shower head runs down his arm and puddles at my jaw when he takes his time assessing the throb in my neck. Confident it isn't going to miraculously snap in half of its own accord, he brings his lips within an inch of my ear.

"If you ever do that again, I'm going to squeeze the life out of you, bring you back, then do it again. And again. And again." His voice grows angrier with every word he utters. "Do you under-stand me?"

He seems off, as if he is more annoyed I gave up my fight than that I rejected him.

My assumptions are proven accurate when he snarls, "You don't live in hell for years to give up the instant you escape. You fight. You maim. You kill if you must, but you *never* give up. Gods were born to fight, Megan. Cowards weaken."

When I sheepishly nod, somewhat agreeing with him, he stands to his feet. His clothes are drenched, showcasing his impressive frame in eye-catching detail. Even with our encounter dominated by violence, it doesn't alter the facts. He is a beautifully tormented man. The overhead lighting glistens in his diamond-shaped eyes, and the scruff on his jaw enhances the sharp lines framing his face. Even his hair is more alluring from being misted by the shower water.

He stands over me in all his six-foot-plus glory for the next several minutes, seemingly conflicted. I understand his struggle. He was on the verge of killing me, and all I am doing is staring up at him in admiration.

I think my daddy was right. There's something terribly wrong with me.

Dexter's deliberation doesn't reach the conclusion I am hoping for when he orders, "Shower then straight to bed. Sleep naked. I want nothing between us when I get back."

When my eyes rocket to his, curious as to where he is going, he says, "I've got a virgin to fuck out of my system before I claim her in a way she's never been claimed."

14

DEXTER

My trek to an overflowing bar two blocks up from the motel I left Megan at slows when a text message sounds from my jeans pocket. My hands visibly shake when I lug out my phone. I nearly killed her. Megan's pulse was nearly decimated because of me.

Usually, I'd feel no remorse, but even a man as emotionless as me can't deny the sensation thickening my veins right now. Her denial angered me. It stripped my veins of blood and left me to die.

But that isn't the reason I nearly strangled her.

I was stuck in a debilitating blackness. I knew where I was and what I was doing, but the person I was doing it to wasn't the person I saw when my hand curled around Megan's throat.

I thought Megan was Cleo.

I'm unsure if Megan's rejection was the catalyst of my break-down or if it's the way she's snaking herself beneath my skin. Whatever it was, I'm losing control—and not in a good way.

I could pretend I was teaching Megan a lesson about what

happens when something I'm dying to taste is brutally stripped away from me, but then I wouldn't have let go. I would have killed her.

Perhaps I should have. I should have fucked her like her eyes were begging me to, then killed her. It wouldn't be the first time things have occurred in that order. I'm sure it won't be the last. But for some fucked-up, annoying-the-living-shit-out-of-me reason, I can't hurt her.

The more her pulse flatlined, the louder the voices in my head shouted. They weren't screaming murderous thoughts. They were begging for mercy, pleading for me to give her one last shot.

I'm not a merciful man. If you double-cross me, expect to pay your penance in blood. But Megan didn't double-cross me. She merely denied me. I don't know why. I read the thoughts streaming from her eyes. I smelled the erotic scent of her cunt.

She wanted me.

She still does!

She must be playing a game I don't participate in. Her loss. Instead of being bedded by a god, she'll be fucked by a peasant. If the idea didn't grate my nerves, I'd laugh. Just the thought of her with another man has me seeing red. It triples the adrenaline surging through my veins and has me actively seeking my next target. I need to work this girl out of my system, and the best way to do that is to put another woman in her place.

As my strides lengthen, I drop my blurry eyes to my phone's screen to discover who my message is from. It isn't Nick's security personnel seeking additional proof Megan is alive. It is a reply to a message I sent nearly an hour ago.

Moose: *Vicar exterminated. Send taxidermist.*

My dad's reply is just as short.

Big Bear: *Call me. Now.*

An additional text quickly follows the first.

Big Bear: It says delivered. Don't keep me waiting, son.

I toss a curse word into the night air before hitting a soon-to-be frequently dialed number and pressing my cell to my ear. When he is in game mode, my father's contact with the outside world is borderline extinct, so his quick reply isn't a good thing. He is either without a target or reminiscing about an old game. Neither scenario is more appealing than the other.

"You owe me thirty seconds." My father's deep chuckle pelts down on me. When I was a child, his laugh scared me. Now, it sparks morbid curiosity. "What happened with Vicar?"

I wait for him to finish shooing people away from him, no doubt women eager to take my mother's place, before replying, "He hunted without an invitation. My target was not his to contain."

"Dexter... son."

I don't know which greeting agitates me more. He only calls me Dexter when he is disappointed in me. He used 'son' when he wanted to taunt my mother.

"I know hunting was never your thing, but you are aware of the rules. The game is the target, not your fellow player's."

"I wasn't hunting—"

"It's her, isn't it? The pretty blonde you escaped with? Does she remind you of your mother? Is that why you've taken such an immediate liking to her?"

I'm a little lost on a reply—not the mother part—that is accurate. What did Dr. Nelson call it? *Oedipus complex,* where a son sees his father as an emotional rival because he sleeps with his mother. It is the part about Megan being blonde. Her hair is a little mousy, but it isn't light enough to call her a blonde.

I stop combing my internal dictionary for an adequate term to describe Megan's hair color when my father asks, "She's younger than your usual toys. How old is she? Sixteen? Seventeen?"

I'm filled with sympathy for Megan's mute state when my mouth refuses to cooperate with the prompts of my brain. I have no clue what my father is talking about. Megan is immature, but I know for a fact she isn't a teen. Her cock-stiffening curves could never be confused with someone who's barely a woman.

With my mouth refusing to cooperate, my ears have no trouble picking up my dad's faint murmur, "She doesn't have your mother's dark hair and molten eyes, but she is around the same age your mother was when I sliced you from her stomach."

Her screams lit my dreams for the next three years, I mouth at the same time my father vocalizes it.

"Do you remember when I shared her with you, Dexter? It was only the quickest touch of her jiggling breast as she lay motionless next to you, but I'm certain you'll never forget it. How old were you then?"

He says, "Four," at the same time I say, "Three."

"Three... four... close enough. One touch wasn't sufficient though, was it? You wanted more. I could see it in your big, beady eyes when you watched me claim her."

"It was enough..." *Enough to spark a manic psychosis.*

It was at summer camp when I was thirteen that I discovered not every child sleeps in their mother's bed. To me, it was normal, almost as routine as being woken in the middle of the night by my father's grunts of ecstasy.

It didn't matter if I was two or twelve, my father never fucked my mother unless I was lying beside her. It was the ultimate way to display the power he had over her. He could do anything to her, even in front of her son, and she would never say no.

Her submissiveness is one quality she and Megan share. The other is the fact they're both orphans. My mother was a misfit runaway. Her foster parents' wish that she abort me was what sent her to sunny California with a backpack full of clothes and a four-month rounded stomach.

My mother often preached that my father stole the light from her eyes, but over the years, my father exposed that wasn't the truth. He saved her life, and in turn, he saved mine.

My mother's foster parents wanted her to abort me so I wasn't born addicted to drugs. After seeing how careless my mother was, my father decided to raise me as his own before I had even left my mother's womb.

The rehabilitation methods he forced upon my mother were barbaric but effective. From the stories I heard, I only shook uncontrollably the first twelve days of my life.

Although my mother's first few years as a parent were rocky, she stepped up to the plate when my father granted me permission to attend middle school. She didn't wear a frilly apron, nor did she cut my sandwiches into heart-shaped designs. She just told anyone and everyone that my father was her abductor and that she was a prisoner in his luxury mansion in the hills of Malibu.

Everyone thought she was hilarious. Even I laughed along with them. Her story was utterly ridiculous. How could anyone be held 'captive' in a multi-million-dollar estate by a much-loved and revered member of society, be forced to wear clothes in excess of four figures per piece, and be draped in diamonds?

No wonder no one believed her. Her story didn't make any sense. She was sick. Kind of like Megan.

Kind of like me.

I was fortunate to have my father's guidance to see me through my dark days. He thickened my skin and proved I wasn't what was wrong with society. Society is the one with the issues.

I'm pulled from my thoughts when a drunken patron stumbles into me while navigating the eight-foot-wide sidewalk. If I could look past my arrogance, I could take responsibility for some of our collision. My steps have never been so wobbly.

"Sorry, sugar," she murmurs with a hiccup before her bare feet gallop across the cracked concrete to catch up to her friends a few steps up. She is lucky she is with company, or I would have passed on my dislike for drunken idiots.

Her slur doesn't just break me from my thoughts. It halts my dad's reminiscing mid-lecture as well. "Geez, Moose, you let me get carried away again. See what happens when you get locked away for years at a time? I reminisce instead of discussing business."

His last word should fill me with worry, but his use of my nickname keeps it at bay.

A chair creaks. He must be in his office. "I'll send the taxidermist to Vicar's playground..."

I wait, knowing there's more.

"But..."

Told you.

"You owe me. Vicar wasn't just a member of my association. He was also a friend."

"What do you want?" My voice is thick from lack of use.

My father sighs heavily, either pondering or hopeful. I realize it is the latter when he asks, "Was Scarlett present during extermination?"

"She was." When his sigh turns into a moan, I quickly add on, "But I doubt she is anymore."

Glass smashing resonates down the line. "You let her go! My god, what's the matter with you?" His sneer is delivered with a memory, a vision of being slapped over the head while hearing the same screamed words on repeat.

I shake my head, ridding the confusion. Usually, the vision is accompanied by my mother's voice, but today it was presented with my father's. This is even more proof that I need to get Megan out of my head. She is fucking with me, making me an idiot who can't see the entire picture.

I practically sprint to the bar. My fast strides chop up my words when I say, "Scarlett won't talk. Joseph called me Moose—"

"I don't care if he called you Jesus, you don't leave witnesses. Ever!" A rustle sounds down the line as if he is cupping the receiver. "Send Micha. We have more than just a body to clean."

His message isn't for me. It is for his right-hand man, Charles.

"Dexter..." My father drawls my name in a long, derogative slur, ensuring I can't miss his fuming anger.

"Yes," I answer without pause.

I do not cower from persecution. I encourage it. His retribution will make me a better man. It will strengthen and condition me for the cruelty of life. He didn't beat me when I was young to be mean. He did it so no one else could ever break me. I don't feel pain. I absorb it. Even the slice of Megan's blade when it skimmed across my skin didn't register. If it weren't for the faint trickle of blood dribbling down my neck, I wouldn't have realized she nicked me.

I freeze. *Nick.* Is that why Megan denied my advance? Because she didn't want to cheat on Nick? If so, I'm even more annoyed I succumbed to the voices in my head. Nick may have millions of dollars in his bank account, a wife with model looks, and the standard one son, one daughter combination every American family strives to achieve, but he isn't half the man I am. He's not even one-tenth!

I was certain Megan's obsession with Nick had shifted to me. She barely reacted when she saw his photo earlier tonight. I put it in my glove compartment as a test. She passed.

Well, I thought she did.

Maybe I can't read her as well as I thought I could? That annoys me even more than her pulse weakening under my touch.

I stop imagining the life in Nick's eyes vanishing via my grip when my father asks, "Is your new pet pure, son?"

My throat works hard to swallow a lump before I answer, "Yes."

I don't need to see my father to know he is smiling. I can feel his gleam from where I am standing.

"Bring her to the stables. It is time for you to repay your debt." He pauses to dramatize his last sentence. "If you're not here by sundown Sunday, I'll send out the vultures."

With that, he hangs up the phone, confident I will never go against his command.

I won't. Even a man as powerful as me knows I am a mere peasant when it comes to a god like my father. I will obey his rules. I always have. Meaning, in just under thirty-six hours, Megan will go from being hunted by the authorities to being hunted by Death himself.

15

MEGAN

*T*hree hours, fifty-seven minutes, and twelve seconds. That's how long I've been staring at the clock, waiting for the creak of the motel room door to announce Dexter is back. The birds have chirped, and the sun has begun its rise, yet I've not slept a wink.

My woozy head isn't the only thing to blame for my lack of sleep—it is being without him, my protector, the man who killed to keep me safe.

It was only when inspecting the bruise circling my neck did the reason for Dexter's psychosis come to light. He wasn't mad I turned him down before attacking him with my blade. He was dispersing the energy that blazes through your veins any time you kill.

It took me days to come down from the high I felt when my father sucked in his last breath. The adrenaline that arrived with his death was merciless. So much strength surged through me, I was able to hang him from the second story beam in our barn.

I didn't want his death to look like a suicide. I wanted him to hang like the rodents in the western movies he watched. He said they were cowards, and a hanging was too upstanding for them. Since he never expressed a more heinous way to die, I had no choice but to hang him. I had considered burying him with my mother, but even with bugs replacing her eyes, she looked peaceful, so I didn't want to disturb her. *Especially not with him.*

My muscles ached for days, but the visual of him hanging lifeless in the barn where he had buried my mother was beautiful. Nearly as wondrous as the blood splattered on the rim of Dexter's hat.

Dexter stood up for me.

He killed a man for me.

And what did I do to thank him?

I treated him like every other vile man I've crossed paths with in my life.

I thought Dexter wanted to use and abuse me. I was wrong.

When I tried to hurt Nick's baby, he retaliated with as much violence. The fumes from the cloth held over my mouth burned my airways, but it was nothing compared to the effect of Nick's betrayal on my heart. He told the police I wasn't his girlfriend and begged the judge to issue a restraining order so I had to keep my distance from him. He acted like he hated me when all I had ever done was love him.

If that wasn't bad enough, he sent me far, far away to a place more interested in medicating than helping me.

Dexter would never do that. He dumped my pills to ensure my thoughts remain lucid and clear. He wants me to make my own decisions.

He might even possibly love me.

My assumptions weaken when a giggle sounds through my ears. It isn't the big, vociferous laugh I've grown accustomed to the past two days. It's dainty and cute, similar to a giggle a female would make when a prickly chin is dragged down her neck.

With my heart pounding in my ears, I turn toward the pattering sound of steps. Thick curtains are drawn across the window, blocking out the early morning sun, but it isn't dark enough for me to miss a visual a thousand years won't wrench from my mind.

Dexter isn't alone. A pretty brunette is in his arms, and his tongue is rammed down her throat.

I try to look away, but one image stops me before I get too far. Dexter's wintry blue eyes. He watches me over the brunette's silky mane, his bloodshot eyes locked with mine. His gaze is so penetrating, my mouth feels every lick of his tongue.

A tingling sensation builds low in my belly when he steps closer, bringing his eyes level to mine. I stare at him with an equal amount of shock and disgust. The image of him kissing another woman should fill me with rage, but unlike when I watched Nick and Jenni, I'm not seeing two people. I'm only seeing one. Dexter.

He is kissing her, but he is tasting me. He samples my mouth with long, devoted licks and vicious bites, her purrs are barely heard over my throaty moans. The sensation ripping through my body is intoxicating, making my head as woozy as the red drink I consumed with dinner. I am hot, sweaty, and utterly breathless.

When Dexter's guest switches her attention to dragging his shirt over his head, Dexter's eyes drop to my feverishly thrusting chest. His chest puffs when he notices I am sleeping naked as requested. I even stripped the mattress of bedding to ensure there wasn't a thing between us.

The ache of my nipples doubles when his tongue darts out to replenish his kiss-swollen mouth. He knows the sharp points at the end of my perky breasts are for him. He is aware I'm ready, willing, and able. He just needs to push her away, to choose me over her.

Realizing she has competition, Dexter's guest doesn't stop at his shirt. She falls to her knees before her hands dart to his belt. Anger roars through my body when she rubs her palm along his erection straining his zipper. She is mistaking his excitement as a consequence of kissing her.

It's not. It's for me. I did that to him. She's just an obstacle.

One I plan to get rid of.

When Dexter's penis leaps from his boxers, I shoot my eyes to the side. I hate that I am missing out on seeing the veins pulsating in his penis, but I can't stand watching the brunette's mouth create an O before she narrows toward his glistening tip. It fills my head with horrible, depraved thoughts and has my hand sneaking across the mattress in search of my razor.

My attention is only diverted for a second. The slump of a body on the mattress secures my utmost devotion faster than lightning brightening a black sky. Unfortunately, the crash wasn't Dexter pushing the brunette off him. It was from him dumping her onto the bed I'm sitting on.

She giggles, the alcohol leaking from her pores a great explanation for her immaturity.

She's drunker than my daddy every Fourth of July.

Eager to get the party started, her hands dart up to the buttons of her shirt. Even though I hate her with every fiber of my being, my anger isn't as palpable as it could be. Her extremely generous breasts are displayed in their full glory, yet Dexter's attention remains focused on me.

His cock thickens with every second we stare at each other. It is as if *she* isn't even in the room. It is just him and me, one criminally insane patient with another.

I want to say we use our time well, communicating nonverbally, but that isn't the case. Dexter's eyes are too glazed to convey his thoughts, and the excessive adrenaline from his adventurous night is still apparent.

I lose his gaze when the brunette scoots up the bed to ease her jeans down her thighs. I clamber away, wanting to ensure not an inch of her skin touches mine. She's pretty, and her scarcely covered body increases the throb of my pulse, but that's because I'm angry. *Isn't it?*

Before my back can brace the headboard—or my head can work through half the confusion bombarding me—Dexter hooks my ankle and drags me down the mattress. The brunette startles as much as I do when my naked breast grazes her forearm.

"Holy Mary, Mother of Joseph!" she squeals in fright before darting off the bed.

Unlike me, Dexter lets her escape. He's too busy biting behind my knee to voice an opinion on her abrupt exit.

From the way the brunette squirms, you'd swear she was the one enduring the bite-lick-suck routine Dexter is doing to my skin. His bite is painful, but with each one bringing him closer to my throbbing vagina, I'll happily accept the tenderness.

A grunt of frustration rolls up my chest when he floats past an area weeping with want. He chuckles against my skin, the flutters of his breath on my stomach doubling my heightened state.

When the brunette's eyes collide with mine for the quickest second, I nudge my head to the door, giving her marching orders. She ignores me, too mesmerized by the image of Dexter's tongue circling my nipple to move.

I can't blame her. The feeling of him sucking my hardened bud is more phenomenal than anything I've ever felt. Even being scrutinized by the watchful eyes of the brunette doesn't dampen my excitement. The fire brewing low in my gut intensifies with every graze of Dexter's teeth and marvelous swirl of his tongue.

After devouring my left nipple with as much eagerness as he bestowed on my right, Dexter raises his eyes to mine. They are even glassier up close. They aren't the usual bloodshot eyes you expect a drunk man to have. They are hazier. Unhinged. Devastatingly beautiful.

The intensity in his eyes overwhelms me when he brings them to within an inch of my face. He rests his forehead against mine, our breathing intimately shared. He doesn't say anything. He just endlessly stares, frying my brain more effectively than the pills he removed from my stomach earlier.

I want to say something. I want to express the crazy sensation annihilating any thoughts that don't include him, but no matter how hard I fight my lips to move, not a sound escapes them.

Regrettably, the brunette doesn't suffer the same fate as me. "Oh," she purrs, breaking an intimate connection that shouldn't be broken by a third party. "When you said you wanted to play a game, I didn't realize you meant this." Her eyes rake over our practically conjoined bodies, only stopping when she reaches Dexter's jeans huddled around his ankles. "I like her, Dex. She's *real* pretty."

My eyes snap to the unnamed female. Her shortening of Dexter's name annoys the shit out of me but not as much as her sneaky steps toward our bed. One, she is *not* Dexter's friend, so she has no right to give him cute little nicknames. And two, my inability to share was one of the reasons I was expelled from school—that and the fact I set a girl's hair on fire.

When the dark-haired lady rakes her nails across the muscles in Dexter's back, I smack her in the hip with my foot. She laughs, assuming I'm being funny. I'm not. If Dexter's naked body wasn't weighing down my limbs, I'd remove her from my room with one of the many wicked thoughts streaming through my head.

She won't be laughing then.

Her teeth rake her lower lip as she connects her eyes with mine. Her stare fills me with anger.

I know the look she is giving me.

I know the ghastly ideas tainting her mind.

They make me want to slit her throat.

With a smile of a woman not worried about her safety, her hands continue their exploration of Dexter's body. She drags them up his splayed thighs before dipping them ever so slightly when she reaches his backside.

I hiss at her in warning. She stupidly ignores me. It is a bad move on her part. The last woman who ignored me ended up with thirteen stitches in her scalp.

"Hey, Dex?" She sounds like a whiny child disappointed she lost her favorite toy. "Are you going to share?"

Dexter smiles an evil grin... or is it an angry one? I haven't learned all his smiles yet, so I can't be sure. "Sorry. Can't. This one needs to stay pure." His last sentence is delivered via a growl. "If she didn't, I'd already be inside her."

Before I can seek further clarification, Dexter rolls off me.

Now I want to kill everything and everyone.

I haven't worked through one-tenth of my anger when the brunette murmurs, "What if I promise to be gentle? You'd like that, wouldn't you, sweetie?" The sheer dishonesty in her tone secures my utmost attention. I don't know this lady, but I do know she is a liar. "I'll fuck you nice and gentle while Dex fucks me hard and fast. How does that sound to you?"

I growl at her, baring teeth. Ignorant of the fury reddening my cheeks, she scrapes her nails up my thigh. My leg instinctively kicks out, partly in anger, partly due to natural reflexes.

A pained groan rolls up her chest when my foot smacks into her nose. My hit wasn't an accident, but that's the defense I take when she roars, "What the fuck! Do you have any idea how much my nose cost?" She glares at me over her pencil-thin nose that isn't as pretty as it was moments ago. Fury ignites in her narrowed gaze when she spots the curl of my lips. "You did that on purpose." Angered by my halfhearted shrug, she takes a page from Dexter's book by gripping my ankle and dragging me down the bed. "I'll show you what I think of stuck-up bitches!"

Her clutch on my leg barely budges me an inch.

My foot, on the other hand, it has perfect aim.

"Argh!" she screams in a grunt when my kick to her chest sends her sailing across the room.

She lands on the floor with a thud, her angry roar barely heard over Dexter's chuckle. He appears entertained by the show as if this was his plan all along.

Dexter's laughter doesn't linger for long. The brunette's angry shout nips it in the bud quickly. "You stupid bitch! What the hell is wrong with you?"

"What did you call her?" Dexter yells, his furious tone launching my heart into my throat.

Blind to the absolute fury radiating out of Dexter, the brunette stands to her feet, rolls her shoulders, locks her slitted gaze with mine, then sneers, "I called her a bitch."

"Not that part, the bit before it." Dexter stands to his full height. It is even more impressive when he's fuming in anger. "The 'S' word. The one that implies you *think* you're better than her?"

The brunette laughs. "Puh-leeze. I *know* I am better than her. She grunts like an animal, for crying out loud."

"She's mute," Dexter informs her, shocking me with the understanding in his voice.

The snarky bitch drops her brown eyes to mine. The mock in them boils my blood. "You're mute." She's not asking a question. She is taunting me. "Aww, sweetie. Are you okay? Did naughty men do *really* bad things to you that turned your brain to mush?"

She talks to me like I'm a child, goading me in the same manner the girls at my school did when my mother arrived to pick me up without her clothes. "Is that why you're stupid? Did your daddy play the banjo on your vag—"

Her ridicule is stopped when Dexter's hand flies wildly through the air. He backhands her so hard, she crashes into the wall separating our room from the one next door.

Her hand darts up to cradle her reddening cheek as she slumps to the floor. I watch in reverence when Dexter bridges the gap between them, his steps drawn out and dangerous. "There you go with that word again."

Pain erupts in her eyes when Dexter fists her hair. He drags her to my side of the bed, his clutch strengthening with every painful howl she releases. Our room's floor space is minimal, but I'm certain it feels like being dragged down a football field to the brunette.

When they stop in front of me, Dexter yanks her head back, forcing her eyes to align with mine. "Tell her you're sorry." He barks his order so violently, the window in our room rattles.

The brunette's split lip quivers, but not a peep seeps from her mouth.

"Tell her you're sorry!" Dexter roars, maddened by her delay.

"I-I-I'm sorry," she stammers as fresh tears leak from her eyes.

The blood streaking her teeth matches the anger thundering through Dexter's body. He is colored with rage, the clenching and unclenching of his fist as mesmerizing as his naked form.

"Say it again," he demands, unsatisfied with her pathetic attempt at an apology. "If it doesn't sound sincere this time, I'll remove your tongue with my teeth."

Her throat works hard to swallow at the same time my body tightens with excitement. "I'm sorry. S-S-So sorry." The tear gliding down her purplish cheek heightens the sincerity in her tone.

I stop watching a blob of moisture slip off her quivering jaw when Dexter connects his eyes with mine. "Happy?"

His top lip twitches when I nod. He was hoping I'd say no. I should to teach her a lesson, but I'm not a monster. She'll pay for her sins soon enough. If the blackness filling Dexter's eyes is anything to go by, it will be sooner than expected.

"Get dressed." Dexter jerks his head to the shirt the brunette discarded in a hurry only minutes ago.

He growls my name when I shake my head, refusing his request.

I am not wearing her clothes!

His vicious rumble simpers to a purr when I slip off the bed and head for the bathroom to gather the outfit I was wearing earlier. Some of his simmer is from me offering an alternative to his suggestion, but most of it is from my budded nipples scraping his forearm when I slipped by.

When I return to the room dressed in a baggy white tee and knee-high socks, Dexter tosses a set of keys into my chest. "Wait for me in the car."

The brunette squeaks out a sob, hearing the words Dexter didn't express as loudly as I did. She is crouched on the floor next to his feet, his grip on her hair enough to keep her from speaking. If she hadn't degraded me, I might have felt sorry for her. It is a pity empathy was the first thing my father stripped from me when my mother died.

After gathering my meager possessions, I head for the door. Before I lower the handle, Dexter calls my name. "I'm going to need that."

He doesn't need to say what he is referring to.

The dip in his tone tells me everything I need to know.

When I spin around to face him, the brunette shakes uncontrollably. Plea after plea spills from her mouth as I slowly pace back toward them. I'm glad she's found her voice again, but it's a little too late for clemency. She was mean to me, and Dexter is going to ensure it will *never* happen again.

"Good girl. Now go wait for me in the car," Dexter suggests when I hand him the razor clutched in my hand. His voice isn't the one he used on the brunette. This is a special voice. One he'll only use on me from here on out.

The brunette's pleas amplify with every step I take to the door, but by the time I cross the threshold, there's nothing but silence.

It is a beautiful noise when you have several voices screaming for attention at once.

16

DEXTER

*T*he eyes of a little lamb, the core of a warrior, and the heart of Satan all wrapped in an enticing package. Those were the thoughts I had when handing Megan the blade I used to silence Lucy's taunt. I should have cut out her tongue before killing her to teach her how detrimental words can be to a person's sanity when used the wrong way, but her brutal collision with the wall left me short of time—unfortunately.

From what I sampled before Megan's big, consuming eyes secured my attention, her tongue was mighty tasty.

I didn't take Lucy to my room with the intention of having a threesome with Megan. I wanted Megan to experience the fury I felt when she chose Nick over me, to show her what she missed out on from denying me, but she derailed my campaign in less than a second.

I expected her to pluck the brunette's eyes out of her sockets with her nails, or at the very least, hide in the bathroom for the next several hours. She did no such thing. She blew my challenge out of the water in a way I never anticipated.

She surprised me.

My little skitzo isn't just all shades of fucked-up. She makes me use the left side of my brain—the creative, experimental side that hasn't been exercised in years.

If I didn't have sirens wailing in the distance and a father demanding a virgin to hunt, mount, then display in his trophy cabinet, I'd be exercising that side of my brain right now. I'm as hard as fuck, the taste of Megan's nipple in my mouth and her head resting in my crotch equally responsible. Just a couple of inches higher, and her pants of breath would be enough to get me off.

I suggested Megan hide because Lucy's screams meant meddlesome guests spotted me slipping into my car where Megan was waiting. The authorities are looking for two people, so it was best to keep her hidden.

That issue became non-existent when I swapped my GTO for an old truck some geezer left idling at the gas station two hundred miles back, but since I like having Megan close to me, I made her stay.

Sue me.

I TRAVEL another hundred miles before the heaviness of my eyelids becomes too great to ignore. I'm cutting it close to thirty-six hours without sleep, but that isn't the reason I'm pulling over for some shuteye. The vicious twang in my lower back won't take no for an answer, much less the cotton wool lodged in my throat.

Since he is dead, I'll never get confirmation, but I'm fairly confident if I hadn't killed Joseph last night, he would have gutted me like a dog. He wanted Megan, and he was willing to do anything to get her—including drugging me.

That's why my head was so woozy. It wasn't a mental breakdown or coming face to face with whiskey after a prolonged stint of absence. It was Joseph's weakness for fair-skinned women with big, innocent eyes.

And perhaps the adrenaline Little Ms. Psycho's attention overdoses me with.

Megan is making me deranged—even more than usual. If I weren't relishing the high, I'd be pissed. But alas, you can't be both angry and turned on.

Well, normal men can't be.

"COME ON, Megan, I got us a room."

I dig a room keycard into her thigh, endeavoring to wake her up. She moans before burrowing her head more profoundly into the truck's bench seating.

"Megan..."

I dig the card in harder this time.

Still nothing.

Pissed at the delay, I jog to the passenger side of the truck, hook her ankle, then drag her out of the vehicle. I intend to let her fall to the ground, but before she gets halfway there, my arms dart out to catch her. I still can't hurt her. I want her to bleed via my knife while lying naked in front of me, not some gravel rash ooze that would only satisfy my craving for a few seconds.

Two stitches in my back pop open when I pull Megan to my chest before striding to our hotel. Cautious our truck may have been reported as stolen, I parked several miles away from our hotel to make sure we remain under the radar. Now, I'm wishing I wasn't so cautious. Megan isn't heavy, but the weight of her closeness is enough to kill a man.

I want her beneath me, but I'll be dead if I touch her. One sniff, and my dad will know she isn't pure. He requested her untouched, which means I must deliver her untouched.

Obeying my father's command isn't foreign to me. It's how I survived my last twenty-eight years, but the adrenaline that pools in my brain when Megan is close is just as hard to ignore.

The fiendish glint in her eyes is magnetizing, but the way she looks now—a perfect, limp little doll—makes a switch inside of me flick on. It's one I haven't used in an incredibly long time. My impish heart breeds evil faster than it pumps blood, but when Megan is in my arms, she slows it down.

I buried desires deep inside me years ago thanks to my father's demands. He was looking out for me, ensuring I saw the world for what it is instead of how it made me feel. It was for the best. The world is brimming with cruel, sadistic people. I'm merely staying one step ahead of the pack.

AFTER GRIPPING Megan's ass with one hand, I wave a hotel keycard across our room door. I kick the heavily weighted door shut, then merge deeper into the affluent-smelling space. The hotel clerk had to shuffle reservations to grant me the room I requested. A double would have been adequate, but a king deserves to sleep in surroundings matching his reign. That's why we're not staying in a standard dime-a-dozen motel on the side of the highway. We've got the presidential suite. It's the least I can do, considering this weekend will be Megan's last with a pulse.

I lay Megan on the massive bed in the left wing of our suite before tugging off my boots, shirt, and jeans. Once I am naked, I set to work on undressing Megan. I want her scent embedded in my skin even more urgently than I want to sink my cock into her fragrant, enticing cunt.

"Shh," I tell Megan when she slaps my hands away in the process of removing her blood-stained shirt from her body.

It's not her blood. It is Lucy's blood that Megan removed from the razor blade before cradling it in her palm like a precious gem. Since she is without the floral dresses she donned every day the past two months, the razor has become her security blanket. It makes her feel safe.

I'm glad. I doubt she's felt safe in years.

Once I have Megan's shirt and panties removed, I attempt to pry open her fingers so I can dump the razor on the bedside table. Her grip is so rigid, if I weren't afraid of having my eyes gouged out in the middle of the night, I'd leave it in her hand.

"Megan, it's Dexter, open your hand."

My veins double their thickness when her hand pops open without delay.

Smirking at her submissiveness, I pluck the knife from her palm, dump it with her clothes, then jog to the other side of the bed to dive beneath the sheets. Dissatisfied that I'm on one side of the bed while Megan is on the other, I drag her to my side by her elbow. She releases a frustrated groan. My body hears it in a completely different light.

"Sleep," I instruct her when my cock bracing against her curvy ass rouses her more than our two-mile hike through the woods. "You need your rest. You have a big day on Sunday."

The hum she releases thickens my cock, but she does as instructed.

Her training is going well.

THREE HOURS PASS, and I'm still awake. It isn't Lucy's final plea for clemency ringing in my ear that has prevented sleep, nor is it the throb in my lower back. It is the ache in my cock. Megan's hair is overdue for a wash, so her fruity scent can't override the delicious smell of her cunt.

It's teasing me, taunting me, begging to be consumed.

If I trusted myself, I wouldn't hold back.

I don't trust myself.

Rightfully so. That's like asking me to claim someone's life but not watch their soul fade from their eyes. It is *never* going to happen.

I want to put my tongue on every inch of her before smearing her virginal blood on the walls of her pussy with my cock. My cock roars to life just at the thought of her staring up at me as I claim her as she's never been claimed. I might even give her a taste, make her lick her blood from my cock.

She'd do it. She is a good girl who would always put my needs before her own. If I told her to jump, she would always ask how high.

It is a pity I can't do the same for her. There is only one game master. In this game, it is neither Megan nor me. It is my father.

Realizing I'm never going to sleep with a raging boner, I slip out of bed. I could tiptoe into the bathroom to rub one out like a true psychotic, but all the inspiration I need to take care of my dilemma is right in front of me.

I'd be a fool not to take advantage of the situation.

After wrapping my hand around the base of my cock, I lower my eyes to Megan's pert nipple. It is budded and hard, as if aware of the scandalous situation occurring. I do a long stroke, sending a zap of pleasure down my back for a change instead of the constant throb of pain.

I press my thumb against the vein feeding my cock before

quickening my pace. My eyes scan Megan's naked body as crazily as my hand pumps my shaft. I imagine her lying before me, her hazel eyes shining up at me, her mouth open and ready to catch my spawn. She'd be wet—absolutely saturated with need. I'd gather up her excitement with my tongue, flicking and biting the tight bundle of nerves between her thighs with the reverence of a starved man. When she comes, she'd call my name. It would be a husky and raw cry, her throat clutched by the throes of ecstasy.

I can hear it now, her quickening breaths, her frantic gulps. It's as if she's kneeling before me, waiting for my cum to slide down her throat. She would struggle to swallow everything I offer her, but she wouldn't spill a drop—she'd consume every last one.

She's a good girl like that. She follows instructions well.

"Don't you, my little pet?"

As the urge to come overwhelms me, I close my eyes and flop my head back. My active imagination continues inspiring my pursuit to release. Shockingly, not one of my visuals include my mother. This beauty's hair is lighter, more mousy-brown than a dark storm cloud. Her eyes are flecked with gold and green, and her body is so compact I can palm her entire breast with just one hand. She's a pretty little thing, a doll who likes her coffee as sweet as mine and her lifestyle just as dangerous. She would let me kill without regret. She may even encourage it.

The visual of Megan's approving eyes when she handed me the razor to end Lucy's life pushes sperm up my shaft. I continually pump my hand, not caring where my spawn lands. They can have my DNA. It won't pin me to anything. I'm cautious like that. I didn't wipe every inch of Lucy's mouth, body, and cunt with bleach for no reason. Only Megan makes me heedless. Only she compels me to swap the pieces on the chessboard for a more stacked deck.

Just the thought of mixing things up has my strokes quickening.

I nearly come for the second time. The only reason I don't is because Megan isn't the only one who should be reserving energy. My dad invited me to his stables. That means only one thing. He wants me to hunt Megan with him. He doesn't hunt for an hour or two. He likes to draw out the game, easily making it a three-day expedition.

When my cock goes limp in my hand, my eyes pop open to survey the damage. There isn't any. Not an ounce of my spawn is splattered across the bed. It's pooled in a puddle in the middle of the bundled-up shirt Megan is holding under my half-masted cock. She caught my sperm as rapidly as the sadistic thoughts streaming from her eyes snagged my attention weeks ago.

"Did you like that?" I ask before I can stop my words. "Did you enjoy watching me stroke my cock?"

She nods without shame, her eyes widening with lust.

Her pretty hazel eyes aren't the only things gleaming uncontrollably. Her pussy lips are drenched, and her widely spread thighs ensure I can't mistake the cause of the seductive scent filtering in the air.

"Lie back," I demand, my voice rough with ecstasy.

Like a good little pet, she does as requested without protest. My cock twitches with eagerness for a second round when my eyes absorb her bare mound. She is so wet, evidence of her excitement pools in the crevice separating her ass from her cunt.

"Join your feet together at the base, then fan open your knees."

When she does as instructed, I touch her before I can stop myself. It is only brief but long enough a dangerous switch inside me turns on. She is a virgin as claimed, her attached hymen ending any doubt I never truly had.

I'm tempted to defile her right now, to rip the little strip of membrane stopping me from claiming her altogether. The only reason I don't is because of him—my father. If it weren't for him,

I'd be dead. I most likely wouldn't have left my mother's womb breathing, much less survived my first two years.

Even after years of allegiance, my father rarely seeks retribution, so the least I can do is give him this. He let me track Shelley across the country without a single gripe, and he didn't voice concern about the long game of cat and mouse I played with Cleo, as he knew it made me happy, so how can I deny him this?

I return my eyes to Megan. She is watching me eagerly, trying to read me as skillfully as I read her. "Are you saving yourself?"

She nods without pause.

I should shut down our conversation. I should fuck a thousand women in front of her, but since I've always been as inquisitive as I am fucked-up, I ask, "Who are you saving yourself for?"

Her lips twitch, but not a word spills from her mouth.

I work my jaw side to side before grinding out, "Are you saving yourself for Nick?" My words are practically growled, my body announcing there's only one answer to my question.

My head slants to the side when Megan shakes her head. I am equally pissed and relieved.

She better not be lying to me.

"Then who are you waiting for?"

Panicked by the fury slicking my words, her heart rate quickens. I see her mind race a million miles an hour before the faintest squeak parts her lips, "*You.*"

I take a step back certain I heard her wrong. She doesn't speak. She's mute. But I swear that was the word I heard.

"Me?" I confirm, my tone half-wrathful, half-hopeful.

She pauses long enough the tick in my cock extends to my jaw before nodding. She didn't delay because she is lying. She's terrified about my growing hesitation.

She should be. I'm torn between wanting to slit her throat and kiss the living shit out of her.

Every alpha wants to bang his chest and claim his prize when he is chosen as the cream of the crop. I am no different. I want to devour her until she is dripping with cum and blood. I want to throw her against the wall and fuck her until every grunt she releases sounds like howls of pain. But I can't.

I've only known her a few short weeks. I can't put her above my father. She is a woman. She will never outrank a standard man, let alone one as powerful as my father.

The gleam brightening Megan's eyes dulls when I say, "Close your legs and get under the covers."

Tears well in her eyes as she scampers up the bed, but she remains as quiet as a church mouse. She's a good girl like that. She does as she's told even if it kills her.

Because she is so tiny, the duvet hides her seductive curves within seconds. It doesn't douse the fire roaring in my gut, but it stops stacking it with additional wood.

After dumping the DNA-riddled shirt into the lit fireplace at the side of our suite, I return to my side of the bed. My hands itch to return Megan to my side, but a new voice—one I'm certain I've never heard before—stops me.

It is the voice of reason.

17

MEGAN

J wake up smothered by Dexter. His pulse is as frantic as it was last night when he brought himself to ecstasy, and his skin is misted with as much sweat. There is just one difference. The moans he is releasing now aren't pleasurable. He sounds frightened.

"*Ugh!*" I grunt while nudging him with my elbow.

He stirs for a moment, his moan switching to a pained groan. I roll over, giving me a bird's-eye view of his handsome face and rippled body. The deep groove between his brows and the vicious snarl of his lips reveal my assumptions are accurate. He is having a nightmare.

Recalling the violence Ashlee reacted with when I woke her during a nightmare, I cradle Dexter's twitching jaw before soothing him like a mother would a child. I hum a joyful tune while running my fingers through the dark hairs furled around his temples and down his clenched jaw. It feels natural to take care of him. It feels right. He took care of me last night, so it is only right I return the favor.

Although I would have preferred our night end with Dexter pleasing me as he had pleased himself, I slept well. I don't recall the transfer from our car to the hotel. I felt so safe curled up on Dexter's lap like a cat being stroked by its owner, I slept like a baby. I feel the most revived I've ever been. I feel like a million bucks.

The pleasurable hum thrumming through my body dulls when Dexter suddenly snatches my wrist. He tears it away from his face, his hold so firm it feels like my wrist is about to snap in two.

"*Oww.*" I release a painful groan, wordlessly advising him he is hurting me. I like having his hands on me, but not like this. This is the touch of hate—not love.

"What was that?" Dexter growls, glancing past my shoulder with the eyes of a madman. "Who are you?" He appears to be awake, but his eyes are so lifeless, he may not be.

I hum a few more chords of the "Hush Little Baby" lullaby I was singing earlier, hoping the gentle tune will draw him from his nightmare.

With each note, Dexter's grip on my wrist tightens. By the time I reach the mockingbird part of the song, his fury is uncontained.

"Stop it!" he screams, shaking me. His anger is so white-hot, spittle flies out of his mouth and lands on my cheeks. "Stop it!"

He drops my wrist from his grip so he can slap his head. He hits himself so hard, I'm certain his brain is rattling in his skull. If he keeps increasing the intensity as he is, he will kill himself.

I put myself in the line of fire by launching over his skull to protect his brain with my body. The first few pounds of his fists on my back cause pain to surge through me, but it's nothing compared to the excruciating roars erupting from Dexter's mouth. He sounds like a wild animal. Like his heart is being torn in two.

It takes several more hits and many distressed cries before the scent of my skin removes him from his nightmare.

"Megan..." The horror in his voice makes tears prick my eyes. He nestles his nose between my breasts before inhaling deeply. "Megan."

No words. Even if I could build up the courage to speak as I did last night, there is not a single word I could express right now. I'm too scared. I am not frightened of Dexter. I am petrified of the absolute horror radiating from him when he peers up at me.

Realizing no words will ever comfort him, I return to running my fingers through his wild hair. I gather the droplets of sweat beading on his temples before working on returning the color to his cheeks.

Within a matter of minutes, he is back asleep.

WHEN I AWAKE several hours later, I am alone—again. While scooting across the monstrous-size bed, I take in the opulence I failed to register twice last night. It is beautiful, but nothing could have taken my focus off the splendid image I first awoke to, not even a room fit for a queen. And although my second awakening wasn't filled with sunshine and unicorns, it was just as important as the first. It connected Dexter and me in a way I've never experienced. He needed me. I was there for him.

I just hope it wasn't in vain.

After snapping at the voice in my head to shut up, I stand from the bed. The high thread count sheets feel like clouds caressing my skin when I gather them around my naked form to view the opulence surrounding me. I pretend I'm exploring, but in reality, I am hunting for clues to where Dexter went. He wouldn't leave me defenseless. He cares for me.

I freeze when undoubtable evidence is presented before me. Dexter is sitting at a large, rectangular table, eating a croissant from a pile of many. When he notices me standing at the end of the table gawking at him, he jerks up his chin, requesting me to join him.

I do, albeit hesitantly. It isn't because I'm not hungry—I am starving. It is the look Dexter is giving me. He seems put off by my approach instead of appreciative.

Dexter's eyes lift to mine when I fall into the chair next to him with a sigh. I am so confused. Last night, he looked at me like I had granted his every wish. His look this morning isn't one-tenth of its strength. Since I was medicated for so long, I've never had to handle the emotions I've dealt with the past three days. I'm sure over time, things will settle down, I just wish they would move along more quickly. Being this confused can't be healthy. I am more imbalanced now than I was at Meadow Fields.

Dexter doesn't help the situation when he drags my hair away from my neck with a quick brush of his hand. He sucks in a sharp breath when he spots the faint bruise extending from one ear to the other. It isn't a disappointed gasp. It is similar to the ones he released last night before streams of cum rocketed from his cock.

"We'll ice your neck after we've eaten. See if we can lessen the bruising." His voice is hoarse, either from the dry croissant he is attempting to swallow or remorse. I'm unsure which.

After nodding in agreement, I pluck a Danish pastry from a basket in the middle of the table. My calorie-laden breakfast drops onto the gold-rimmed plate in front of me when Dexter snatches my wrist. My teeth gnaw together as a jolting pain rockets up my arm. Although his hold isn't as painful as it was last night, the inch-wide bruise banding my wrist makes it seem as if it is.

"Who did that?" he asks as his wild eyes dart between my wrist and face. "Who marked you?"

I hide my hand under the tablecloth when he abruptly stands from his chair. Wood scraping across marble floors sounds through my ears when he pushes back from the table like a man in a hurry. I don't know where he is rushing to, but he won't get far if he continuously paces the same three steps.

Several minutes pass with him wearing a hole in the carpet before his eyes return to mine. They are even more desolate than normal. "Was it someone at the hotel? Did someone here hurt you?"

He stops shoving his fingers through his hair when I nod. "Who?" His one word is delivered so violently, it sounds like an entire sentence. "Was it the bellhop? Concierge? Who?"

He whispers threats under his breath, promising harm to the person responsible for my injuries. He will cut them, then castrate them before smashing their teeth in with his bare hands.

His pledge of protection excites me until I realize who they're directed at.

I drop my eyes to my plate, ensuring he can't see my eyes. With Dexter so caught up on plotting the demise of the person responsible for my bruise, he leaves me undisturbed for several long minutes.

I want to say I use the time well. Unfortunately, that isn't the case. My stomach is too twisted up to do anything. Even more so when Dexter places his hand under my chin to raise my downcast head two seconds later. "Who hurt you..." His words trail off when he spots the dishonesty in my eyes. He releases a growl so deep, two towns over hear it. "Don't lie to me, Megan."

When I remain quiet, he raises his hand as if he is going to hit me. It is a ploy to force me to answer him, but it frightens me so much, I start humming a tune before I can stop myself.

Dexter's hand falls from the air like a bomb, the joyful lullaby weighing down his arm as if it is made of concrete. He takes a step back, equally sickened and remorseful. "I hurt you? *Me?*"

His throat works hard to swallow when I hesitantly nod. I don't want to hurt him, but I also don't want to discover the repercussions if I lie to him.

It takes a few seconds for him to read the honesty in my eyes. When he does, he goes into a violent rage. Dishware clatters to the floor as a painful roar erupts from his mouth. "You lied! You're a liar!" He shreds the dining room apart, not the least bit concerned he is damaging the hotel's property.

I understand his quest. I underwent the same form of therapy when I discovered Nick's son was born healthy. I spiked his fiancée's tea with so much misoprostol, she should have bled out on the table. I was so angry at Jenni and Nick, I took out my fury on their unborn son.

What I did was wrong. Nick's son didn't deserve the brunt of my fury.

Dexter shouldn't forget the effects of his childhood, either. I'm not a shrink, but I've spent enough time with them to analyze that Dexter's condition is a result of his childhood. From his reaction to a lullaby, it may have even started when he was a baby—perhaps even in the womb.

It's not absurd to think this way. Some people are born to lead. Others are born like us.

We're not broken.

We are unique.

I wait for Dexter's outrage to subdue before standing from my chair. His violence touched every inch of the dining room, leaving only the chair I was sitting in unscathed.

He balks when I remove his hands from his face so I can crawl into his lap. Because of the difference in our heights and frames, it isn't a hard feat. It's just foreign. I've never wanted to nurture someone as much as I do him. My daddy said I am like my mom, that I don't have an empathetic bone in my body. Dexter proves he was a liar. I care about him so much I'll do anything to stop his pain.

Anything at all.

Dexter's heart pounds in my ear when I nuzzle into his chest. It's so furious I'm afraid it will burst my eardrum. Its frantic pace adds to the danger looming in the air but in a calm, nurturing way. He'll never hurt me. The way he left me unscathed during his violent uproar proves this without a doubt.

I don't care what the many doctors' diagnosis is. I know the truth. Dexter is my protector. My lover. The man slowly reviving my veins with blood. It might be a little murky, but it is still life-saving blood all the same. He will take care of me, and I will do the same for him.

Dexter's tormented eyes bounce between mine when I raise my hand to his face to remove the strands of hair stuck to his temples. After clearing them away, I glide my fingers down his cheeks and across his plump lips. I comfort him without the lullaby I used last night, finally recognizing the tune is partly to blame for his psychotic break.

I caress him for what feels like hours but is more minutes, and just when I think he will never return my affections, his hand traces the bumps of my spine. He draws me closer to him with every contusion he glides past. His silence should be off-putting, but it isn't. He doesn't need to express gratitude for my comfort. I would do it even if he requested that I stop.

It is what a woman does for the man she loves.

18

DEXTER

"We need to leave within twenty minutes. We cannot be late."

Megan stops peering at herself in the mirror to shift her remorseful eyes to me. She isn't looking at me as a psychotic maniac with no grasp on life. She's peering past the layers, seeking the source of my disturbing behavior.

She will be searching a very long time.

Nearly twenty-nine years, to be precise.

"There's no need to put in an effort, Megan. My father won't judge you on how you look." *He'll be too busy formulating how you bleed to assess the clothes you're wearing.*

She sets down the makeup kit I had delivered this morning before standing to her feet. Instead of wearing the clothes I purchased for her when we escaped Meadow Fields, she has on the knee-length skirt and three-quarter-sleeve knitted jacket. The instant I spotted the ensemble in the boutique store of our hotel, I knew it was designed for her. The subtle palette adds to her innocence, and the green foliage enhances her diamond eyes.

My father will be pleased when he sees her. She is the very essence of pure.

After placing her hand on my chest, Megan gives me a look that reveals she's nervously excited. When I told her we were going to visit my father, she misunderstood the situation entirely. She thought I was laying down foundations. I am—somewhat— just not in the way she predicted.

She knows of my secrets, of my inability to keep a rational head when in the depths of a nightmare. For that alone, she will never be my pet. This is the exact reason why I never slept in a woman's bed. I try to maintain control over every aspect of my life, but there are some things I can't regulate, such as my dreams.

I guess the same could be said for Cleo's dad when he killed Shelley. Maybe it was just an accident, and no one was at fault as Megan suggested last night. When it's your time, it's your time. That's what I've been continually telling Megan the past sixteen hours.

Argh! I'm talking like I have a cunt between my legs.

I need to get this woman out of my head. She is making me unhinged. Even more than usual.

My reaction to the bruise circling her wrist was all the indication I needed to know it's time to finalize this part of my playbook. I don't pursue women who remind me of my mother because I am infatuated with her. I hate her so much, I hurt women who look like her because I can't hurt her. Every tear they shed, every scream ripped from their throat, I pretend came from her.

My manic behavior is disturbing but is easily excused. Many years ago, I was diagnosed as having Sadistic Personality Disorder, among other comorbid mental illnesses. In laymen's terms, I'm several shades of fucked-up. I don't just have one mental illness. I have many.

Aren't I lucky?

I laugh at my hilarious inner monologue. It isn't a smart thing to do. Megan is giving me that look again, not the sympathetic one, the one she gave me in the cabin days ago. She's looking at me with love in her eyes.

I snatch her hand off my chest before raising it to my mouth. When the vein in her neck flutters in excitement, I draw my lips over my teeth, halving the impact of my bite. I don't do it because I'm an upstanding guy who buys a dozen roses for a first date. I do it to weaken her eagerness. She wants me to bite her. Not just her wrist, her entire body. I don't answer to anyone's pleas. I do what I want when I want.

Except when it comes to your father.

Feeling my qualm slipping, I ask, "You ready?"

Not waiting for Megan to answer me, I head for the door. Recalling my request for her to wear running shoes instead of the strappy shoes she's been getting around in the past few days, she tugs them on before shadowing me to the elevator bank. With our suite the entire top floor of the hotel, the elevator car comes straight to us—the important guests.

We ride the first ten floors in silence. The tension firing in the air is electrifying. It has the same dramatic edge that kickstarts my pulse before every hunt but in a unique way. It is a foreign feeling that is extremely hard to explain. If I had to put it into words, I could explain it as if I've swallowed the antidote for crazy—like that's even possible.

After pushing aside the unexplainable as a consequence of arriving to a hunt with the target in tow, I continue counting our descent—only thirty-four floors to go.

My wish to evade the confines of an enclosed box triples when the elevator comes to a stop at the twelfth floor. Because the uniformed officer is deep in conversation with a plain-clothed detective, he doesn't immediately notice Megan and me standing at the back of the empty car.

I have a cap hanging low over my eyes, but Megan's face is completely exposed. She looks identical to the photos every news agency in the country has been broadcasting hourly since our escape, and she knows it.

A vein in her neck pulsates as her eyes calculate the distance between her and the officer's gun. She'll never make it in time. His gun case is clipped shut, meaning she'd be shot by the detective before she could remove the gun from his partner's hip.

Not calculating the risk as expertly as me, Megan steps toward the officer. Before she gets us both killed, I grab her wrist, pin her to the wall, then seal my mouth over hers.

The squeak she releases when my tongue delves between her cherry balm-flavored lips alerts the officers that they are not alone. They balk before cocking their heads to the side to watch the spectacle of Megan climbing my frame so she can grind against my stiffening shaft.

As my tongue strokes the roof of Megan's mouth, I watch the officers in the elevator's mirrored wall. I'm hoping the presidential suite keychain dangling from my back pocket will enhance my ruse.

It does—along with Megan's hearty moans.

Every stroke of my tongue along the ridges of her mouth triples her husky groans, and I'm not going to mention her prolonged grinding against my crotch. She kisses me like she's starved of taste, and I'm the only man who has ever caressed her in such a way. She kisses me until I forget why we're kissing. Then she kisses me some more.

My tongue doesn't need to continue the exploration of her mouth. The officer's grumbled comment about impatient honeymooners ensured we were left to ride the elevator alone, but no matter how many times my brain commands me to withdraw, my mouth refuses to listen. Megan tastes like heaven and hell wrapped up in one sadistic little skitzo package.

It is only when a computerized voice announces we have arrived in the underground parking garage do my teeth relinquish Megan's lip from its torture. The meow she releases when I place her onto her feet is her heartiest of the weekend.

"Soon."

Failing to hear the deceit in my tone, Megan skips out of the elevator car, my promise lightening her steps. Our hike to a row of cars far away from prying eyes slows when a deep voice shouts for us to stop. Although their demand isn't one you'd expect upon discovering two escaped inmates from a mental institution, it still prickles my skin with hesitation. It was laced with authority, the tone an officer uses when making an inquiry.

"Remain calm," I instruct Megan while tugging her to my side.

When we spin around to face the voice, my intuition is proved spot on. A young officer I'd guess to be mid-twenties has a clipboard balancing on his washboard stomach. He stands to the right of a group of rental cars. He appears to be matching the tags with the guests of this hotel.

Goddammit—I knew we should have left yesterday.

I'm getting careless.

She's making me weak.

I stop glaring at Megan to raise my eyes to the rookie officer. "Can we help you, officer?" I keep my tone friendly, even though I am anything but.

He stops peering at his clipboard to lock his eyes with mine. It is virtually impossible with how low the rim of my cap is. "License and registration, please. No vehicles can enter or exit this garage without being jotted down on my sheet."

He taps his pencil on his clipboard as his smirk increases to a smile. He's not smiling to be friendly. He has Megan in his sights. I'm not surprised. For each day she is weaned from medication, the more beautiful she becomes. The healthy dose of psycho in her eyes has done wonders for her complexion.

"Hey, you look familiar," the officer croons, heading our way. "Are you from around these parts—"

"Should I be concerned about the number of officers here this evening, sir? My wife, she's pregnant. I don't want anything to happen to her and our unborn son."

Megan's eyes rocket to mine as swiftly as the officer's drop to her stomach. He's inspecting her enticing frame for a bump it doesn't have. His gawk only lasts a matter of seconds, but it is long enough for me to advise Megan of our plan of attack.

After slipping me the razor from the hidden pocket of her dress, Megan clutches her stomach. Her throat-curdling cry startles the officer's legs into gear. He gallops across the oil-stained concrete, his keys jingling on his hip with every step he takes.

He curls his arm around Megan's shoulders then guides her to a bench seat. "It's okay, ma'am. There's no reason to be scared. I'll keep you safe."

His promise causes my eye to twitch.

It also spares him his life.

I smack him over the head with a fire extinguisher attached to the wall instead of slitting his throat as planned. I don't know why I offer him clemency. I've never given anyone a pardon before, much less a member of law enforcement. Perhaps it was his last-ditch attempt to show Megan not all men are evil? He may very well be the last gentleman she will encounter in her lifetime.

"Grab his keys," I demand of Megan while nudging my head to his belt. My voice is high with the adrenaline it usually exerts when I've killed, but my thirst for blood isn't close to being quenched.

Soon, I tell myself.

Once Megan has the officer's keys, I hook my arms under his sweaty pits and drag him to his patrol car. Recognizing my strategy, Megan pops open his trunk before removing her sweater to clear away the drops of blood the wound in the back of his head left on the concrete.

After a quick glance at the clipboard balancing on his chest, I slam the trunk shut. As suspected, police located the stolen truck yesterday morning. Although they haven't linked its theft to us, I'm not taking any risks. I've amassed enough the past four days, I can't possibly fit any more in.

My eyes stray to the passenger door of the cruiser. "Jump in."

Megan glares at me like I am insane. It is a look I've been given numerous times in my life.

"We're only taking him for a little ride until we can switch cars."

Her glare grows, wordlessly expressing her demands.

"I promise," I growl through clenched teeth, more peeved at her fondness for the officer than her demand for less carnage.

After Megan slips into the passenger seat, I get behind the steering wheel. I take the exit of the underground garage forcefully, ensuring the sizable speed bump issues the officer the hit I am unable to give him. *Yet.*

With flashing lights and a loud siren, we travel twenty miles at a record-setting pace. Safeguarding the promise I made to Megan, I take advantage of our mode of transportation by pulling over a Ferrari roaring down the freeway. It is only right I confiscate his car for his bad judgment. The laws are there for a reason. If every Tom, Dick, and Harry did what they want, when they want, the country would be overrun with people like Megan and me.

Nobody wants that. Not even me. There's a certain uniqueness that comes from being batshit crazy. Not everyone can be this remarkable.

"Tie their shoelaces together."

Megan slants her head to the side and arches a brow. The low hang of the sun bouncing off her shining eyes makes it harder to look annoyed.

"It will be funny. When they try to run, they'll trip over." I barge her with my hip, adding some playfulness to my request. It is either barge her or kiss her again. Considering we're only five miles from my father's estate, I settle for the friendly vibe instead of a passionate one.

With a roll of her eyes, Megan does as instructed. I knew she would. She's a good little pet.

While she knots the officer's shoes with the Ferrari owner's loafers, my eyes drift to the speedster's Rolex. "Shit, we're going to be late."

I yank Megan away from the police cruiser before slamming down the trunk. She lands in the Ferrari's leather-stitched seat with a thud when I toss her inside. She grunts, unappreciative of my manhandling. She'll thank me when she discovers my father's dislike of tardiness.

When I floor my foot on the gas pedal, the tires fail to gain traction the first ten seconds. Thankfully, it doesn't take long for us to be weaving through the traffic surrounding us.

We arrive at my father's estate with barely a minute to spare. I don't care that it is by the skin of our teeth. A second early is still not late.

As I guide the Ferrari down a gravel driveway I've traveled many times, Megan's eyes go crazy. Just like many before her, when I referred to my father's estate as the "stables," she envisioned a rundown country estate. That isn't the case. Not in the slightest.

The grandeur of his home is as extravagant as a palace. Large clay bricks hold up the four-story, twenty-two bedroom, sixteen-bathroom design on over twenty-five hundred acres of estate. It is the derelict stables in the middle of his hunting ground four miles from here that gave it its title. This is where he brings his favorite pets, the ones he plans to keep longer than a night or two.

Confusion slides my foot from the gas pedal to the brake.

Is that why he asked me to bring Megan here? Does he want to make her his?

Before I can answer myself, a man emerging out of the hatch above the main entrance stairs steals my focus. My father gallops down the stairs of his palace, his smile big enough to compete with the moon.

Megan grunts, requesting to know if the man with snow-white hair and black-as-death eyes is my father. With my throat closing up, I nod, answering her question with as many words as she used to ask it.

She smiles as if pleased. She shouldn't judge a book by its cover. Not all stories between the covers are fiction. Some are factual.

My father is a brilliant man. He obtained his substantial wealth in a way many hope to emulate but will most likely never achieve. He writes books. I'm not talking hearts-and-flowers romance stories women like Megan enjoy reading. I'm talking blood and gore, psychological thrillers with missing women and frenzied maniacs who love the scent of blood and crave their next kill like a drug.

His stories have been adapted into major motion pictures. His name is well-known amongst celebrities, politicians, and even the president of our great country. He has them all fooled, believing the words he pens are fiction. I know for a fact they are not. Every story he has written is a true story, even the one that includes the death of my mother.

As Megan is aided from her seat by Charles, my father's long-term butler slash deviant, my father jogs to my side of the car. He greets me with the eagerness of a man many years younger. His excitement about his upcoming hunt is beaming out of him.

"Moose." He ruffles my hair like he did when I was a child before pulling my head down to his chest, which is no easy feat considering I am four inches taller than him. "I didn't think you were going to make it on time. I had my stick ready."

He's not speaking figuratively. He has a broom stick with a nail stuck in one end. If you are a couple of minutes late, you're struck in the head with the non-sharp end of the stick. If you are tardy by five minutes or more, you're hit with the nail end. The amount of hits and the strength used is determined by my father on the spot. There is no sense to his madness.

"Who is this?" my father questions when Megan stops at my side. He isn't asking in interest. He sounds annoyed.

"This is Megan. My pet." My last two words are whispered but delivered loud enough both Megan and my father hear them.

"This isn't who I am waiting on," my father snarls, snubbing Megan's offer of a handshake.

His rejection should relieve me, but all I am feeling is concern.

"Who is this woman, Dexter?"

My worry grows. The quick revert from Moose to Dexter is a telltale sign his paranoia is at an all-time high.

"This is Megan." I speak slow as if he is hard of hearing. "She helped me escape—"

"No. No. No. No. *No!*" He tugs on his hair, sending the perfectly straight strands into spikes. "She is *not* the woman we discussed over the phone." His hand falls from his hair so he can click his fingers together. Charles arrives at his side two seconds later. "This is your pet."

He slaps the silver tray Charles is balancing on his palm three times before pivoting away from me. His psychosis lapse is nothing new to me, but Megan appears a little unsure how to handle it. She floats a few steps back before fixating her eyes on the ground.

It takes me several seconds glancing at the photo to recognize the blonde-haired, blue-eyed woman peering back at me. It is the goth-lover, Ashlee, before she went to the dark side.

"She escaped at the same time as us, but she isn't with us," I explain to my father. When he roars like an animal, I quickly add, "I could get her for you."

That secures his attention.

"You can?" He sounds like a child being promised a bike for Christmas.

I nod while deliberating how to deliver my next sentence. "But she doesn't look like that anymore. She's... ah... impure," I settle on.

Anyone would swear I admitted to lacing his drink with arsenic for how loud he gags. "She's not innocent?"

"No." I drag out the short word dramatically. Ashlee's photo makes her look like a preacher's daughter. She certainly isn't one of them.

Well, not anymore.

"But she is?" My father steps closer to Megan, his interest now notable. He trails his eyes down her frame partly hidden by my body, loitering on the modest length of her skirt longer than her eyes. "She looks pure, just in a different way." He returns his eyes to mine. "Is she like us?"

He doesn't mean mentally challenged. He's asking if she's a

fighter. He likes his targets to be innocent but with a hostile edge that will push the hunt into overtime.

It takes a mammoth effort, but I squeak out, "Yes."

My father smiles a grin like Hannibal in *Silence of the Lambs* before holding out his hand in offering to Megan. She takes it, although hesitantly. She is good at reading people. She knows she is amongst greatness.

Her eyes rocket to mine when my father leans in to take a deep whiff of her hair.

"*It's okay,*" I silently mouth when his nose trails down her neck, over the bumps of her erratically heaving chest, and past her quivering stomach.

She squeaks when he thrusts his nose between her thighs to authenticate her purity, but since she trusts me, she doesn't slap him away as predicted.

Although disappointed by her lack of gall, I'm appreciative of her submissiveness.

My father growls, his stamp of approval delivered without words. "Who would have known? The lack of purity these days had me wondering if women were born devirginized."

He laughs, prompting me to mimic him. I either laugh or be subjected to torture. Nobody wants the latter, not even a madman like me. I prefer delivering the punishments, not being on the receiving end of them.

"Charles!" my dad barks.

Like magic, Charles appears out of nowhere.

"Take..."

"Megan," I fill in.

"Megan to her room and order her some supper..."

"We've already eaten."

My father continues talking as if I never did, "Then draw her a bath. Let's relax her muscles before exhausting them."

When Charles places his hand on Megan's back to guide her into my father's manor, her eyes stray to mine.

"Go on," I say, demanding she follows Charles's lead.

I'm not going to lie. It isn't easy for me to do. She killed for me. She maimed for me. She would go to the ends of the earth for me. But everything she has or will do for me, the man standing next to me has already done.

"What time will the show begin?"

My father stops watching Megan's reluctant retreat to shift on his feet to face me. His pupils are massive, his excitement palpable. Although he doesn't like my deep snarl, he isn't stunned by it. Hunting has never been my thing. I like a slow, panther-like game, the watching from afar before creeping up on them unaware. I don't like my women reeking of fear, sweat, and blood before sleeping with them. I like them smelling that way once I'm done with them.

After absorbing the low-hanging sun for a few seconds, my father returns his eyes to mine. "An hour. Possibly two."

His eagerness to get the hunt underway isn't surprising. He's on the brink of a mental breakdown. That's why he's acting so maniacally. Megan is his ticket out of Crazyville. She will give him the relief he needs without requiring him to move a piece on his chessboard.

He'll just destroy mine instead.

"Are we doing it here or at the stables?"

My father's lips quirk. "We? You're joining the hunt?"

Ignoring the bile burning my throat, I nod.

"Good." My father smiles, welcoming the challenge. "We'll do it at the stables. I don't want to scare my little pet too soon."

His reply would make most people assume he is referring to Megan. I'm not most people. But I am confused.

If he already has a pet, why does he want Megan?

My unasked question is answered when my father curls his arm around my shoulders to guide me into the house. "Come, son. Let me introduce you to your new mother."

MY FATHER'S choice in captive is nothing out of the ordinary—early thirties, big worldly eyes, slim frame, and naked head to toe. Her hair is the same burned charcoal color my mother's was, and her nipples are a similar shade of brown. She is pretty, but with her eyes brimming with fear instead of psychotic tendencies, she is demure. Boring. *Nothing like Megan.*

"Please," she whispers when we return to the hall. I assume her plea is for me until she adds, "I did as you asked. I won't disobey you again."

Now my father's desire to hunt makes sense. He wants to punish his latest plaything for disobedience by showing her what will happen if she doesn't follow his command to a T. He could hunt her instead of Megan, but since she is nearly an exact replica of my mother at the age she was before he killed her, he's giving her one final chance to make amends.

He offered the same mercy to my mother.

She didn't conform.

I can only hope Megan doesn't follow her footsteps.

19

MEGAN

"*N*o! Not a dress. Wear pants. Thick pants."

Dexter snatches the dress out of my hand before moving to a closet in the far corner of the room. It is stocked with an assortment of women's clothing. His father must have bought out an entire boutique as these outfits are for all shapes and sizes.

After handing me riding pants, a long-sleeve shirt, panties, and a blazer, Dexter heads for the bathroom I just exited. My body is well-pampered, but the soothing oils Charles placed in the water did nothing to ease the knot in my stomach.

Dexter's dad is a handsome man, but something about him is off. His greeting... let me just say, I've never been greeted like that, not even after spending five years in a mental asylum for the criminally insane.

"Where are the panties you wore today?" Dexter asks after a quick search of the bathroom floor fails to locate them.

I shrug, unsure. They were there five minutes ago.

"Are they in your dress?" The urgency in his tone shocks me.

He's acting as if my underwear is a priceless treasure. "Then check!" he shouts when I once again shrug.

I jump to his command. My wish to please him so dire, my towel falls from my body.

Air hisses through Dexter's teeth when I spin around to face him a few minutes later. It isn't my nudity sparking his response. It is showing him my empty hands. "He's so sure he is going to win he's already claiming trophies."

His words aren't for me, so I don't reply, but when a deep scowl mars his handsome face, I move toward him, wanting to ease his pain as I have several times the past twenty-four hours.

"Don't," he warns, stopping my steps midstride. "Get dressed. *Please.*"

His unusual plea floods me with worry, but it doesn't stop me from following his command.

Once I am dressed, Dexter guides me out of the room. His family estate is beautiful. The hallway is lined with paintings. They're artistic pieces that need more than a quick glance to adequately appraise them. I think they're nudes, but the women's bodies are contorted in odd angles.

"Did you drink the bottle of water I sent to your room?" Dexter asks when we are halfway down the hall, drawing my eyes from a painting of a woman without a head.

I nod.

"And the pills? Did you take them?"

This nod is harder to deliver than my first one. I hate lying. I took two of the four tablets Charles offered me. The other two are stashed under the pillow in my room.

My eyes shoot to Dexter when he guides me outside. When he said we were going to play a game, I figured it would be held in the den I walked by earlier.

"We play outside. Zip up your coat." He tugs up the zipper before I get the chance.

I jump out of my skin when his father arrives at our side two seconds later. His steps were so agile, I didn't hear them. He smiles as if pleased by my skittish response.

Dexter's father is attractive with platinum blond hair and dark, dangerous eyes. He is fit for a man of his age, which I guess would be early sixties. Unlike the buttoned-up shirt and black trousers he was wearing earlier, he has on a plaid shirt, dirty jeans, and boots covered with vibrant splotches of blood.

I stop trying to decipher if the blood is human or animal when I'm overcome with a bout of dizziness. I clutch my temples, circling the throb there. It doesn't begin to stop me from swaying. If anything, it makes it worse. I feel like I am moments away from collapse.

Sensing my unspoken worry, Dexter scoops me into his arms. I only know it is him because of his virile, manly scent. The wooziness inflicting my head is so blistering it has blurred my vision beyond recognition.

"Where is Charles taking her?" Dexter asks, his words shake by his gallop down a set of stairs. His hurried movements double the throb in my skull and force my eyes to taper closed.

"That is not how this game works, son. Locating the target is half the fun."

Target?

When I am placed down on a cool, plastic surface, I beg my eyes to open. No matter how hard I fight their heaviness, they refuse to budge. They feel like they're being taped down with the same sturdy material currently binding my wrists together.

"She can't run if you tape her ankles. I thought you liked taking down your targets when they're on the move?"

Dexter's words sound like they are delivered underwater. They're barely audible.

"Who is that? What are they doing here? This hunt was supposed to be just me and you. You didn't say you were bringing in additional hunters!"

A scuffle sounds through my ears before Dexter's dad replies. I can't hear a word he is speaking. A black hole is creeping over me, swallowing me whole. I can't move or scream. I can barely breathe through the weight on my chest.

Horrible thoughts bombard me—none of them are pretty. I'm scared and feeling oddly alone, considering I am surrounded by people. I can hear their footsteps, smell the adrenaline slicking their skin, but I am the loneliest I've ever been.

A tear stops trekking down my cheek when a callused finger sweeps it away. "Remember what I told you, Megan. You didn't escape hell to give up now. Gods fight. Cowards weaken. No matter what you hear or see, remember who you are."

Dexter's deep timbre fades when a motor kicking over vibrates through my body. My stomach lurches into my throat, tires rolling over an uneven surface, activating an alerted response from my body.

Where am I going? And why isn't Dexter coming with me?

We travel for several miles. I can't tell you exactly how many. With my mind precariously balanced between irrationally panicked and borderline psychotic, keeping count of the number of tire rotations was impossible.

With the dampness in the air growing as rapidly as the heaviness of my eyelids, I can only assume we're in the forest Dexter steered us through earlier today. Although my eyes are shut, I know it isn't as pretty as it was earlier. The leaves will no longer be wilted and orange. They'll be dead and lifeless. I won't misunderstand the moss woven through the willow trees as an extension of their beauty. I'll see it for what it is—vermin sucking the marrow straight from the trees' core.

I am imagining it as a scary and dark place, similar to a graveyard at midnight.

Rain taps on metal when we come to a stop, but it is scarcely heard over the buzzing of bugs and the hoot of an owl. I twist my neck to the side when the creak of a car door sounds through my ears. It is virtually impossible to do since my head feels the weight of ten bowling balls.

"Come on, sweetheart, time to go home," says a voice in the distance, one I immediately recognize. It is Charles, the man who served me sparkling wine and stuffed olives for supper.

His leathery hands curl around my wrist so he can drag me off the tarp-like material Dexter laid me on. With a grunt and a heave, he tosses me over his shoulder. Other than the stomps of his boots on the rain-sodden ground, I hear nothing else. We are in isolation, my screams utterly pointless.

"I laid down a blanket for you in case you wake before he is ready."

Charles isn't talking to offer me comfort. My limbs are so heavy on his shoulder, I doubt he knows I am awake. He is doing it to distract his thoughts from the remorse in his tone, to ensure he doesn't give in to temptation.

"There is a bottle of water for you as well. I loosened the seal so it won't be hard for you to open it."

He lays me down with a groan. Blanket fibers scratch my neck and face. It isn't damp like Charles' shoulder. It must be protected from the rain by a shelter.

"The sedatives will wear off within an hour or two. I suggest you run before they do. It will be best for you to be unaware of what is coming. Don't run for the manor. No one there will help you. Not even Dexter."

The bang of a trapdoor being slammed shut makes my bones jump out of my skin.

"I'll set the timer for an hour. It isn't as long as Mr. Leicester requested, but he'll enjoy the hunt more if he actually hunts you instead of lying in wait. You have no bragging rights to a stuffed bear carcass if you aren't the man who caught it."

He chuckles as if amused. Well, I assume it is a chuckle. The wooziness in my head has me missing half his words. I'd have no trouble filling in the gaps if I could just open my eyes.

Unfortunately, my fight to stay out of the blackness is lost within seconds of Charles leaving me.

20

DEXTER

I don't know why I whispered encouraging thoughts into Megan's ear before Charles took her to the stables. You can run all you like, but no one can hide from death. *Not even Death himself.* The sedatives I forced Megan to take already weakened our game, let alone the four additional hunters my father invited onto his playground.

This is so unlike him. He's never invited outsiders to the stables before. He is on the verge of psychosis. I am seeing the same signs in him I witnessed in myself during the hours leading to my mental breakdown yesterday. But this... this isn't him at all.

He hunts for the thrill, for the adrenaline associated with it. Tonight's game isn't filled with palpable excitement. It is laden with hate, inspired by death. He's not hunting Megan because his thirst for blood is the strongest it's ever been. He is killing for glory instead of need.

I understand his quest. I too have killed for reasons other than an insatiable appetite. I am not judging him. I am merely confused. The man who raised me was a brilliant, cunning man.

He taught me that no one is more revered or important than me. That I was not greatness waiting to happen, I was already great.

That is not the man standing across from me now.

This man is demented. Hyper-sensitized. If I didn't know any better, I might even say medicated. He's not strategizing his game plan for the most direct maneuver. He is wishing for the game to be over before it truly begins. I've only ever seen him unhinged once before. It was when...

"You fell in love with your pet."

I intended to say my comment inside my head, but the words slipped from my lips before I could stop them. I'm glad. If I was having any doubts about my theory, my father's wide eyes and unspoken rebuttal soon take care of them. He's not hunting Megan to forewarn his captive what will happen to her if she doesn't obey his every command. He is doing it to prove he is still in the game, that he is still capable of ruling his sanction with eminence.

He's hunting Megan to prove a point.

"Don't be absurd. My pet will follow this routine. I'm just preparing her for the carnage."

Lies, nothing but lies spill from his lips.

"You know that isn't the way I operate anymore. I didn't just teach your mother. She taught me as well. Most importantly, that people like us can never fall in love."

He pours two servings of whiskey into dusty glasses before handing one to me. His hand trembles so fiercely, brown liquid spills over the rim and onto the floor.

I ignore his nerves. He always gets extra agitated in the lead-up to a hunt.

"She was never going to understand us, Dexter. That's why I had to do what I did. I didn't want her to die, but she was hurting you, so I had no choice."

He tosses down a mouthful of whiskey before suggesting I do the same. The last thing I want is to haze my mind with alcohol, but I need something to take the edge off the pain rocketing through my lower back. I have to be on my game tonight. I am the youngest and fittest here, but I am competing against a man who has hunted for longer than I've been born.

Megan left over an hour ago, but my father can still smell her scent lingering in the air. How do I know this? I can smell her as well. She's not just embedded in my skin. She's underneath it. Never to be removed.

When I place my empty glass of whiskey on the counter, my father nudges his head to the bottle, asking if I want another. I shake my head, amplifying the immediate buzz the whiskey caused in my veins.

"Are you not going to finish yours?" My words slur like I've drunk a gallon of whiskey instead of a measly glass. I wiggle my tongue around my mouth, loosening its uncooperativeness.

When I take a step toward the bar for a glass of water, the room spins around me. The pain zinging my back no longer exists when my hands dart out to steady myself. I accidentally bump my glass off the counter, exposing a gritty substance coating the bottom of it.

Suspicion runs rife through my veins. "You drugged me?" My voice resembles a snake's hiss in the seconds leading to his venomous strike. "You drugged your own fucking son!"

My father steadies my wobbly legs by leaning me into his chest. His whispered words are too low for my thumping ears to hear when he guides me to a mangy chair in the middle of the room. I watch him through kaleidoscope vision when he returns to the group of men standing at the side of his den, gawking at me with concern.

"It's okay," he assures them, his voice brimming with concern. "This is all a part of the detoxification process."

When a man with a receding hairline asks if they should stay to help with my rehabilitation, my father assures him he has everything under control. He plays the part of a devoted father well. Even I'm convinced he is on a mission to rid me of evil.

After seeing out the men I thought were hunters, but now realize are guests, my father returns to the dark nook in his detached workshop at the back of his family manor. The manic glint his eyes held earlier has vanished, replaced with the gleam of a man in the midst of his prime.

"What did I tell you, son? What was the number one rule you swore you'd *never* break again after your arrest?" He flips a chair around to face him before straddling it backward. "You were not to fall in love... *ever again!* It's a trick, a ploy, another way of medicating us. Women do *not* love us. They want to contain us. Control us. They want to stop us from being the men we were born to be! I thought your arrest would have proven that to you."

He scoots his chair closer, bringing his face to within an inch of mine. "That's why I'm doing this. It was not my intention, but I've seen the signs you refuse to acknowledge. I was already suspicious of the indecisiveness in your tone when I asked if she was pure. You couldn't stand the thought of her with another man. You didn't even want to consider it."

He *tsks* me loudly. "That wasn't your only downfall. You got sloppy. You left your hand wide open for the world to see. Your eagerness to put Ashlee in her place left me no doubt about what I needed to do. Then I saw how you looked at her when you thought I wasn't watching." He sounds disgusted like his throat is burning with the same bile scorching mine. "You did the same thing with Shelley. That's why I had to send her away."

My eyes widen in shock. *I knew she didn't leave of her own accord.*

"Don't act surprised, son. We don't share the same blood, but I am still your father. It is my job to protect you from the vile, ill-informed people who think they know better than me. I hated seeing you locked away, but I had no other choice."

He locks his eyes with mine, ensuring I can see the honesty in them.

He didn't protect me.

He had me prosecuted.

"Megan will *never* love you. She will *never* conform to our ways. Our uniqueness makes us unlovable." When I try to rebut, he pushes his finger to my lips. "Lies will only deepen the cuts I place in her thighs."

Usually, the idea of Megan's luscious thighs streaked with blood arouses me, but coming from my father's mouth, it doesn't have the same effect. It fills me with rage and reddens my cheeks.

"You killed Joseph for her."

Because my father's statement is honest, I don't attempt a denial. I did kill Joseph for Megan, and I will do the same thing to any man who dares to touch her.

"That's what I thought," my father murmurs, reading me with an ability he's always had. "She'll ruin you like your mother ruined me. That's why I summoned you here instead of the stables. I am going to do what you should have done the night you escaped Meadow Fields."

He saunters to a dark corner of the room, his steps arrogant and slow. "I am going to disfigure Megan, fuck her, smear her with my cum, then kill her. And just like your beady little eyes couldn't stay off me when I governed your mother, you're going to watch me do it."

Violence roars through me when he yanks a tarp off a square contraption at his right. Megan is curled in a ball in the bottom of a cage. She appears to be sleeping peacefully on a knitted blanket.

A roar unlike anything I've ever felt rolls up my chest when my father pokes her with a stick. He jabs the pointy end into her milky white skin, scratching the little freckle high on her thigh. "Look at the contrasting colors between her skin and her blood. She will bleed beautifully."

My back arches off the couch. My endeavor to get to Megan fills me with inhuman strength, but I barely budge an inch. I am paralyzed from the chest down. My father finds my attempt to stuff his words down his throat with my fists amusing. It brightens his eyes with a sadistic edge and furls his lips.

"Oh, dear lord, you've got the same murderous look in your eyes your mother had when I held you under the water the day you were born." His eyes flicker as if he is recalling fond memories as they drink in the scar on my left brow. "The thought of losing you had her toeing the line for years. She never once went against me."

I suck in a sharp breath, struggling to stay ahead of the debilitating confusion bombarding me. "My mother disobeyed you every chance she got. That's why you killed her. She wouldn't conform. She hurt me, brutally and without sorrow. She maimed me as if I were an animal. That's why I'm fucked in the head because she filled my brain with lies and twisted my beliefs."

My eyes snap to my father when his deep laughter rattles through my chest. It only takes glancing into his evil eyes for the briefest second for clarity to form. It arrives as clear and direct as it did yesterday.

This is just a game to him. I am not his son. I am a token on the chessboard he's been playing the past fifty-plus years. I am a mere pawn for him to fuck with.

It is a pity he underestimated how well he trained me.

I am not the puppeteer.

I am the master—a god!

"Now, Megan!"

My father's neck doesn't even snap halfway around before Megan's blade jumps across his throat in the exact pattern we rehearsed multiple times last night. The scent of her fruity hair hits my senses when she weaves down low to nick the femoral artery in his left thigh.

He immediately buckles to his knees.

The vision of his eyes darkening with death thickens my cock. Those are the exact pair of eyes that tormented my dreams for years, but if it weren't for the hum of a lullaby, I would have never understood why.

The lady crawling onto my lap to nuzzle into my chest broke through the fog. She shattered the wall my father built around my brain without a word escaping from her lips. She made me see things clearly.

My mom didn't abuse me. She loved me. That is why my father killed her. He was jealous of the immediate bond she had with me. She saw past the blackness in my heart and loved me even with my flaws.

My father wanted her to do the same for him, but he went about achieving it the wrong way. He took something angelic and tried to tarnish it. When that didn't work, he removed the one thing she loved and made it an exact replica of him. Me.

I was born this way, but I am also a consequence of my father's obsession. A pawn to be used and abused. He kept me caged because he couldn't fully clip my mother's wings. He could have killed me once his game with my mother expired, but that would have concluded his game in an unsatisfactory manner.

You don't win a game of chess by removing only the pawns from the board. You go after the king. You go against a man as powerful as you.

I was not my father's son.

I was his challenger.

And now, thanks to Megan, I am his successor.

As one game ends, another one starts. There is just one difference this time around. I don't need to cage Megan to force her to love me. I merely need to set her free. I don't mean in the literal sense. I am referring to the dark veins woven around her heart, about letting her express herself without fear of persecution. I'm going to awaken her hunger for blood so rampantly, the only thoughts she will conjure of Nick will be ones that involve his death.

A good soul can cure the evilness in anyone, but only a black soul can utterly consume them.

21

MEGAN

*M*y knees wobble as I carry Dexter to his borrowed car parked at the side of the manor. He isn't overly heavy, but excluding a couple of days ago, it's been a while since I've carried anyone on my back. My father also didn't move as much as Dexter. He was too drunk to do anything, much less fight me.

I should have hated him for wasting all our money on alcohol, but since it kept his focus off me, I supplied him with endless bottles of whiskey. I wasn't old enough to buy it, but some good comes from people feeling sorry for you. They don't want to help you. They merely want to usher you out of their store as soon as possible that they're willing to sell alcohol to a fourteen-year-old child.

Dexter isn't drunk, but whatever his father gave him had him sleeping like a baby for the past several hours. He rambled constantly under his breath. Nothing he said made any sense, but it all followed a similar pattern. That he should have protected his mother. That he should have believed her. And that he will *never* make the same mistake again.

I offered him comfort the best I could, but there's only so much I can do while in the arena that caused his nightmares. If I don't want him to go into a full psychosis, I need to get him out of this place as soon as possible. A two-star motel isn't the best location to unscramble the mess, but it's got to be better than staying here. Being here will harm Dexter more, and the way he patted my hair while promising to fix his mistakes has me more than eager to seek a secondary location.

I like when he pats my hair and tells me I'm a good girl. Not once have I ever been praised. Not even by my mother. I thought it was because of all the hurtful things my father said to her. That she couldn't understand how to give praise because she had never received it. But I'm beginning to wonder if that's the truth. Perhaps she didn't love me like my father always told me. Maybe she was selfish and all about herself. Sometimes that is the only way you can live.

Thankfully, I won't need to worry about that anymore. I'll have Dexter by my side, and together, we will be unstoppable.

I just need to get him far away from this horrible ranch.

If I had left my family ranch when I was old enough to do so, perhaps I wouldn't have been admitted to the mental hospital before the age of twelve. My life has been one doctor visit after another and a ton of medication in between. I can't recall the last time my brain was this clear. It's still hazy, and there's lots of murkiness to sludge through, but it's nowhere near as glum as it once was.

It's so clear, I'm now realizing how silly I was for believing Nick was my savior. He didn't save me from the torment. He pushed me headfirst into it. He was mean and bitter, and he always took *her* side.

That won't be the case with Dexter. He will look after me. He might even love me.

We'll make sure of it.

Just a little bit further, I mutter to the determined voices in my head since my mouth refuses to cooperate with my brain. Through the constant chatter, I can hear the words I want to speak. They're rolling around in my head, but they won't come out no matter how hard I try.

I haven't spoken in years, so I shouldn't be so hard on myself. Everything takes time.

Even murders aren't thought up on a whim.

I hope Dexter isn't too mad when he discovers I didn't take all the pills he gave me. The water served with my supper made me super woozy. I hated feeling like that. My mind was in a haze for years, so I'll do everything in my power not to feel that way again.

I don't want to get in trouble. He said once we killed his dad, we would be free to be with one another. I don't want to lose that chance. I also don't want to lose him. It's scary out here alone, even more so when the wind whistles through the trees. They sound like women crying, like the tormented screams that ripped from my mother's mouth multiple times before she cried enough tears to fill the bathtub.

She cried all the time. Even while cuddling me, her cheeks were drenched. Daddy said the men who visited our house once a week made her upset. I never once believed him. She cried more after he went to check on her. I don't know what he said, but she always yelled the same thing on repeat once he left. "I hate you. I'll hate you till the day I take my last breath."

She did precisely that only two days later.

After shaking off the bad memories like I'm not carrying a man double my size on my back, I continue my journey. It is a slow and treacherous trek, but with a strength I never knew I had in me, we make it to the flashy car Dexter borrowed yesterday just as the man who carried me into the marshland exits the manor.

He warned me not to come back here, but where else am I meant to go? Dexter's father is dead, his son is belligerent, and I don't have a single penny to my name.

"*Ugh*," I grunt when Dexter's slip into the car doesn't occur without him pulling out a chunk of my hair. It reminds me of how I got the chip in my front tooth. As you can imagine, it wasn't pleasant, but since we need to get out of here before our escape is interrupted, I'll save the details for another day.

After slipping into the driver's seat of a pricy sports car, I take off like a bat out of hell. I don't know how to drive a car with this horsepower. We nearly skid out of control, but a quick yank on the steering wheel veers us back toward the main road.

My veins are already doing the weird pulsating thing they did after I hung my father from the beam in the barn, but it feels different today. I don't know if that is because Dexter is seated next to me or because the man I killed isn't related to me by blood.

Whatever it is, it sees me flattening my foot to the floor.

We make it to Motel 6 at a record-setting pace. It is the same motel I wordlessly begged Dexter to take me to after he sharpened the blade on my razor. I'm not a natural-born killer like Dexter. It takes a lot of pushing to get me to that place. My father hurt me for years, but it was only when he told me I had to pick between my one true love or him did I snap.

The same can be said for Dexter. If we didn't kill his father, I wouldn't be here for him to love.

That isn't something he ever wants to face.

I hope.

After gathering up a bundle of bills from Dexter's wallet and the switchblade that's still coated in his father's blood, I peel out of the driver's seat and walk up to the main entrance. Since we needed to perfect our ruse, we didn't have time to discuss the semantics of our crime, but with our last run-in at a motel still in the forefront of my mind, I keep my head down low and my eyes peeled to the ground.

"A king or two singles?" the clerk asks when he detects my presence.

I drift my eyes back to Dexter slumped in the passenger seat of our borrowed ride, unsure of how to answer. The last motel we stayed in only had one bed, but it was very expensive, so is it pretentious of me to assume he wants to share a bed again?

The last time I shared a bed with a man who was passed out saw him leaving the next morning in a hurry, and I didn't see him again for months.

I don't want that to happen with Dexter, so instead of gesturing my head to the king-size bed in the pamphlet on the counter, I point to the two-single suite instead. It makes me sad. Even though I shouldn't, I like sharing a bed with Dexter.

"That'll be eighty," the clerk says before he tosses a clipboard onto the counter wedged between us.

I slowly peer up at him, unsure of what to do. The last time I put my details down at a seedy motel like this, the bad man found me. He took me to visit a prison before he dumped me at a hospital with no windows. I don't want to go there again. I'd rather die than be poked and prodded like they did to me my first several months there. They didn't touch my ungodly area like Lee wanted to, but what they did was far worse. They taunted me and called me names.

I should have killed them.

Perhaps Dexter will when you tell him what they did to you.

Mistaking my hopeful nod to the voices in my head as reluctance, the clerk locks his eyes with mine. "If you don't want to fill in the form, the room rate is double." He drags his eyes down my body. It makes my stomach flip, and not in a good way. I want to vomit even more now than I did when Dexter went over his plan to make his father pay. "I've seen how much girls like you get around these parts. I'm sure it won't cause too much of an indent in your takings."

I hide my daftness of his riddle with a smile before tossing two one-hundred bills onto the counter, snatch up the key he's dangling in front of me, then spin around. He can keep the change if it removes his sleazy eyes from me.

I make it almost to the door before the clerk shouts for me to stop. My blade feels heavy in my hand when I hear the stomps of his boots as he creeps up on me. I'm not overly good at reading people, but his vibe is off. It reminds me of the bad man we ate spaghetti with only two nights ago. He wants something from me I'm not willing to give, and just like Dexter's father, it will cost him his life.

As he stalks my way, I feel his beady eyes drinking in my body. Unlike when Dexter watched me with the same heavy-hooded and glazed-over stare the past two hours, it doesn't cause a good tingle between my legs. It makes me want to barf on the dirty tile floor.

I try to yank away from him when he pulls up a section of my hair to sniff it. I almost warn him that he'll be in big trouble if he touches me again, but before I can beg my brain to speak the words the voices in my head are screaming, he asks, "What's your rate?"

I'm lost as to what he means, but my naïveness doesn't last long.

"We cater for all types of *travelers* out this way..." he air quotes 'travelers' so I have no trouble understanding the dip in his tone before he tugs me back to him by a rough grab of my arm, "... but I've never seen one with as much innocence as you. Even the way you walk doesn't reflect banged-up insides from being fucked seven ways from Sunday."

As my mouth gapes, the truth smacks into me. He thinks I'm one of those women my daddy visited once a month after my mother died. They wore pretty dresses like my mom, and their lipstick was just as red as her blood seeping into her mattress, but they weren't her no matter how much my father wished they were. He said they were whores and told me I'd grow up to be just like them.

That night I made his porridge extra hot. He couldn't taste the poison I hid in his food the months leading to his death, but I was hopeful it burned when it slithered to his stomach.

"Because I might just let you stay for free for how pretty your hair smells." With his growl loud enough for me to hear it twice, he misses the slightest creak of my razor when I flick it open. "I like the shy, demure girls, but there's something different about you, isn't there?" He grinds himself against my backside. "You're special."

I'm about to show him exactly how special I am, but before I can, a deep penetrating voice breaks through the silence teeming between us. "Is there a problem?" Dexter slants his head to the side as his scrunched brows shoot up high on his face. His words are slurred, but as he stands before me now, you wouldn't know that he had been drugged only hours ago.

I like how strong he is.

I like it very much.

Me too, shouts a voice in my head.

The clerk takes a giant step back when Dexter heads our way. He's scared. I can smell it seeping from his skin and see it dripping from the pores of his sweaty armpits. Rightfully so. He should be scared. Dexter's expression is the same one he wore after trashing our hotel room. Death is dancing in his eyes, and I've never seen anything more entrancing in my life.

"Give it to me," he demands after stopping in front of me, his eyes locked on the sliver of silver shimmering in my hand. I haven't had the chance to slice it across the clerk's face yet, but he grabbed me hard enough to mark, so shouldn't retaliation be anticipated, much less sought?

When Dexter arches a brow, reminding me I haven't answered him, I shake my head. I don't want him to be mad, but he taught me that sometimes punishments must be handled in-house.

I wasn't meant to kill his father. We only practiced my ballet routine on repeat in case Dexter couldn't get to me before his father. We had no clue he would drug his own son.

My father was a terrible man, but the only drugs he ever gave me were the ones prescribed by doctors in white coats. I like to pretend he did that because he cared for me, but as the drugs wear off, so does the fog in my head. My father never did anything if it didn't benefit him in some way, so although he told me he killed my mother for me, I know that isn't true. He did it for himself.

Just like I killed him for me

It was him or me, and for once, I put myself first.

I don't get the chance this time around, though. With a brutal shove, Dexter pins me to the wall by my throat then snatches the blade out of my hand. I squirm in an instant. I don't know if it's a nervous wiggle or the one that usually follows a heap of inappropriate thoughts.

When the tingles racing down my spine cluster in my ungodly womanly parts, I assume it is the latter.

"If you want to play the role right, you need to go the full hog." Dexter strays his eyes from the man who was sniffing my hair only moments ago to me. "She doesn't want to be wined and dined. She wants to be consumed, devoured, and possessed. You don't win her by sniffing her hair like a man without a dick. You show her how bad it will be without you before giving her a taste of the darkness that comes with you." I assume he's trapped in the terrifying throes of a psychosis until he says, "Megan looks sweet and innocent but beneath that persona is a devil so evil not even Satan could taint it." He returns his eyes to the motel clerk. "So do you think you have what it takes to bed a woman like that?"

The clerk stupidly nods.

It will be the last thing he ever does.

Well, so I thought.

A nanosecond after his second head bop, Dexter loosens his grip on my throat. As I suck in some much-needed breaths, he drags over the chair the clerk was sitting in when I entered the reception area. He places it between the frozen clerk and me, then he heads for the roller blind covering the main window at the front of the motel. His steps are still not as smooth and fluid as normal, but the clerk doesn't pay his unsteady footing any attention. He's too busy flaring his nostrils hoping he will permanently capture the scent making the air hot with humidity.

As he hides us from the world, I watch Dexter with eagerness, confused yet somehow unpanicked. I've handled my share of broken promises, but until Dexter does something to lose my trust, I will continue to believe I am safe with him. He killed for me. He can't earn my trust any better than that.

"Then what are you going to do to achieve that?" Dexter asks as his eyes bounce between the clerk and me. There's an edginess to his eyes. He's clearly still under the influence, but the gleam in his dark gaze doesn't appear to be solely based on the drug his father gave him. There's something much deeper to them. Something more unbalanced. "You've got her here, so now what do you want to do to her?"

My eyes rocket to him when the clerk replies, "It isn't what I want to do to her. It's what I want her to do to me." He smiles like I'm not seconds from gouging his eyes out with one of the sharpened pencils on his desk before he mutters, "I want her to suck my dick."

Dexter smirks. "Good choice... I've been wondering myself how soft her lips are." With a lick of his lips, he nudges his head to the clerk's pants. "Well, go on, what are you waiting for? Flop it out."

"I don't need to pay first?" the clerk asks, apparently well-versed on the protocol for sanctioning a woman to hell by making love to her with no plans to place a baby in her belly.

"You want to pay?" Dexter asks, his voice still on edge. "Because from what I saw earlier, you seemed like you wanted to take? If I hadn't showed up, you probably would have taken her right on this dirty floor. Am I right?"

The clerk's head shakes like a bobblehead toy. "No. Of course not. I can pay." His tone dips, concealing his deceit before he mutters, "If you need me to pay."

"I don't need you to do anything." Dexter steps up to him until they're chest to chest. "Except get your dick out. I am sure my girl is dying to see it. You're just her type." I didn't notice the clerk's similarities to Nick until Dexter points them out. "Golden blond hair, baby blue eyes. You even have calloused fingertips. Let me guess, you play guitar during your free time."

"How'd you know?" People think I'm slow because I'm mentally unwell. If that is the criteria for assessing someone's intellect, this man must have spent years in mental asylums.

"Just a guess," Dexter mutters before returning his eyes to me. They're blazing ten times brighter than the lightning in the sky, and they expose he is hungry—for blood. Mine or the clerk's? I'm not sure, but I'm confident we're about to find out when he adds,

"We usually charge by the hour, so you better hurry up if you want your money's worth."

When the clerk's hand shoots down to his zipper, I spin away. I don't want to see his penis. I don't want to see anyone's penis.

Except Dexter's.

Since that isn't a lie, I don't argue with the narky voice in my head.

"Oh no, you don't, Megan. You're going to want to watch this." Dexter gives me no choice but to obey his snapped command when he stands behind me, cranks my neck back to the clerk, then forces my eyes open with his index fingers and thumbs. They burn like the fiery depths of hell I'll be forced to live in when the clerk yanks his penis out of his pants. It's hard and glistening at the tip like Nick's was every time he put it in *her*.

"Now?" Dexter asks, his voice extra throaty.

The clerk stammers out, "She needs to remove her pants before getting on her knees."

I try to shake my head, but I can't. Dexter's hold is too firm, not to mention the buckling of my knees when a second after he pulls my pants to my knees, he rams his foot into the back of them. The cracks in the filthy tiles rip up my knees when I tumble to the floor, but before a whimper can escape my lips, Dexter yanks my head back then wordlessly gestures for the clerk to step forward.

I grunt and hiss at him in warning. If he brings his cock anywhere near my face, I will bite it off.

I wonder if that's the point when Dexter whispers in my ear, "Not even spineless men bow, Megan, so if you didn't like what he was doing, you should have forced him to his knees. There's no quicker way to do that than to make them *think* they have the control."

When Dexter pulls my hair away from my face to fist it at the back of my head, the veins in the clerk's penis throb in anticipation. He shouldn't be so eager. The gleam in Dexter's eyes had me confused, but that isn't an issue anymore. I now comprehend what he wants me to do, and since I want to make up for taking the glory of his kill away from him, I'll do exactly as asked.

Dexter's throaty garble makes my thighs shake more than the image of the clerk sliding his cock in and out of his hand when he asks, "Are you ready?"

I swallow before nodding, then, just as images of the woman Dexter brought to our hotel room two nights ago flash before my eyes, I lock gazes with the clerk. He has no idea what is coming for him, but Dexter understands. I can feel the heat of his penis on the back of my head. Feel the energy teeming through him. He's as excited as I am because we both know this is only the start of our night. Once I do this, there will be no one left between us. Not our fathers. Not Nick. Not even Cleo. It will be just us and the revenge we plan to get no matter the cost.

"Now open your mouth like a good girl, Megan. Spencer has a surprise for you."

My jaw falls open, and I struggle not to gag when Spencer pushes his cock deep into my mouth, but just like the precious pet Dexter told me I am yesterday, I keep my teeth sheathed behind my lips until Dexter signals otherwise.

Then, there's no holding back.

22

DEXTER

The pounding of my temples clears away when Megan gnaws her teeth through the motel clerk's veiny shaft without the slightest bit of remorse. She bites him with a viciousness that only took a handful of compliments to unearth yesterday.

Her munch ends when Spencer stumbles back with a roar. "What the fuck!"

He backhands her so hard the sweet scent of her shampoo overtakes the ghastly smell of his tainted blood. He thought he had the makings of a king, that he could play the game of a master without even a pawn left on the board.

Megan will teach him otherwise.

Not only is his dick limp enough to ensure it won't be pressed up against the curves of anyone's ass anytime soon, but Megan doesn't back down when she's against the odds. The Vicar and Lucy's attempts to belittle her didn't see her clambering away like a coward, and this fool won't this time either.

Megan is up in the clerk's face in an instant, her wish to gut him more on par with what I was anticipating when I took Lucy back to our hotel with the hope I could fuck a little 'skitzo' from my thoughts with a woman only half as beautiful as her but a whole lot saner.

"Now, Megan," I demand, my voice as rough as it was when I ordered for her to slit my father's throat. It's not only raw from the arsenic my father tried to poison me with, but it's also rough from the endorphins pumping through my veins.

Like all good little pets, Megan immediately obeys the command in my tone. She stabs her thumbs into the clerk's eyes, scratching the corneas enough for the putrid scent of his piss to linger in the air. He should be grateful I disarmed her while still plotting my game plan. If she had her blade, it would have been slit across his throat by now.

I removed her security blanket as a test. She passed, which lessens my agitation about waking up to discover her ass being ground by a man with oddly similar features to Nick.

"Take him down, Megan!" I scream, frustrated by her lack of strength. When she tripped on her pants huddled around her knees, Spencer used her tumble to his advantage. He pinned her to the wall across from his desk, then crept his hand toward her neck.

He almost has her at an advantage—almost—because before he knows what's happening, Megan wrangles an ankle out of her pants, then pops a knee into his groin.

I slouch back in the chair with a grin, more than happy to watch the spectacle unfold from a distance. As Megan claws her nails down his face, all I see is Nick. The rage, the anger, the years of abuse Megan suffered because of him is unleashed in the most brilliant way. She gives it her all, prompting me to wonder if she too is thinking about him.

She wants revenge for the way he treated her. As much as me? I don't know, but I am determined to find out.

I do know one thing, though. She can now express herself without fear of persecution. I've awakened a beast. Her hunger for blood is rampant, and I plan to expose it even more so—*after* I fix the problem that has my head murky with more than the medication my mother tried to force down my throat from the age of eight to eleven.

"You're taking too long," I mutter under my breath while standing from my chair and marching across the room. "You don't always need to play with your pets, little doll. Even rapists are taken down humanely, so why are you toying with him?"

Before Megan can answer me, I drag her switchblade across the clerk's jugular. A stream of red lines his neck from one ear to the other. The gaping wound isn't the reason I'm smiling, though. It's from the spurts of blood that coat Megan's face and the wide-eyed look she gives me when I smear the still warm byproduct of the man now slumped at her feet onto her top lip. She goes from disgusted to turned on in zero point five seconds, and even quicker than that, I answer the screaming wails of the voices in my head by sealing my mouth over hers.

I thought the drugs I snorted to forget the naïve virgin my father wanted to corrupt had me mistaking the taste of Megan's skin, that her mouth couldn't have been anywhere near as scrumptious as my fucked head was believing, but as I slowly emerge out of my father's shadow, I'm learning not all his teachings were correct.

He said the women who taste like heaven are discarded imps of hell, that God sullied them purely to take down his competition. They were conceived to destroy us, birthed to force governance, and that only the strong could see past their tasty mouths, succulent tits, and dripping cunts that could only be more appetizing when smeared with virginal blood.

That's why he took down the innocent and hunted the pure. He said that by doing God's work, he made the playing field even and that it gave more chance for boys like me to live a normal life.

Stupidly, I believed him. My mother did force pills down my throat, she let the doctors poke and prod me for days on end, and she didn't care when the pills made me bedridden for a week, but only because if I was braindead, my father's teachings were pointless.

A vegetable can't respond, much less participate in a hunt with targets only a couple of years older than him.

My mother hurt me, but in a sick and twisted way, it wasn't to be cruel. A lullaby doesn't excuse the torment I was forced to endure under her and my father's watch, but it assured me that you can't nurture a boy to be a killer. He's either a murderer or not. There are no in-betweens.

Although, I am beginning to wonder if it's the same for women. Megan's eyes are too innocent to portray the iniquity of a murderer and her skin too soft to believe it was scorched by Satan's touch, but there's a killer hidden inside her. It's stronger than the evil my father instilled in me because it was derived from pure evil, embedded by the men who were supposed to teach us right from wrong.

We were tainted by our fathers, then left for slaughter. Except now, he's slumped on a dirty barn floor while my fingers are inching toward a heat growing warmer the closer my fingertips get.

Megan's cunt smells decadent, and although I'm dying to corrupt it as no man has, there's one little matter I need to take care of first.

Megan hisses into my mouth when I strip away the thin, half-moon disc of skin at the front of her opening. If I hadn't seen the truth in her eyes when I asked if her father inappropriately touched her, I would have never believed he hadn't instilled the same cruel acts of purity my father forced on his little pets.

Even at an age not appropriate for a man in his sixties, his pets were groomed to ensure they upheld the utmost wholesomeness until well into their teens. Bike riding, gymnastics, horse riding, and even swimming were off the agenda. They sat on poufy cushions, washed with only the slightest spray of water, and never wore undergarments that would scratch or erode the skin my father was fascinated with, but even then, it was rare to find an untouched woman with an intact hymen.

My father saw them as gifts, a treasure to hold onto for eternity, and that is precisely what he would have done with Megan if he discovered what I had unearthed in our hotel room only two nights ago. She would have been his pet, his little doll. His plaything.

Now, she'll forever be the woman who took him down.

I'd laugh at the absurdity a man of such wealth and power was taken down by a woman with the mental capacity of a fifteen-year-old girl if I weren't concerned the same thing is about to happen to me.

I toy with women.

I break them then slowly piece them back together.

I do not lick up evidence of the pain I'm causing them with my tongue before promising it will feel good soon. Megan is making me soft, but until the adrenaline of watching the light fade from my father's eyes wanes, I'll let her get away with it.

"Just a little more pain," I whisper down Megan's ear while scissoring the two fingers I slipped inside her when she bit my chest to conceal her howled sob. "Then I'll make it better. I'll fuck you and mark you before covering you with my cum. Then when people look at you, they won't see a poor, scared little girl. They'll see a warrior. A misfit. A fucking skitzo who should have never been misunderstood. You won't apologize again once I'm done with you. But they will. Every single person who has done you wrong will be on their knees, begging for their lives."

My promise brings Megan out of the trenches and sees her clawing from the dark hole I pushed her in. The walls of her tight cunt stopped fighting against my fingers. She opens up for me, and her obedience is rewarded in the most brilliant way. Instead of stuffing my cock inside her as it begged to do when she crawled onto my lap with the blood of my father dripping from her hands, I walk her to the desk that the clerk would still be sitting behind if he hadn't danced with the devil and lost.

Once I have the beaten wood cleared away of pens, clipboards, keys, and a half-consumed sandwich, I plant Megan's backside on top before pushing her back so her shoulder blades brace the battered material.

I *tsk* her after taking in the mess she's made of her panties. They're flicked with droplets of blood, but that isn't the only thing they're exposing. They are drenched through and erotically exposing her delicious cunt to my hungry-yet-on-the-verge-of-psychosis eyes.

"Is this for me or him?"

Megan doesn't talk, she's as mute as I wish I had been when my father suggested I come up with a punishment for my mother when she arrived one minute late the night he made me convince her that I believed her, but I swear she mutters, "You," before a terrifying memory almost strongarms me into another debilitating relapse.

I told my mother to pack her things and meet me at the big grandfather clock on the second floor at precisely twelve midnight. When the clock struck twelve, I thought she had skipped the flames.

I stopped thinking she wanted what was best for me when she hustled onto the second story landing only a minute later.

Her punishment was severe that night, and I never saw her again after it. Don't get me wrong, she was present, there was just nothing inside her but a ghost of a woman.

After shaking my head to clear it of the dread weighing down my senses more than the drugs my father laced my drink with, I snap off Megan's panties to survey the damage firsthand.

The quickest crack of the elastic of her panties against her silky skin causes it to pinken with heat. It also doubles her erotic scent.

"I told you I wouldn't need to see your cunt to know it's dripping." I scrape up some of the mess with my index finger before popping it into my mouth. My cock knocks at my zipper when the combined taste of her arousal and blood activates my taste buds. She tastes delicious. Pure. And she's so fucking unhinged, I'm about to drag her to the depths of hell right along with me. "Remember you asked for this," I mutter on a groan before I curl my hand around her throat, pin her to the desk, then burrow my head between her legs.

I lick up the droplets of blood my hand missed when I ripped at her with the bestiality of a savage from her thighs before I snake my tongue up to her soaked slit.

"Still," I bark out when the weaves of my tongue have her squirming enough to loosen my grip on her throat. She's a tiny little thing who could easily slip out of my hold, but I like them frozen in fear and too scared to move. It's what makes them perfect little dolls who do as they're told and don't make a sound no matter how bad the punishment.

Not a squeak popped from my mother's lips when my father

punished her the night she mistakenly believed I was on her side. He was cruel, and his bite was more vicious than normal, but she kept her eyes locked on me and her face free of tears.

Her stance to show me she wasn't afraid had my father seeing red. He whipped her, beat her, then tightened his grip on her throat so firmly, her eyes almost bulged out of her head.

She died twice, but it still wasn't enough for him. He brought her back again and again and again until the wrong victim snapped.

That was the first *and* last time I struck my father.

His punishment was vicious but oh so worthwhile.

It made me the man I am today.

It made me stronger—strong enough to know that if I don't weaken my grip on Megan's neck, more than a man striving to emerge from the thick cloak of sedation will crack. Her neck will as well.

Against the better judgment of my deviant head, I loosen my grip. After watching her over the frantic thrusts of her breasts long enough to know she isn't close to passing out, I grip her ass, drag her to the edge of the desk, then devour her cunt like I was dying to do when I rid it of every strand of wiry hair.

I bite at her clit a little harder than I should. What can I say? I fucking love the taste of her blood. It is almost as enticing as the dripping wetness leaking from her center. It's so entrancing, it takes everything I have to remember not to sink my teeth into her heated skin with the same cruelness she instilled on the clerk.

I wouldn't hold back if her virginal blood wasn't enough to keep my cock hard for a week.

I never understood my father's fascination with virgins. Yes, they're fun to manipulate, and there's nothing wrong with a woman answering her man's every whim, but it is a boring game that loses steam a lot faster than a hotheaded woman who'll fight you every step of the way.

A true master bends the spine of a disobedient woman. He does not alter his game plan for her.

Well, he didn't.

While ignoring the incessant ring of alarm bells in my head, I spear my tongue into Megan's salivating cunt. I've lapped up all the goodness coating the outside of her clenching pussy, so now I must concentrate on getting more of the addictive substance keeping my blood thick with adrenaline even without me recording a single worthwhile kill in the last twenty-four hours.

"Fighting it will only make it overwhelm you more," I growl against Megan's dripping folds when she fights against the waves of destruction threatening to pull her under. "You're meant to feel out of control, blinded by hunger. You're supposed to feel like you're tripping the fuck out." I lick her slit with a long, prolonged drag of my tongue before curling it around her throbbing clit. "Because this is a high you want. This one is safe. It is the safest mind fuck there is."

The wobble of her slim thighs doubles when I hit her clit with back-to-back flicks of my tongue. It's calloused from where Shelley tried to gnaw it off. She didn't realize it was me under the mask of the New Year's Eve ball she attended the year before her death. If she had, she wouldn't have fought me like she did when I snuck into her house for the first time to watch her sleep. It adds a nice amount of pressure to the strikes I'm hitting Megan's clit with and has her grunting like a wild animal only seconds later.

"Give it to me," I growl into her throbbing cunt when she steals the glory before all the thunder rolls in. She keeps clamming up like what we're doing is eviler than executing the perfect ruse to undo years of torture and lies.

I freeze when a disturbing notion pops into my head.

Don't worry, this one isn't as murderous as the ones it handles day in and day out.

"Whatever he told you is a lie." I wipe at my mouth with the back of my hand before locking my eyes with Megan's. The specks of gold in her hazel eyes appear even brighter since they're swamped by her pupils, and the wish to come is written all over her face. "We weren't designed to react a certain way. How we feel, respond, and treat people is taught to us. We just lucked out when we got fuckers more interested in screwing with our heads than the doctors in white coats they took us to when their tactics worked."

Dad must have drugged me with the good shit as I've never spoken this way before. I didn't mean it is untrue, it's just unusual for me to be so forthright. "Feeling good isn't a bad thing. Did you feel good when that piece of shit dropped to the floor like a bag of shit?" I nudge my head to the clerk slumped in a pool of his own blood during the 'piece of shit' part of my reply.

When Megan nods, I ask, "Did it feel as good as it did when I had my head burrowed between your legs?" She instantly shakes her head, swelling my cock to the point it's painful. "So, what's the issue? If it makes you feel good, why shouldn't you enjoy it? We're not here for a long time, Megan, so I plan to make the most of it."

When I attempt to step back, she curls her feet around my ass and tugs me back in. It isn't the same rueful yank she did when kicking Lucy away from the bed I wanted to desperately sodomize her on, but it is a clear indication she doesn't want me to go anywhere.

I'd relish the thought if she weren't looking up at me with the same gaga eyes she had when I returned to the cabin to collect her.

"What did I tell you about looking at me like that, Megan?" I don't give her the chance to answer. I backhand her clit, which sends a faint moan bouncing around the dead-silent office. "Don't ever look at me like that. I am not your savior, Megan. I am a man who was used and abused and caged for years, but my wings have never been fully clipped, and neither have yours."

After tugging her off the desk, I spin her around then push down between her shoulder blades. Her ass is primed and ready to go. It is drenched with evidence of her arousal, but instead of being the cruel man I was raised to be, I shift my focus to her clenching, wet pussy.

"If there has ever been a good time for you to speak, Megan, it is now. Because once I have you, there will be no turning back. Not for Nick. Not for Cleo. Not for anyone." The possessiveness in my voice is shocking. I've never heard it have this type of edginess before, and it didn't even hitch when I mentioned *her* name. I shouldn't be surprised. Unlike Cleo, Megan is a good little pet. She does as she's told, and even if she could talk, I doubt she would. "Final warning, Megan. The board has been cleared. Only the king and queen remain."

When she peers at me over the waves of brown locks falling in front of her face, I lose all rational thoughts.

She wants to be claimed.

Marked.

Fucked so hard that killing my father won't be the highlight of her night.

So, with my mind blank and my wish for revenge a distant memory, I line up my cock with the entrance of her clenching cunt, then drive home.

A grunt unlike anything I've ever heard before rumbles in my chest, and the walls of her pussy clamp around my twitching shaft. She is so fucking tight and grunting like a feral pig, even with my cock almost fully sunk inside her, I can tell it's coated with her virginal blood before I even commence withdrawing it.

"If they thought I had lost my mind earlier, they had no fucking clue." A pleasing zap shoots through my shaft when my eyes drop to watch my cock retreat from Megan's pussy that is hugging it so fiercely, she's causing herself more pain than pleasure. "My cock is dripping in your blood. I've never seen a more erotic sight." When she arches back to take in the visual thickening my cock to the point it is painful, I say, "Nuh-uh, the only way you'll get to see is when you're cleaning up the mess with your tongue." I stuff my cock back inside her, grunting when my warning increases the wetness between her legs instead of drying it up. She likes the idea of pleasing me, so much so she'd lick her virginal blood off my cock if I demanded her to.

The knowledge sees me adding a flick to my hips during my third and fourth plunge. I'm not usually worried about my little pets coming when I'm between their legs. My father taught me that women were solely created for our pleasure, but this feels different. I want Megan's cum to be drenching my cock as much as her virginal blood.

"Grip the edge of the desk and lift your ass a little higher." Megan jumps to my command, which sees her awarded with another two inches of my cock. "Does that feel better?"

She doesn't answer me, but her moan is the equivalent of a million words. It tells me everything I need to know and then some.

Faster.

Harder.

Take everything I want.

I could fuck her to within an inch of her life, and she'd still want more.

"This isn't going to last long," I warn, too caught up in a hysteria I haven't faced for years to care that I'm about to make a fool of myself. "But you don't need to worry. Once we've buried the clerk in the woods and let the world know you killed my father, I'll take my time with you. We can fuck until your cunt is so raw, not even the lashes of my tongue will soothe it."

The fact she doesn't even flinch during my confession that I planned for her to take full credit for my father's murder sees me pumping in and out of her so rapidly, within minutes, my balls draw in close to my body, and the rush of endorphins I've been chasing for years slam into me at once.

I fuck Megan with everything I have. It is a manic, consuming romp that has sweat dribbling down my cheeks as rapidly as blood oozed from my father's wound when Megan's switchblade raced across his clammy skin. I grind, grunt, and grip her like a madman, but no matter how hard I fuck her or how loud the voices in my head scream for me to come, it never eventuates.

I want more.

I need more.

And for some really annoying reason, I can't achieve that by myself.

I need her, and my fucking god, I swear she will pay for that *after* I've made her come. *After* she's screamed my name loud enough for it to ring in my ears for eternity but without a syllable escaping her lips. *After* I've ensured she's protected from the imps, monsters, and men like our fathers who ridiculed and shamed her.

Not before.

Never before.

Only after.

A squeak I'd give anything to turn into a word pops from Megan's mouth when I withdraw my cock, flip her over as if she is weightless, then bury my head back between her legs. The amount of blood that coats my tongue when I spear it inside her almost has me on the brink of a manic episode. It makes me disturbed, deranged, and one hundred percent certain I'll never need to feast again after gorging on her cunt, but some good comes from the manic undertakings of an insane man.

If Alice had a man like me helming her dream, perhaps it wouldn't have taken her so long to tiptoe down the rabbit hole.

"*Yesss,*" I grunt against Megan's drenched slit when she bucks and rears against me. She is wordlessly howling like a banshee, and the banquet I plan to devour even more than her blood floods my tongue as she is overcome by a climax. "You taste like such a good little pet." I lick her, stick my tongue deep inside of her, then swivel it around her nervy bud. "Pure and evil mixed together. The perfect palette."

I continue to toy with her clit and tease her cunt with flicks of my tongue until the raging tornado that's made her a blubbering mess subsides, and a new type of hunger takes hold. This one is more violent than any she has previously encountered. More deviant.

It's the demands of a woman who has suddenly realized she is a woman.

She's hungry for my cum, and I'm now ready to give it to her.

"Lay back and open your legs wide for me." My voice is gritty. It is very much deranged. "I should be mad that you forgot to fetch our belongings." I slap her pretty little cunt that's swollen from its earlier pounding with the back of my hand before saying, "Because now I have no proof to show Nick." A flare darts through her eyes, but since it is more in panic about being exposed than the mentioning of Nick's name, I let it slide. "So I guess he'll just have to take my word. He'll do that, won't he, Megan? He'll believe your cunt has never been as wet as it is now. That it's never looked so thoroughly claimed."

She nods without pause for thought, pleasing me more.

"Because if he didn't..." I slice my thumb across my jugular to finalize my statement.

When the earlier flare darting through her eyes augments, cum races to the crest of my cock. She no longer wants to bed Nick. She wants him dead.

As do I.

"I'll give you everything your twisted black heart desires, little doll, but first, we have one small matter we must take care of..."

My head nudge to the clerk's slumped body ends when Megan falls to her knees in front of me, confident even with her blood smeared on my dick, I'll taste better than any revenge I could serve her. She looks me in the eyes as she licks my cock clean, then as I pat her hair, she takes my engorged knob between her lips and sucks me deep. Her hand trembles more now than when it skidded across my father's throat.

I like that she's scared.

Unsure.

But even more than that, I love that she's so eager to please me, she will do something she is convinced will send her to hell.

When she takes me to the very back of her throat, her gag is the equivalent of a thousand words spilling from her lips. Her nipples harden, and the drawing of my balls in close to my body is undeniable. I'm desperate to come, to coat her throat with my seed, but more than that, I want to continue watching the woman behind the skitzo in her eyes emerge.

She's not a twelve-year-old girl being pumped with drugs that will do her more harm than good. She's a woman in every sense of the word.

And so fucking evilly corrupt, it will take more than a little bit of virginal blood to quench her thirst for blood.

I don't mind. I'll give her everything she wants and more because if it weren't for her, I'd still be my father's puppet.

I may even give her my last name.

23

MEGAN

*T*he flicking embers of a raging inferno stop dancing in my dilated eyes when Dexter grips the ankle tucked under my bottom and drags me to his side of the bench seat of the hotel clerk's truck. After what we just did, my skin should be bubbling with blisters like it did when my mother made the bath-water too hot. I should be melting in the flames of hell, but for some silly reason, all I'm feeling is joy.

My body is aching, and my stomach hurts from how many times it clenched while trying to ignore the tingles bombarding me from all sides, but I feel more alive now than I did when my father told me he killed my mother so she couldn't hurt me anymore.

Back then, I thought I was going to be free, but like almost all the lessons in my life, I soon discovered it was a lie. Not even after hanging my father from the rafters of my family ranch was I free. Up until thirty minutes ago, I was controlled and manipulated.

I didn't kneel in front of Dexter because I wanted to sanction him to hell alongside me. I wanted to make his eyes light up like the sky did for me when he made me voicelessly scream like my mother did when her 'friends' came to visit. I wanted to make him feel good even with his skin hot and clammy, and from the way his nostrils flared when the clerk stuffed his penis into my mouth, I was certain I knew the perfect way.

Mine once did the same anytime Nick was with *her*.

They won't anymore, though.

She can have Nick. She can keep him for eternity.

As we will Dexter.

"No," Dexter snaps out in a groggy tone when he mistakes my head bob as me burying my head between his pecs to get comfortable. "No sleep. Not yet. Once we've put the steps into play, then you can rest but not before."

My achy lips raise against his chest when he pats my bottom like he did at the cabin days ago. His tone would have you convinced he's angry at me, but his nurturing gesture proves otherwise. Don't get me wrong, he was angry that I parked the car he borrowed yesterday at the front of the motel we were planning to stay at, but his anger only lasted as long as it took for him to work out another way of getting rid of our DNA from the crime scene.

Fire destroys many things—even pesky genes that could expose the truth.

"Do you remember the plan?" After taking a moment to relish the possessiveness in his tone, I peer up at Dexter, then dip my chin. "You need to be faster this time, Megan. If you're slow, you'll—" When I drop my head, irked by the word forever tossed at me in my teens, Dexter's foot slips from the gas pedal to the brake. I'm anticipating for him to comfort me or offer me some kind of apology, so you can imagine my surprise when he pulls me onto his lap then curls his hand around my throat. "Charles may look old and kind, but he is a murderer in every meaning of the word." As I dig my nails into his hand in an endeavor to loosen his grip, he snarls, "He carried you into the woods knowing my father's plan to hunt, desecrate, and kill you. He is *not* who you think he is. He could know you for years and still kill you on command."

I realize not all his words are for me when I spot the direction of his gaze.

He is peering past me instead of at me.

Dexter's grip loosens when I stop fighting against him. He still holds me firm enough for my lungs to scream in protest, but not with a firmness that will kill me anytime within the next two minutes. When I rub at the groove embedded deeply between his dark eyes, the torment in his eyes weakens. Within seconds, it goes from a raging tornado to a summer storm. Then, it switches to a sun shower.

"He knew her for years," he murmurs more to himself than me. "But he didn't even blink when he entered the room covered with splotches of her blood." His laugh is as tormented as my insides feel when he mutters, "He just washed her blood off her as if she was a child, spoon-fed her, then tucked her into bed." My heart squeezes painfully in my chest when he locks his eyes with mine. "He deserves to die."

Since I wholeheartedly agree with him and also believe he's asking a question more than stating a fact, I nod. Even if his recent confession wasn't swaying my opinion in his favor, Charles deserves to die. I just wish Dexter would entrust me to serve his punishment on my own.

Oh well. At least we get to be a part of it.

I nod to the voices in my head that suddenly don't seem as irrational as they once did before lowering my hand from Dexter's brows to his lips. They're still plump and red from how many times he kissed both my lips and the constantly hot area between my legs, and tasty enough for me to agree to massacre an entire village just to taste them again.

"*Oww*," I whimper on a sob when Dexter makes his mouth look nowhere near as appealing by showing how savage it can be. He sinks his teeth into the delicate skin on my wrist firm enough to mark before he lowers them to my elbow.

When I attempt to yank away from him, he digs his teeth in firm enough my skin rips under his incisor teeth. After licking up the dribble of blood seeping from his recent bite mark, he mutters, "We have to make it look real. Charles will never believe you got away from my father without some battle wounds." I bury my head into his chest to hide the tears threatening to spill down my face when he grips my thigh with enough strength to bruise. "But this type of pain can be good too, Megan. You can find pleasure in it if you stop wrongly thinking it hurts."

I want to tell him that it does hurt. That I'm not making up the pain ripping through my body, but before I can, he steals the screams of the voices in my head demanding immediate retaliation by slipping his hand underneath the grubby shirt he stole from the clerk.

"See, you're saturated. You wouldn't be wet if you didn't enjoy it."

My quivering breaths rebound off his chest when he slips a finger inside my vagina. His fingers aren't as thick and veiny as his penis, so my body doesn't instantly protest the intrusion like it did when he stuck his penis inside me earlier. It encourages the gentle pumps of his fat digit before the swivel of my hips coerces his thumb to get in on the action as well.

"I knew you'd have a greedy cunt, Megan. That one snippet of attention would have it begging for another and another and another." I shudder like I'm cold when the thumb he used to smear the murky white stuff that pumped onto my tongue earlier into my lip circles the little bud my father threatened to cut off when I learned of its ability to zap you with electricity when you touch it.

I was granted permission to have a bath the day of my sixteenth birthday. The water was super cold, so I was rubbing myself to get warm. I nearly vaulted out of the tub when my hand skimmed over a region of my protruding bones I'd never paid much attention to.

Although certain I was summoning myself to hell, I touched myself down there enough times to contemplate how bad hell could really be when my father walked in, catching me mid-twirl.

I didn't sit for a week after that, and I was never allowed a bath again.

"Good girl, Megan. Concentrate on how good it feels while I... fix... this..." Dexter grunts more than he speaks. I learn why when the coolness of steel brushes against my heated vagina a mere second before it adds to the fiery hotness burning my insides. He cut me with the switchblade. Not enough to make me fearful for my life, but enough to steal my devotion away from the wave building inside my core.

"*Oww.*"

"Shh..." he comforts me, his tone surprisingly gentle. "It's just a little nick. Nothing I can't fix once we've done what we came here for."

When his eyes drift to the driver's side window, I realize he didn't stop because he was mad I assumed he was calling me stupid with a less demoralizing word. It's because we arrived at our destination. Although hidden by a forest that's even scarier in the dawn of morning, the building his father was murdered in is highly recognizable.

"Charles will be waiting by the west staircase. He's *always* waiting by the west staircase." It dawns on me that his last sentence was only for him when he returns his eyes to me. They're filled with hate, but since it isn't directed at me, I ignore the snarky voice in my head reminding me that my switchblade is a mere inch from his cock. "I don't need you to take him out for me, Megan. I just need you to get him out far enough he's away from surveillance. Okay?"

I nod, more than eager to help.

His smile makes me happy about the voices in my head. If the mean doctors in white coats hadn't moved me to a facility capable of handling 'someone like me,' we would have never met, and I'd still believe that Nick was the love of my life.

I know better now.

"Okay," Dexter repeats before he removes his bloody hand from under my shirt and curls it around my jaw. It adds to the smears of the clerk's blood still on my cheeks, but it feels more like war paint than the blood of a dead man.

After dragging his thumb across my lips still aching from stretching to take in his penis, he slips it down my neck and across my collarbone before he stops at the bouncing flesh my father said were the devil's spawn.

"You look like heaven and hell." He brushes his hand down the back of my nipple, peaking it more before locking his eyes with mine. "Now let's show them how wrong they were when they thought either one of us was angelic." He nips at my lips sharply enough to draw blood before he pulls back, tosses open the driver's side door of the truck, then slides out with me still in his lap. "It's time for the hunter to be hunted."

He pats my backside in a way that shouldn't feel good considering how many times I was spanked as a child but does before he sets me down onto my feet. He then moves for a crate on the far corner of an old building. When Dexter explained aspects of his father's teaching, I thought he meant they hunted figuratively but learn otherwise when he tosses off the lid of the wood box. It's filled with a range of instruments. Some look like fun, like the ax you toss at a fair to win a prize, but others look like they came off the set of an action movie.

Once he is loaded up and ready to fight, Dexter spins on his heels to face me. I nervously squirm when he takes his time drinking me in. It can't be a good squirm. I look like a wretched mess—even worse than I did after sewing my mother's eyes shut and scrubbing her mattress clean of her blood. The clerk's shirt is stained with the blood that seeped from his neck, my feet are muddy from trekking across an abandoned parking lot to the clerk's truck after walking through the gasoline Dexter poured over the motel's office to make sure it was well lit before firefighters arrived, and the cut Dexter placed at the top of my thigh has blood leaking down my leg.

"Perfect," Dexter mutters under his breath, shocking me. "You look every bit the part of my father's victim." I yearn to comfort him when he murmurs, "My mother bled the exact same way for almost a week once he was done with her." He shakes his head as if ridding it of horrible memories before adding, "Charles will believe you evaded his capture, and forever wanting to be in his good books, he will take you straight back to him." He smirks, mindful that even with my brain a little mushy from the medication I was forced to take, I know exactly where that scenario will lead us—straight to Dexter, who will be lying in wait, waiting to take out Charles.

"*Ugh*," I grunt when Dexter stops my endeavor to comfort him by pushing me away.

"We don't have time." His tone seems nowhere near as harsh when he curls his hand around my jaw and scrapes his thumb over my top lip. "But once we've done this, I'll take the pain away. I promise." His pledge seems off. It has an edge of deceit to it like he did when he said we'll leave Meadow Fields together. I thought he was going to leave me alone, and in a way, that is what he did when we first left. He sent me out in the big bad world alone. "Hey..." he murmurs on a grunt when he spots the stupid tears pricking my eyes. "What are those for? Who are they for?" He scrubs at my tears with more violence than he used when he slit the hotel clerk's throat. "They better not be for him, Megan. You better not be crying for him."

Before I can determine whom he's referencing, he grips the back of my head and pulls me forward with so much force, my front tooth almost cracks again when our mouths smash together. Before a wince of pain can escape my lips, his tongue slides across my top lip before he plunges it inside my mouth. His kiss is hungry and urgent—a similar kiss to the one Nick gave Jenni when she returned home from school in New York for the first time. It was like he was desperate to keep her, that he'd do anything in the world not to tell her about the baby I thought I was carrying.

It makes me happy that it seems as if Dexter wants to keep me around. Not enough for me not to whimper when he pulls away, though. I could be kissed by him for days and never grow tired.

Daddy lied when he said kisses were Satan's tormentors.

They're much too yummy to be anything bad.

After biting my lower lip hard enough to leave a mark, Dexter shifts on his feet to face the manor in the distance. "We need to move quickly, but once this is done, I'll fix the injustices he did to you. He will regret the day he hurt you."

Once again, I don't know who he is referencing, but once again, I'm too caught up in his wish to protect me to care.

Besides, if he believes they hurt me, they probably did and deserve to be punished accordingly.

After staring at the manor long enough for goosebumps to

race across my forearms, Dexter shifts his eyes back to me. "Are you ready?"

I nod, press my lips to his like a peck will keep him out of a psychosis for another thirty minutes, then pivot on my heels and race toward the manor. With my body aching from the naughty activities Dexter and I undertook at the motel, my hobble toward the large residential property hidden by a thick forest is more convincing of the victim I'm meant to be playing. It reminds me of the times I ran and hid from my father in the thick scrub that surrounded our family ranch. It wasn't brimming with trees wide enough to hide the forest men my father always warned me about. It was merely overgrown because my father cared more about watching sports and drinking than maintaining the property he inherited. But I always loved the freshness of the air out there.

It didn't smell like death like my bedroom.

It didn't matter how many times I cleaned my room, it always smelled disgusting.

That might have something more to do with the bodies hidden in the walls than my inability to clean. My mother said I needed friends, and to her warped and twisted mind, dead friends were better than no friends.

I stop recalling her brushing the hair of a little girl who wasn't much younger than me before placing her into the wall of my room when the creak of a door being roughly yanked open sounds through my ears. Charles is standing at the foot of the entryway. He is next to a shovel and tarp that wasn't there earlier, and his expression is somewhat confused.

"What did I tell you, sweetie? Coming back here won't do you any good." He steps out of the doorway, closes it behind him, then peers up at a window on the top level. When the light switches off, he shifts his focus back to me. "If you scare his little pet, he'll be even harder on you." He nudges his head in the direction I just sprinted from. "Now go on, get back out there."

Recalling Dexter's demand for me to bring him out of hiding, I shake my head then stomp down my foot, wordlessly announcing that I'm not budging unless forced.

Guilt creeps into my veins when Charles hesitates for the quickest second before he steps closer to me. He seemed kind while taking me out into the forest to be hunted. He laid a blanket down for me and loosened the water bottle's lid so I wouldn't struggle, but that doesn't excuse the fact he drugged me before he left me to fend for myself. And it most certainly doesn't justify Dexter's claim that he knew his father was going to force him to watch me be assaulted.

Dexter said Charles is his father's right-hand man. He knows everything bad he does, and more times than not, he encourages more violence. Dexter's father likes to show off.

My father was the same. That's why he let the men take my mother into her room when she didn't want to go. He said he was sharing as all good little girls should. It made my skin crawl when he said comments like that, but since the winds whipping up through the floorboards hid my shivers, he never knew how much his comments scared me.

"You need to go back. Defying him will only make your punishment worse." A grin curls on Charles's lips when his eyes drop to the smear of blood on my knee. It isn't a nice smile. It's vindictive and cold, and it has me desperate to slide my switch-blade across his jugular like I did his master only hours earlier.

The only reason I don't is because within a nanosecond of gripping my arm, he marches me straight in the direction Dexter is lying in wait. "If you do as you're told, he will let you live. He has a pet in training, and you'll be a good reminder to her of what happens if she doesn't follow the *rules...*" He chokes on his last word when our entrance into the stable-like building sees him confronted with the image of his master lying on the floor in a pool of his own blood. "What did you do, and where is Moose—"

His words are interrupted for the second time. This time, it is compliments to Dexter bracing the barrel of a gun at the back of his head. "So you did know what he was planning to do?" Charles shakes his head, which switches Dexter's tone from manic to downright enraged. "Don't fucking lie to me, Charles! He doesn't hunt when he has a pet already on the hook, especially when she looks *exactly* like my mother. He parades women in front of her, shows her what disobedience costs, then fucks their almost-corpse in front of her." His finger inches back the trigger with each word he speaks. "The game hasn't changed since I was a kid. Only his victims altered." He walks in a circle until he is standing in front of Charles. "Because he already fucked my head, he switched his cruel tactics to women."

"He taught you how to survive—"

"He taught me how to hate!" Dexter screams in Charles's face. "How to maim, cheat, and steal! He taught me how to be heartless enough to kill a man while staring into his eyes and not feel an ounce of remorse."

"Dexter—" Anything further Charles is planning to say is cut off by the boom of a bullet racing out of a gun. It lodges deep into his skull, stunning him so much, he remains standing for almost three whole seconds before he eventually slumps to the ground with a thud.

*a*s the smell of a recently fired gun lingers in the air, a sense of calm washes over me. I thought my head was muddled from the drugs my mother forced down my throat during my prepubescent years and the nightmares that used to keep me awake in my teens were just that, nightmares, but the more the cloak of sedation wears off, the more I realize I was played for a fool.

He maimed me.

He manipulated me.

And now, the man who groomed my father so he knew exactly how to groom me will be buried in the same shallow grave as him.

My father is classed as a national treasure. He would have had a state funeral that would have seen the who's who of Hollywood elite in attendance, but now, once I expose him as the monster he truly was, there will be no one at his grave. Not even the man he once called son.

"Grab his legs. We need to move him closer since half of his face exploded."

Megan grimaces for the quickest second before she hoists Charles off the ground by his legs and assists me in moving him closer to my father. If her strength wasn't already an aphrodisiac, seeing her scoop up remnants of his brain and dump them next to his no longer recognizable face surely is.

She is a fucking skitzo with no sense of morality.

A perfect little doll for me to keep for eternity.

Megan's eyes light up like a Christmas tree when I say, "Should we burn this place down too?" After winking at her eagerness, I add, "It will make the process of identification harder but their trip to hell faster."

She moves for the gasoline tins at the back of the stables before all my reply leaves my mouth. She wasn't as eager at the hotel because she was worried about sleeping guests getting caught in the flames, but out here, she has no concerns. Anyone here deserves to die, and if they don't, they'd be wishing they were dead anyway.

In a way, we're being humane.

Once the barn is well lit, we make our way to the manor. We're far enough out that by the time flames are noticed, it will be too late to salvage anything. But the quicker we commence this half of our ruse, the faster some of the anger burning me alive will subside. I'm not a man known for dallying, so you can imagine how frustrating the past several years locked up in a mental hospital have been.

My wings are finally expanding, and Megan will soon learn that hers weren't hacked off years ago. They were merely clipped.

"Grab anything you need for a couple of nights on the road. It's a long drive from here to Ravenshoe when you have to take all the back streets."

Megan's wide eyes shoot up to mine. Confusion is all over her face. I don't know why she's confused. I said I would make Nick pay for how he treated her, and although I am rarely an honorable man, when I say I am going to do something, you can be assured I will.

"No pants," I push out with a grunt when Megan tugs down a hideous pair of riding pants from the closet in my room. I went without physical contact for years, and although I said I wouldn't need to feast again after eating Megan's cunt doesn't mean I won't want to ravish her at every available opportunity.

Pants create an obstacle. The hotel clerk learned that the hard way.

My steps into the bathroom to gather Megan's shampoo bottles slow when I notice two little pills on the chair Charles used as a table to serve Megan supper. I've played my father's games for years, so I knew of his intention to drug Megan. I just had no clue his twisted punt would shift his focus to me.

"Why are there pills here?" When Megan clambers back with a frightened step, I step up to her so fast, my brisk movements waft her hair off her face. "You were told to take them all. The tranquilizer he gave you was strong enough to take down a horse."

Her wild eyes bounce between mine as her lips quiver, but not a single word I see firing through her skitzo eyes escapes her lips.

"You could have failed."

The angst in my voice frustrates me more than Megan ignoring a direct order. It isn't from realizing she may have failed at killing my father since her senses were weakened by mind-numbing medication, his day was coming no matter what. It's the fact he would have sodomized her in front of me like he did my mother for years on end. That he would have ripped at her like a savage without a heart.

He would have hurt her, and there wasn't a single fucking thing I could have done about it.

Just like what happened with my mother.

I can't tell if angst is highlighting my tone or fury when I shout, "You were told to take them all!"

I feel the spiral coming.

I feel it raining down on me too hard and fast for me to combat.

But no matter what I do, and no matter how hard Megan wordlessly pleads for forgiveness, it swamps me in a matter of seconds. I'm no longer Dexter Elias. I am the monster I was groomed to be. The imp from the bottom of the ocean.

I am Megan's worst nightmare.

But instead of taking my anger out on her, I know a way I can hurt her without touching her. I have the means to rip her heart out and make her regret the day she ignored my direct order. She'll never defy me again.

Good. Because a king can't rule if even his queen doesn't listen.

"Come with me."

Megan follows me down the hall, up a flight of stairs, and to a locked door at the end of the hall I paced when I was forced to test my mother and she failed. The door is locked, but with my anger at an all-time high and psychosis making me think I am invincible, I kick open the door with my boot, then thrust Megan into the room with a woman who looks eerily like my mother.

"No, please," the woman begs when I hook her ankle and drag her down the stripped-bare mattress. I want to rip at her clothes like a savage, to watch tears pool in her eyes as I strip her of her modesty, but since my father always keeps his little pets naked and ready, there's nothing for me to claw at. So instead, I brace my knee between her stick-thin thighs, then backhand her with enough force, her begs turn into faint whimpers.

"This is what would have happened to you," I scream through flaring nostrils and lungs that are begging for air. "This is what he would have made you." I thrust my hand at the limp, lifeless woman sprawled before me. She's bruised and malnourished but still pretty enough to arouse any man's cock. "This is what you would have become. A discarded little toy too fucked in the head to fight, but not brain dead enough not to know that seduction is the *only* thing you've got going for you."

When I drift my massively dilated eyes to Megan, I'm not surprised to see her features are hardened with anger. Not a single word I spoke was a lie. Not only would she have become my father's latest project to torture into submission, but she is also aware the woman lying before us with swept open thighs and glistening pussy lips will do *anything* to stay alive.

She'll even fuck the man whose father tormented her to within an inch of her grave.

The switch-up of her sobs to moans is proof of this, not to mention the creep of her hand toward the zipper in my trousers.

When my father's latest plaything rubs my cock through my pants, Megan sees red. She pulls at her hair while grunting like a feral pig before she lashes out in the only manner she knows how —with extreme violence.

I don't know where the salt lamp comes from, but within a nanosecond of it landing in Megan's hands, she smashes it into the face of the unknown woman. She doesn't stop at one hit, though. She rears it back over and over again until my worries of this raven-haired woman not representing her become a thing of the past. My father's little pet's face is caved in, and although DNA is easy to manipulate once it is in the system, facial scans are a little harder to bypass.

We don't need to worry about that now.

"I think she's dead." The easy deliverance of my words exposes my psychosis ended as quickly as it started. I'm not surprised. Killing has a way of pulling you out of the darkest pit, not to mention when someone kills because they're jealous.

When Megan's rage subsides, she stammers back with wide eyes and a dropped jaw. Her eyes dart between the bloodied salt lamp in her hand and the woman lying faceless on the bed in front of her for several long seconds before she pulls her hands out from beneath her murder weapon of choice.

"Nuh-uh," I mutter on a groan when she peers at the door like she's seconds from racing through it. "If you make a mess, it is only right that you clean it."

She looks at me with begging eyes for three heart-thrashing seconds, glances at the door, then steps back toward the bed. Anyone who's ever accused her of being slow has no clue what they're talking about. I often speak in riddles. If you're not smart enough to understand my riddle, you're not smart enough to associate with me. End of story.

Megan is smart. She knows my comment about cleaning up her mess has nothing to do with the bludgeoned woman lying dead in front of me and everything to do with the mess her rage caused to my face. It's splattered with blood, and although I'd usually relish the thought, since it isn't Megan's blood, it is suddenly nowhere near as appealing.

After cleaning her hands on her shirt, Megan raises them to my face. It only takes her a handful of swipes to gather up the droplets of blood, but before it can join the numerous DNA samples on her shirt, I say in a gravelly tone, "Now lick it."

She hesitates for only a second before doing as asked.

She's a good little pet like that.

Although I didn't have to fuck my father's pet to get across my point, Megan was taught a lesson.

She is training well.

"Did you like that?" I ask, my voice extra rough like it's as cut-up and bleeding as the unnamed woman's face.

My cock hardens to the point it is painful when Megan bobs her head.

"As much as my co—"

She shakes her head before I get all of my question out.

Such a good little doll.

"Now on your knees."

My plan to mimic Megan's dental records with the unknown woman is almost left for dust when Megan immediately falls to her knees. My dick wasn't the first one forced between her lips, but we all know it will be the last.

"Look at me." I help the strands of hair sticking to her sweaty temples to fall back with the rest of her locks when she obeys my command, then I drag my thumb over the curve of her thin brow. Her eyes are hazy, but I'm not sure if that is compliments to her recent trudge through the dark or from the drugs Charles gave her.

An hour ago, I didn't care she'd been drugged because I assumed she had taken all the pills I'd left for her. Now, I care—probably a little too much.

The scent of hair that's in bad need of a wash fills my nostrils when I grip her chin to lift her head higher. She's grubby, covered with blood, and a range of bruises are mottled over her body, so now is not the time for her to suck my dick.

I just need my head to get the memo because instead of stepping back to count the number of molars in the now-deceased lady's head, I dip my thumb into Megan's mouth and groan when she sucks down on the bloody digit like she's starving.

"Wider." I kick her knees with my boot until I can wedge my foot under her bare cunt. I feel the vibration of her moan more than I hear it when I rub the toe of my boot against her swollen pussy. She'd be sore from how cruelly I took her, but forever eager to please, she fights through the pain by grinding down instead of cowering away.

I dip my thumb in and out of her mouth enough times to quell the urge to whip my cock out and stuff it between her pouty lips, then I nudge my head to the door. "Go grab your things. I'll meet you at the truck."

When disappointment crosses her features, I drift my eyes down her body before shifting my focus to the faceless woman. Her body is as nicked as Megan's, but I have a handful of marks I need to replicate before she'll come close to being Megan's twin— most notably, her once cracked tooth.

"Megan," I say, stopping her slow walk to the door. Once she pivots around to face me, I drop my head to her torso. "Leave the shirt."

Like the good little pet she is, she removes her only article of clothing without a peep, peers at me with a twinkle in her eyes that announces she's noticed my body's reaction to her nakedness, then she spins on her heels and skips out of the room, aware I'm about to become the fiend from her nightmares but only to protect her.

To a woman as unhinged as Megan, that is the equivalent of telling her you love her.

25

MEGAN

I can't believe you did that!
        Why not? It was fucking awesome.
That's because you don't want her with Dexter.
Who said? I like Dexter.
That's right. You like him, but the rest of us love him.

I bang my hand on my forehead, telling the voices to shut up. I'm already shocked about my earlier callousness. I don't need them making me feel worse. Although I will admit, I liked the part where they admitted they love Dexter too.

I just hope he isn't mad at you. Who wants to marry a psychopath?

Marry? I reply to the kind voice in my head. *Do you think he wants to marry me?*

I can't see her. Hell, I can barely hear her through the ruckus of screams in my head, but I swear I see her nod. Her agreeing response pleases me greatly, so much so I consider her suggestion that I medicate before it's too late.

He wants to love you, but not even Daddy could love you without medication.

I want to tell her to shut up and call her a lying bitch, but in all honesty, nothing she said is a lie. My father didn't associate with me until I was heavily sedated for the first time. He said the medication makes the holes in my head not as obvious, that they siphon out some of the goop, but Dexter said the medication is what makes me stupid, so I really don't know what to do.

Lucky for me, I don't have access to anything anyway. Dexter tossed my prescription into the marshland bordering the road.

I bet we could find some.

I usually like this voice in my head. She's the only one who's nice to me, but today, she's more annoying than helpful.

See? She whispers like she doesn't want the other voices to hear her when an orange canister falls out of the pocket of a jacket I yanked out of Dexter's closet. *I knew there would be some here somewhere.* As I roll the pills in the canister back and forth, she adds a final plea to her campaign. *It will make the rest of them quiet, then it will be just Dexter, you, and me.*

I'd rather it just be Dexter and me, but one competitor will always be greater than five, so instead of listening to the alarm bells sounding in my head, I listen to the voice instead.

One dose won't change much.

Not badly anyway.

"WHAT'S WITH THE DRESSES?"

When I drift my eyes from the scenery whizzing by my window to Dexter, I catch his scan of my dress for the third time in the past hour. We've been traveling down a dusty road the past two hours. Although most of Dexter's handsome face is covered by a low-riding cap, and a scruffy chin is hiding his cut jaw, we still need to be cautious. Our last victim's body only showed weeks of abuse. Mine has the marks of someone abused from birth. It isn't something that's easily replicated.

"I get the ease of access, and they're as feminine as it comes, but it would be lucky to be twenty out. You'd have to be cold."

I shake my head. I don't feel the cold like normal people because I'd rather be cold than covered with blisters.

"Did your father not want a girl? Is that what it was? Were you defying him?"

My brows scrunch as I contemplate his questions. I started wearing dresses simply because they were the only clothes I had access to, but as the middle-of-the-night visits to our ranch increased and our access to funds plumped out with them, I could have switched things up. I just didn't. I don't know why.

With a grunt, I wave my hand over the bag of clothes I packed in a hurry, wordlessly announcing I can get changed if he wants me to. I'll do anything he wants. I don't want to be in trouble. Especially since I stole another kill from him, and we won't mention my little slip-up earlier.

I thought medicating would lessen the voices, but all it did was triple them.

Dexter peers at me with quirked lips. He will never admit it, but I know he was planning to kill the woman in the attic. He rambled about her several times during his paralysis, commenting how she was a similar height and build to me and that by pretending she was me, we could make it to Ravenshoe before they'd realize they're still searching for two perps.

It was a brilliant plan that was almost ruined by jealousy.

My outrage wasn't my fault. I couldn't hold back my anger for a second longer. She was touching Dexter like Lucy did, but I wasn't close enough to kick her away, so I had to come up with another way to get her to stop.

The salt lamp wasn't the best solution, but it stopped her from touching Dexter, and since that was my goal, I don't feel sorry about what I did. I'd do it again if it's the only way to keep people's grubby hands off Dexter.

He is mine, and I'll kill anyone who says any different. Even the snarky voices in my head giggling about how much trouble I'll be in when Dexter finds out I borrowed some of his outdated medication. I tried to bring them up the instant they started riling me, but no matter how hard I shoved my fingers down my throat, I didn't gag. My fingers aren't as long as Dexter's cock, so they didn't come close to the back of my throat.

"Megan..." Dexter growls in a gravelly tone, drawing my focus to him. "You're giving me that look again. The one I warned you about." I almost drop my eyes to my hands balled in my lap. Only 'almost' because as fast as panic settles in, I remember when Dexter warned me to keep my thoughts to myself. It was before we knew we'd been duped, before I found out that your one true love is meant to love you back.

It was before I killed his father and gave him my virginity, so I can look at him like that now because he is mine, and I am his.

Forever.

"You're going to have me committed before the end of the month," Dexter mutters under his breath before he zooms down a side street so fast my head knocks into the window from the brash movement. "Come here." Before I can obey him like I always will, he yanks me across the stitched leather seating, then pulls me onto his lap so my torso faces the steering wheel and my backside is nestled against his penis. "Hands on the steering wheel. Eyes on the road. If you take them off for a second, we're dead. Understand?"

When I nod, he flattens his foot on the gas pedal. My heart rate accelerates as fast as our speed when we zip down the narrowed back road at a pace way too fast to be safe, yet nothing but excitement bursts through me. Dexter's hands are no longer on the steering wheel. One is on my breast, and the other is creeping toward the area I covered with a pair of panties simply to soak up the little droplets of blood still trickling from both my vagina and the cut Dexter placed high in my thigh.

"I'd fuck you now while we race to hell..." He squeezes my breast firm enough for a squeak to pop from my lips when I snap my eyes to his. Only once I return them to the road does he go back to fondling them with only the littlest bit of pain. "But you're too swollen to take me now, so I'm going to toy with your clit for a little bit and bite your neck. Then, once you're drenched from multiple orgasms, I'll stuff my cock inside you *real* deep. Will you like that, Megan? Do you want my cock inside you again?"

His hot breaths hit my neck when I rapidly bob my head. I've already been sentenced to hell, so I may as well have a good time until Satan arrives to collect me.

"Good. Now open your legs a little wider."

As the needle on the speedometer edges toward the red zone, Dexter slithers his hand up my thigh. After scrubbing his thumb over the cut he inflicted earlier near the edge of my panties, he slips past the damp material then gently strokes his fingers over my labia.

"Eyes on the road," he grinds out when they almost flutter shut in response to him slipping two of his fingers inside me. It felt too good not to respond, and the voices in my head were shouting too loud for my brain to follow any other prompt but theirs.

As trees whizz by at the speed of light, we bob and weave over numerous water-filled potholes, and Dexter pumps his fingers in and out of me in rhythm to the swaying movements of our borrowed ride. I want to say at a pace that drives me crazy, but since we already know I'm well past sane, I'll keep my thoughts to myself.

As his thumb circles my clit, Dexter growls against my neck, "I want a mess on my pants. If there isn't a mess, I'm going to hurt you until there is one. Do you understand me, Megan? I want a fucking mess."

The slickness coating his hand soon overtakes the sloshy ground flicking up under the tires as we race into the blackened night. There's as much wetness oozing from my vagina now as there was when Dexter had his head buried between my legs, but from the scent alone, I know no blood is intermingled with the wetness. It is all from the excitement cresting in the lower half of my stomach.

It feels dangerous.

Deranged.

Very much like Dexter.

It is so blinding, as the shake of my thighs reaches my lips, I loosen my grip on the steering wheel then sink deeper into Dexter's body. I like being cocooned by him, but even more than that, I'm desperate to feel the rush of euphoria wash over me again, and I'm willing to die to achieve it.

What doesn't kill me will only make me stronger. My mother taught me that, and my father ensured I understood what it meant before I was close to becoming a woman.

When Dexter drags some of the wetness from my vagina to my clit, my nipples harden as a shiver runs up my spine. I'm shaking all over and on the verge of falling off more than a cliff. My insanity isn't in question. My sanity is.

As screams I'd give anything to release roll up my throat in silent roars, I fully let go of the steering wheel then surrender to the madness pulling me under.

"Yesss," Dexter hisses into my ear before he sinks his teeth into my neck.

His bite returns my voice. No words come out, but the grunts and moans seeping from my lips can't be denied. They're as loud as the fireworks sparking before my eyes, and as rough as the callous on Dexter's tongue when he licks up the droplets of blood his bite forced to leak from my skin.

I'm so overwhelmed by the sensation roaring through me not even the voices in my head can be heard. There's no one but Dexter and me and his multiple pleas for me to turn the fucking steering wheel.

"*Now,* Megan!" he roars. "Turn the fucking steering wheel now!"

As I yank on the steering wheel to skid us around a bend in the road, Dexter hits my clit with three quick flicks. I shatter like glass on a concrete floor. A tsunami of tingles envelops me as the wave in my belly breaks. As we careen toward a large tree, I grunt and groan like I'm in the midst of being resurrected, but not once do I brace for impact.

My body is too consumed shaking through the most revitalizing experience it's ever faced to worry about our imminent collision.

Unfortunately for me, I've only shook through half of the shudders making me squeal like a banshee by the time our sail off the road finds a mark.

When we hit the tree with enough force to launch me out of Dexter's lap, blood gurgles in my throat, and the obvious crack of my ribcage whistles through my clenched teeth. I'd be out the windshield and sailing over the muddy grounds if Dexter's grip on my waist wasn't firm enough to mark. He holds me in place when the truck's excessive speed is brought to an immediate halt by a massive tree trunk.

Our heads rock forward before they whiplash back with the same level of aggression.

Then despite the giggles roaring up my throat, everything goes black.

By the time I wake, the sky is once again dark, I'm sleeping on a makeshift bed on the floor, and the unusual scent of chlorine is filtering in the air.

As I slowly flutter open my eyes, I take a second whiff.

Or is it...

"*No!*" I internally scream at the voice in my head. They're quieter than they were earlier today, but I'd rather them be completely silent. My head is thumping too much to deal with them, not to mention the ache in the lower half of my body. "*He wouldn't bring me here. He loves me. He wouldn't hurt me like that.*"

The conviction in my tone is sideswiped when my eyes finally follow the prompts of my brain. I'm waking in my nightmare, except it's not blurry like it is in my head. It's as clear as the moon lighting up the night sky.

As my eyes drift between the numerous photographs of Nick plastered over every inch of my room, I slowly sit up. It takes everything I have not to vomit when I realize I am alone. Not only is Dexter's absence proof of my silly ways, but the removal of every article of clothing is also extremely confronting. Dexter went on a rampage like he did at the hotel, and I wasn't lucid enough to comfort him.

I thought you loved him.

"I do!" I desperately want to scream back. "I just... I just..."

Chose to be a whore!

While pulling at my hair, I leap to my feet. As I shred the evidence of my whorish ways from the walls, I tell the voices in my head on repeat to shut up. They don't know what they're talking about. Dexter loves me, and I love him. He wouldn't abandon me. You don't do that to someone you love. You stick by them. That's why my mom could never leave. She stayed for me, and in the end, it was her love for me that got her killed.

He wanted to take me. The man who came to visit my mother once a week wanted me, but my mom said no, that I was too broken for him to fix.

As memories flood my head instead of grogginess, I spin around and around. The rush of dizziness my brisk movements cause my head don't alter the facts. The man who came to visit my mom once a week wanted to take me. He said I was pretty and reminded him of his daughter. He also promised to take care of me.

As more than my head spins in the aftereffects of my twirl, I move into the room that was once slated to be a bathroom. It was gutted during a remodel when I was a child, but with my mother's death lessening the number of male visitors we had and my father's backside never leaving his favorite recliner, the build was never finished. So instead of a fancy bathroom, I closed the walls and made this room a study.

I could only sit in here after coating the walls with bleach. The smell was too ghastly, and even though I knew the girl in the wall was dead, I swore sometimes I could hear her tapping.

Even the voices in my head are shocked in silence when I notice the wall that covered the little girl is no longer filled with drywall. A giant hole is right near the place she was laid to rest, and a heap of police tape adds a pop of color to the once bland room.

He didn't want you, screams a voice in my head once they get over their shock.

"*Yes, he did,*" I argue back. "*But my mother said she would go with him instead.*" I shake my head to make sure memories come through instead of nightmares before muttering to myself like it is perfectly sane to talk to the voices in your head. *"When they went into her room, I thought they were packing, but when they came out, only he left."* My nails dig into my palms when I confess. *"He visited a lot after that, and every time he did, Mom always made the bath super hot, or she hurt me so bad I couldn't leave my room."*

Where was your father when that happened? That was the quieter one of the voices. The one who promises me I'm not as evil as the rest make me out to be.

Although I shouldn't play their games, I march out of my room, race down the hallway, then point to the end of a rickety stairwell. My father's recliner is in the exact spot he left it, covered with rubbish and scraps of the food I poisoned.

Except his chair is no longer empty.

Someone is sitting in it.

Someone who looks *really* mad.

Told you he's cranky.

I whack my forehead with my palm two times to shut up the snarky voice before galloping down the stairs two at a time. Even if he's really mad, Dexter is still here. That means something.

My frantic steps skid to a halt when I spot an orange canister with a white lid in Dexter's hand. He's gripping his prescription bottle so tightly the plastic shell is splintered and on the verge of cracking.

"When did you take them?" he asks once he detects my presence, his voice deadly low.

I shake my head, stupidly trying to lie. I know his stance on medication, but I needed something to take the edge off. I had never killed with a clear head before, so I was struggling not to spiral again. Medication is my crutch. It numbs me and makes me unresponsive, but it's also all I've ever known, so it's not an easy thing to give up when you're barely holding on.

I don't know why I bothered trying to deceive Dexter. He knows me well enough to know I'm lying.

"When. Did. You. Take. Them?" he repeats, his words separated by big breaths.

When I hold my index finger in the air, indicating one night ago, he throws the pill bottle across the room so forcefully, the air wafting off his arm blows a lock of hair off my face. "They fuck with your head, Megan. They make you stupid."

I stomp down my foot, super mad that he called me stupid.

I'm not stupid.

"Yes, you are!" he denies to my angry snarl. "Because that's the type of shit that makes you think you're invincible. That has you willing to crash into a fucking tree to get off." He weaves his fingers through my sweat-damp hair, grips a fist full of my locks, then yanks my head back. "It is the type of shit that gets you killed!" After bouncing his eyes between mine for several long seconds, he mutters, "How many were you hearing?" When my brows pull together, he asks, "Voices, Megan? How many voices were you hearing?"

I almost act ignorant to his interrogation, but when his grip on my hair tightens enough to rip several strands from the roots, I blink an incalculable number of times instead.

"So more than the standard three you're used to hearing?"

After taking a moment to appreciate his personal understanding about my 'condition,' I nod. He grinds his teeth together so loudly it overtakes my stomach's worried gurgle. When I crank my neck back to peer at him, frantic to tell him that the number has returned to the standard three, he pushes me back with so much aggression, I skid across the rubbish-lined floor.

"Go shower. You smell like shit." When he spots the faintest shake of my head, he locks his eyes with mine then snarls, "You either wash off the skank seeping from your pores, or I will fuck it out of you." When I rise to my feet, he steps closer to me. "But it won't be like it was in the motel or the truck because by the time I'm done with you, you won't be breathing. That..." I wince in pain when he grips my thigh hard enough to reopen the cut he made yesterday. "... will seem like child's play." Nothing but hurt beams out of him when he snarls through a clenched jaw. "So go and fucking shower before I do something I can't take back."

26

DEXTER

*W*hen the shower switches off, I wipe at the sweat careening down my face before acting as if I didn't spend the last twenty minutes searching Megan's house top to bottom for any medication she may be hiding.

I'm pissed.

Peeved as fuck.

I thought Megan understood me because she too was emanci- pated from the normality society demands, that we're wired the same way, but after discovering two pills missing in a canister with my name on the label in the bag she packed, I'm beginning to wonder if we're anything alike.

She killed my father's little pet, but perhaps she only did that because the voices in her head coerced her to. Maybe the rage that burned her alive had nothing to do with jealousy and everything to do with her being medicated

If I were being honest, I'd admit I'm not overly pissed about her self-medicating. Everyone handles trauma in their own way. I am more concerned about the warnings the voice I ignore more than I listen to is hitting me with.

It is the voice of reason.

It's telling me that the whole basis of Megan's craziness is the medication she was forced to take for years on end.

If that's true, I'm more fucked in the head than I thought.

Obsessions are meant to be reciprocated and screwed up. They're meant to make you the most unhinged you've ever been and come with a heap of fucked-up shit you'd pretend didn't exist just for the briefest glance from a pair of skitzo eyes.

I thought I had that with Megan, that our uniqueness was what would meld us together.

Now I have no fucking clue which way is up.

Little Ms. Sunshine with the psychopathic eyes might not be screwed in the head at all, and for some reason, the acknowledgment of that frustrates me more than my reason for traveling thousands of miles in the direction opposite to the one I had planned to take when Megan's lips circled my dick after she licked off her virginal blood.

I wanted to protect her, but now it appears as if the only way I can do that is by letting her go.

Over my dead body.

I whack my head three times, hating the stupid thoughts constantly flooding it of late. It was my belief I could be more than I was born to be that saw my mother killed. I can't make the same mistake twice.

My thoughts shift from my past to the present when Megan enters the room in nothing but a towel. Her hair is drenched and hanging heavily down her back, and her skin has been scrubbed raw.

She took my comment literally when I said she smelled like

shit. She didn't, but if I didn't assault her verbally, I might have assaulted her physically.

Usually, I wouldn't hold back. If a woman's disobedience needs punishing, I'm more than willing to cross that line, but since she unearthed the truth for me and freed some of the mess inside my head, I can't take the same route this time.

"Not a dress. Wear pants." Megan's eyes stray from the floral dress she was about to slip on to me. They're as pleading as they were when she silently begged for me to shower with her instead of dumping her favorite shampoo onto the moldy shower floor and leaving the bathroom as quickly as I entered it. "You won't need to be easily accessible. *Well, not for me anyway.*" I was meant to say the last sentence in my head, but it's clear from Megan's expression that I spoke it out loud. She looks as distraught as my mother did when she realized I had set her up. I told her it was time for her to be free. That she didn't have to follow his rules anymore. I lied. As I do now too. "It's time for you to go home, right? Back to Nick. That was the plan all along, wasn't it?"

Megan shakes her head so fiercely she becomes unsteady on her feet. "*Ugh,*" she grunts when I push her away with the same aggression I used when I discovered her canister of blandness.

My shove is brutal, but it barely slows her down. She's up in my face in an instant, and even quicker than that, she falls to her knees and wraps her arms around my thigh.

"Begging will do you no good. It's too late for that now."

She once again aggressively shakes her head before she clutches me even tighter. "*Uhn.*"

When the wetness of her tears seeps into my pants, I fight the urge to shift her silent begs into screams of mercy. It's a fucking hard feat, even more so since her towel slipped from her body when she raced my way.

The skitzo in Megan's eyes will never fully wane, but there's no denying her beauty, and when the scent of her blood is intermingled with her fruity shampoo, she's even more beautifully deranged.

But it's just the pills, right? She's not fucked in the head like me. She could have a normal life if I can look past my father's teachings and understand that not everyone is born to be like me.

Well, as normal as someone who has killed can. That's a 'condition' that is rarely correctable.

Hating that I'm trying to talk myself out of my decision, I peel Megan off me then bark out, "You need to get dressed. We only have days before our plan is upended for months on end."

Rise Up, the band both Megan's obsession and Cleo's mate are a part of, is going on a final world tour. They leave for the European leg late next week.

My steps away from Megan wobble when the faintest murmur leaves her lips. It could have been a grunt, but the thickening of my cock doesn't agree. She spoke, and if the prickling of the hairs on my nape are anything to go by, she did it to deny me.

I spin around to face her, my footing so unsteady my words crack out of my mouth as loudly as the creak of my bones from my abrupt twist. "What did you say?"

Her drenched hair falls from her face when she sheepishly tilts back her head. The determination in her eyes is surprisingly strong for how hard her lips are quivering. I realize that's more from the effort it takes for her to deny me again than fear when she whispers, "No."

"You're denying me?" After charging across the room, I hoist her to her feet by a rough yank on her arm, then spit in her face, "*Me! I* fucking saved you! *I* stopped you from becoming a braindead idiot." *I'm still trying to save you from becoming a braindead idiot.* "You cannot deny me. I am a fucking king."

"My king! We're one and the same. If you are the king, then I am a king. If you hate, I hate. If you die, I die. I am yours, and you are mine, and I'll kill anyone who tries to take you away from me." She breathes in three times in a row before she whispers, "Even you."

Her voice shocks me. It's sweet and soft, a serenade a billionaire would pay out the eye to hear over and over again, but my bewilderment has nothing to do with the fact she's finally spoken. It's the fanning of her arms as she steps away from me that has me frantically grasping for reality. She's naked. Exposed. And although the erotic scent lingering in the air exposes that her cunt is dripping, it isn't the wetness I'm paying attention to. It's the streams of red rolling down her midsection and the deep cuts in her stomach that spell out my name.

She carved my name into her skin.

Marked herself in a way no man could ever deny who she belongs to.

And she did it without a single ounce of medication teeming through her veins because I made sure every morsel of substance in her stomach was deposited onto the bathroom floor before she entered the shower.

She's medication free.

Unhinged.

And oh so fucking perfect.

Megan tightens her grip on her switchblade when I mutter, "Give it to me."

Her stance only lasts as long as it takes for me to point out that her X looks like a T.

When she drops her eyes to check her handiwork, I grip her hand clutching the blade firm enough to snap several bones, then shoot my other hand up to squeeze her neck. "Let me fix it." They're not the words streaming through my head, but since they're far less dangerous, I run with them. "We don't want people thinking you're obsessed with Detter. What type of name is Detter, anyway? No one would call their kid Detter. Not even someone as crazy as you."

Her eyes flare like I complimented her before she bobs her head. It should be impossible for her to do with how hard I am gripping her throat, but like the good little skitzo I am now confident she is, she manages just fine.

"Back on the bed. Feet together and knees spread wide." I don't need to see her cunt to know she's turned on by the rapid shift in my mood. I can smell her arousal in the air. I merely want to make sure the slits in her stomach are as pretty as the one between her legs.

"You didn't hold back, did you?" I ask after inspecting how deep her cuts go. They'll scab up nicely, which means they will be seen for years to come.

Megan shakes her head like she didn't wholly derail my plans with a handful of words before she props herself onto her elbows so she can watch me fix the X in my name.

"Shh. I'm barely touching you," I mutter when the slightest whimper rumbles in her chest from the switchblade digging deep into her skin. It switches to a moan when I add, "Yet."

Air hisses between her teeth like a snake when I lick up a droplet of blood before it can roll over her almost bare mound.

"Waste not, want not," I murmur against her blood-stained skin before hitting her stomach with another long lick, this one a little lower than the first.

When the combined taste of her arousal and blood warp my senses, I dump the switchblade onto the bedding before burying my head between her legs. I bite her clit with the viciousness of a beast before suffocating it with the undivided attention of my tongue. I lick, suck, and fuck her delicious cunt with my mouth for several long minutes, completely oblivious to the fact she's close to detonation with only the slightest bit of cruelty.

I shouldn't be surprised. When you're being bedded by a king, gimmicks aren't needed.

When I inch back so I can backhand Megan's clit, she exhales the breath she's holding in. I can see her wish to scream all over her face. It is as desperate as the throbs of her clit, but for some reason, she remains as silent as a church mouse.

"You won't keep them from me anymore, Megan. I want to hear you scream." I adjust her position so her cunt is displayed directly in front of me. "And you'll do it in between breathless murmurs of my name." I circle her clit with my thumb before slipping two fingers inside her. She clenches around me and once again holds her breath, but within a couple of pumps, the whimpers she can't hold back turn into moans, then they eventually heighten to gruff words. "Louder."

"Ahh..." she meows before her eyes roll into her head. She grunts, sweats, then tremors. I have her on the brink, right on the fucking edge of hysteria, then I drag her back from the pit of hell by stabbing my nails into the D on the edge of her stomach.

"Say it."

I pump my fingers in and out of her in rhythm to the rocks of her hips. It's a cruel, deranged finger-fuck that sees her tiny body scoot up the mattress further with every hard thrust of my fingers. Shivers of pleasure rip through her. She shudders, moans, and slicks my palms with her arousal, but doesn't give up the one thing I'm craving even more than the taste of her blood.

"Say it!"

When Megan's head squashes into the headboard, I push down on the lower half of her stomach, curl my fingers upward, then lock my eyes with her sweaty face. As I milk every drop of cum from her body, she screams in hysteria. She's dripping from every orifice and almost incoherent, but it isn't enough.

I want more.

I need more.

I must hear her scream my name.

"Fucking say it!"

Another orgasm rolls through her when I bombard her clit with a heap of attention. I suck the nervy bud into my mouth, graze it with my teeth, then swivel it with my tongue.

Angered about her continued denial, I'm about to bite it off, but before my teeth are halfway exposed, the most lyrically composed ballad fills my ears, "M-m-more, Dexter. M-more. P-please."

As a groan of a satisfied man rumbles in my chest, I scissor the two fingers inside her in preparation to give the ultimate 'more' she's requesting.

"Open up wide. I want to fit all the way in without needing to take my eyes off your stomach."

Megan clamps her hands around her thighs and pulls them back. For someone who would have been forced to forgo any sporting activities to ensure her hymen remained intact, her flexibility is outstanding. I can wedge my large frame between her legs without hindrance, then, even quicker than that, I'm notching my cock into her weeping pussy.

"Arch up. Let some of that blood roll between your tits." After grazing her lower lip with her teeth, Megan bows her back as demanded. The crazy in her eyes ramps up when the blood from her newly crafted X rolls between the gully of her bouncing breasts. "Do you want to taste yourself?"

She nods before scooping up a little droplet of blood on her index finger and careening it toward her mouth.

"Wait."

Her finger suspends midair. Since her obedience greatly pleases me, I'm extra generous with the amount of cum I coat my finger with.

Once my index finger is drenched with evidence of Megan's multiple orgasms, I curl my hand over hers then stuff our fingers into her mouth. The vibration of her moan on the tip of my finger almost sets me off. I can taste her on my lips, her climax streaked with her blood is dancing on my taste buds, and I love that she's as obsessed with her taste as she is me.

It means occasions like this will occur more often, and I'd be a liar if I said I wouldn't let her kill me for that.

27

MEGAN

"And that one? How'd you get that one?" The cramps in my tummy appear nowhere near as bad when Dexter treks his finger down a tiny scar at the side of my nose. We've been comparing battle wounds for the past two hours. To begin with, I was angry we didn't even reach the halfway point an hour into our game, but the longer we play, the more I realize hiding who you are will never end well.

It also taught me that medication wasn't my crutch. It was a cloak. A sedative. A mask I was forced to hide behind. It didn't allow me to be me. It wanted me to conform to what society classes as acceptable.

That isn't me.

We aren't all cut from the same cloth.

Some of us are special.

Dexter is living proof of this.

"K-knife." My voice still sounds so foreign to me. Not because of a lack of use, but because it's been so long since I've used it I keep anticipating a girl's voice, but the one that leaves my mouth is far more feminine and mature. I don't sound like a silly little girl who does as she is told and only speaks when spoken to. I sound like a woman.

Like a woman in love.

After nodding in agreement to the one voice in my head, I work the words I want to speak through my head three times before stuttering out, "I-I didn't make h-his sandwich right."

Dexter traces the scar gentler this time while muttering, "A smidge to the left, and you would have lost an eye."

I grit my teeth when I recall a doctor saying the same thing. I wasn't angry about his assessment of my condition. It was the fact he sent me home with the man I told him had stabbed me.

The system is flawed, and more times than not, it is the victims who get harmed further by it.

After weaving my fingers through Dexter's thick hair, I trickle my fingertip over a scar I noticed when he had his head buried between my legs.

When I lock my eyes with his, I wordlessly ask him what happened.

"That was a broom," he murmurs a couple of seconds later. He rolls onto his back, which pulls my hand away from his scar before saying, "We had recently returned from a hunt. I didn't know my mom had mopped the floor, so when I trekked across it with muddy boots, she struck me over the head." He smiles before he shakes his head. "For how little my mom was, you wouldn't think she was capable of thirteen stitches."

I desperately want to ask why his mother never used her strength against his father, but before I can, Dexter stands from the bed, stuffs his feet into a pair of jeans without any boxer shorts, then shifts on his feet to face me. "Come on. We need to get on the road before the sun completely disappears."

As my eyes dart between his, wordlessly asking where we're

going, I scoot past the outdated candy bars we gorged on when my stomach rumbled louder than Dexter's grunts when he comes. I was starving, and although I would prepare Dexter's food without the special ingredients I forever placed in my father's meals, he's adamant I will *never* cook for him.

I would have been upset if he didn't grin while muttering his comment.

He has a nice smile.

I like it a lot.

And so do we.

"Ravenshoe, remember?" Dexter answers after tying his boot laces. "The band flies out next week."

I freeze, unsure if it is hurt enraging me or jealousy. Rise Up's spouses travel with them everywhere they go, so is Dexter rushing to Ravenshoe to stop Cleo leaving with Marcus or was he being honest when he said he'd make the people who hurt me pay.

I want to believe it is the latter, but I'm not a girl who's ever placed first.

Last is the only spot I'll ever achieve.

"What was that?"

I peer past my shoulder, curious as to what has Dexter's attention. When I see nothing behind me but walls ruined by tape that held onto the paint better than the magazine articles I covered them with, I drift my eyes back to Dexter.

I swallow harshly. He isn't looking at anything behind me.

He's staring straight at me.

"The look in your eyes. What was that?" A mix of anger and disgust crosses his face before he spits out, "Surely, you don't think he should be let off scot-free. He hurt you, Megan. He lied to you time and time again. He should be licking the mud off your fucking boots, and I'm going to make sure he does if it's the last thing I do."

I stare at him in shock.

In absolute bewilderment.

He didn't mention Cleo once. Not even his thoughts veered toward her.

This is all about me and him wanting to right the wrongs people have done to me.

I told you, mutters a voice in my head. *Carving his name into your stomach was the right thing to do. He loves it, and he loves you too.*

Incapable of denying the absolute accuracy of her statement, I dip my chin, snatch up the schedule Dexter printed last night, then hightail it down the stairs to get dressed.

Nick is about to go down but to make it more interesting, I'm going to ensure Dexter's dream comes true as well.

As my mother always said, it is better to wipe the board clean than leave a handful of pawns standing in the aftermath of greatness.

*W*ith a grunt, I yank on the steering wheel of my borrowed ride, unlatch Megan's seat belt, then lean across her fidgeting body to toss open her door. "Pee now. You won't have time later."

We're already cutting it close. The roads out this way aren't as well maintained as the ones I took to Megan's family ranch, and although authorities believe my father's little pet was Megan, I must remain cautious. They're still hunting me—the supposed mastermind of our escape.

I won't lie. When I watched the news reports circulating the country, my chest swelled almost as much as it did when I realized Megan is crazy with or without medication. She's all shades of fucked-up, and I very much look forward to exploring just how dark her craziness seeps *after* Nick grovels at her feet.

Megan doesn't need his forgiveness, she'll never want for anything since she's wholly given herself to me, but every psycho deserves to taste the tears of their victims at least once.

"Now, Megan," I snap out when her ass remains planted in

her seat. "If you don't show up on time, we're fucking done. He'll never say sorry, and I'll have no choice but to kill them all." Her crinkled brows are as cute as the blood I smell seeping into the bandage hidden by her floral dress. "There are a lot of disadvantages with modern technology. Almost every jet in their fleet can be remotely controlled." I've lost her with the computer talk, her cell phone before she was put away was the size of a brick, but I get her back when I make an explosive noise with my lips. "They'll all go down together in a big fiery blaze." I stop imagining the terror on Marcus's face when the plane he's helming commences plummeting back to earth when the alarm on my cell phone buzzes. "You'll need to hold. We don't have time."

After slamming her door shut and acting ignorant to the heat radiating out of her, I pull our ride back onto the road and recommence our last ten miles to Bronte's Peak.

Rise Up thinks they're clever about security, that paying out the eye for big, beefy men to shadow their every move counterbalances my level of smarts.

They're poorly mistaken.

Being a public figure makes them exactly that—public. And since they rarely do anything without their spouses and children, numerous opportunities were presented as to how we could get Nick alone, unarmed, and utterly fucking defenseless, but catching him unaware will be much more fun.

"Remember, in and out as soon as possible. We're not hunting here, Megan. That will come once we have his son." I pull into a parking lot a couple of spots up from the private school Nick's 'little treasure' attends before angling my torso to face Megan. Her black wig is fucking with my head, and the scent of her heated skin has my cock disregarding the fact we're about to add kidnap of a minor to my long list of charges, but other than that, she looks the part of a substitute teacher—*if* she could tone down the crazy in her eyes.

Megan shakes her head when I hold out my arm before muttering, "Test it."

I don't give her the chance to deny me again. I snatch the taser out of her purse, jab it into my sweaty skin, then forcefully make her press the button.

Fuck me.

The surge is as adrenaline-producing as Megan's blood dancing on my taste buds.

"Alright. Alright," I push out with a groan when Megan holds down the taser button a little longer than needed. A second longer and she'd singe the hairs off my balls. "If you hit him in the exact spot I showed you, he'll go down long enough for you to make your getaway." My words are rough. I hate sending Megan into battle by herself, but with McMallian College having only female teachers, I don't have much choice. "This..." I snatch the lanyard out of the hand of the woman gagged and bound in the back seat of her sedan, "... will open the rear emergency exit doors. I'll meet you there in five minutes." When Megan nods, I reiterate, "*Five* minutes, Megan. Not a minute longer."

She shakily nods again, presses her lips to the corner of my mouth, slips out of the car, then paces up the footpath that's blocked at the end by three burly security personnel. Supposedly, all the Rise Up kids attend this school but were absent the past three days. They only returned today to say goodbye to their friends before they jet-set across the country with their parents, endless nannies, and personal tutors.

It's a pity their popularity will be the commencement of their parents' downfall.

With her floral dress, cashmere cardigan, and wedged sandals adding credit to the school credentials in front of her, Megan makes it past the security manning the front door of McMallian College without a second glance.

Their failure to see the evil in her stoic face and forced blandness will cost them more than their job.

It will also claim their lives.

MEGAN

s I stride down a corridor where the chatter of excited children is noisier than the gurgles of my stomach, I wipe at the clump of sweat at the back of my neck. I'm hot all over, but it feels like more than recalling the time I lit a girl's hair on fire because she said I was ugly.

My skin is clammy, and my stomach is twisted up in knots. I honestly feel ill, but I couldn't even take Panadol as Dexter made sure every type of medicine is out of my reach while I showered.

I grunt at a woman approaching me from the other end of the hallway to gain her attention. After pointing at the map showing Jasper's class, I lift my eyes to hers. She's taken aback by my non-verbal question. So much so I'm forced to speak. "It's my f-first day, and I'm running late. Positions are hard to get in this community, and I'm afraid I've ruined any chance of securing a full-time place-ment." I huff. "I'm so angry at myself."

I don't know what shocks me more, the maturity of my reply or the fact I no longer feel as if I am one of the children weaving around us. Dexter said the medication would eventually wear off and that I'd mature right along with their disappearance, but I hadn't expected such a quick improvement.

Neither did we.

After telling the voices to be quiet, I shift my focus back to the woman eyeing me curiously. She hesitates for a minute before she eventually says, "Third door on the left. Your class is already seated. They arrive early." She rolls her eyes as if annoyed by the privileges only certain members of the community get, mutters a goodbye, then loudly questions as to why the hallway isn't vacant. "Class started five minutes ago, and for every minute you're late, I'll add five to the detention schedule."

The hallway empties in two seconds when she claps her hands together.

She reminds me of the principal who snarled at me while taking in the blisters on my hands. She said I did it on purpose, that I'd do anything to slack off.

I hated her.

I still do.

No! shouts a voice in my head. She's the kind one. *Dexter will be mad if we're late. We need to keep going.*

After gritting my teeth, I bob my chin in agreement before walking to the door the witch pointed at. The man manning the door isn't as stupid as the three I bypassed only minutes ago. He doesn't just scrutinize my ID, but he also places it into a scanner to ensure it isn't fake.

"Why are you late?" Think about a man who's been kicked in the throat too many times, then you'll have an idea of how rough his voice is. "Your ID check says you live on Ferris Way. That's a five-minute walk from here. You could have made it on time if you—"

I stuff the taser right where his voice box is, then hit him with a long zap. The electricity surging through his body buckles his legs out from underneath him in half a second, but its paralyzing effects are a little slower on his arms. He snatches up my ankle, which sends me tumbling into the classroom instead of entering with the authority of a substitute teacher.

"Oh no," says a little voice that sounds oddly familiar, even with it being much younger than the one that once regularly woke me in the middle of the night the past seven years. "Are you okay?" A miniature version of Nick crouches down in front of me. He is identical to his father in every way. He just isn't mean. After placing his hand on my sweaty forehead, he says, "Do you need medicine? You look sick."

I shake my head before clambering to my feet. "I-I'm okay." I wipe my sweaty hands down my pretty floral dress before curling one of them around Jasper's. "But I need you to come with me. We're g-going to play a game. You like games, d-don't you?" My voice has reverted to the timid, shy one I was hoping had gone for good.

"Ah..." When he twists his head back to a little girl with glossy brown ringlets hanging past her ears, she stops twisting the arm of a boy double her size to lock her eyes with Jasper's. "Can Maddie come?"

I almost nod when Maddie's dark eyes register as familiar, but then, just as quickly, I remember Noah was mostly kind to me when he spotted me waiting for Nick after their performances at Mavericks. He told me he was sorry that Nick had to leave early, and on more than one occasion, he offered me a ride home. I never accepted because I didn't want Nick to be mad that I went home with one of his bandmates, but I should have because the blisters on my feet the next morning were horrific.

While remembering the time Noah handed me a card for a doctor he promised would help me, I shake my head. "N-not this time. Okay?"

Little tears prick in Jasper's eyes before he gently whispers, "Okay."

I pretend I'm brushing away his tears while guiding him out of the classroom. I more poke him in the eye than clear away the moisture, but I'd rather hurt him a little than have him scream when he spots the slumped form of the man paid to protect him.

When "Jasper" sounds out of the classroom, I double the length of my steps, dragging Jasper along with me. We make it to the emergency exit doors Dexter went over time and time again last night before Maddie's head pops out of the classroom.

She screams bloody murder when she spots the slumped bodyguard, but it is too late. We're outside, mere feet from the car Dexter is helming.

"Quick," I mutter, my heart fluttering with more than excitement. "We're almost there."

Jasper's chubby cheeks bounce as we gallop down the fire escape stairs, but they have nothing on the thud of my heart when a voice I haven't heard in person for years trickles into my ears.

Nick is here.

He's racing up the sidewalk, wearing a tailored suit. His hair is shorter than it was when I last saw him, and his face has aged, but he is very much the rock god you'd anticipate when someone references the sexiest musician of all time.

He's got nothing on Dexter, though.

With my head in agreement with the voice in my head for a change, I nod before continuing my beeline for Dexter. I make it halfway down the footpath when my steps freeze as quickly as my heart.

I'm not second-guessing Dexter's plan. I'm stunned by the horrid words spilling from Nick's mouth.

"It wasn't her. The burned corpse they found wasn't her. It wasn't Megan," he screams down his cell phone while yanking on a tie I'm confident his wife forces him to wear. I'll never do that to Dexter. I like his edgy look. It's sexy. "Because the victim was pregnant! Megan can't have kids. It wasn't part of the report they did when she tried to fake her pregnancy to me." He grips his phone almost as roughly as I grip his son's wrist. "But it is why Col never took her. She was worthless to him. She was worthless to fucking everyone!"

I'll show you worthless.

I startle to within an inch of my life when I'm suddenly clutched at the side and dragged away from Nick. "Not here. This is *not* our playground."

In quicker than I can blink, Dexter sets me into the passenger seat of his borrowed car before he shoves Jasper into the back seat with his real substitute teacher. He was already on the verge of crying from how hard I gripped his arm while his mean dad berated me, but now he's in full hysterics.

"Shh," I snap at him a mere nanosecond before his sobs alert his father to his distress. I'm not overly angry at Jasper. He's kind of cute, and he was nice to me, but I'm feeling so unwell I either snap at him or curl into a ball and cry.

The last time I felt this unwell was when my mom made me a special soup. She said it would make me better, but it hurt me for days on end.

I don't want to feel like that again.

When Jasper's whimpers reach Nick's ears, his head rockets our way so fast I hear the crack of his bones before he pushes out a tormented, "No!"

With his cell phone shattered on the concrete sidewalk and his tendency to run when things get hairy nowhere to be seen, Nick sprints our way.

He reaches us remarkedly quick. Dexter has only just slipped into the driver's seat, and his foot has just braced the gas pedal.

"Please, please, please," Nick begs as he chases the rolling sedan down the isolated street. "I'll give you anything you want," he pleads while staring into my eyes. "Anything at all. Please, Megan. Just don't hurt my son."

His pleads should do something to my insides. They should have my stomach dancing and my heart rate soaring, but nothing happens. He is the blip at the bottom of the heart monitor I was seeking when I tried to claim my life six times the past year.

The flatline.

He means nothing to me anymore, and Dexter means everything.

Once he realizes his chances of mending things between us are null and void, Nick shifts his focus to his son. "Open the door, Jasper. Pull up the lock. It's okay, Daddy is right here. I just need you to unlock the door for me, okay?"

He's almost taken out by the door he's referencing when Dexter veers for a stationary truck. The collision flicks Nick off the back of our sedan and sends him tumbling across the asphalt.

I shouldn't smile when the expensive threads of his suit get hacked up during his tumble, but I do. He threw me out like trash, so it's only fair he gets treated the same way.

"Good girl," Dexter mutters under his breath when I scoot across the old bench seat so I can curl up onto his lap like the kitten my mother never let me have.

As I struggle to ease the pain ripping through me, I consider the events of the past ten minutes. I thought a weight would lift when I confronted Nick and felt absolutely nothing for him, but it hasn't. I feel heavy and weak. Somewhat woozy.

I'm so tired, I only just send the message to Nick's security team telling them where Nick must arrive alone before my eyelids become too heavy for me to keep open.

"*M*egan." I slap her harder than intended before shaking the shit out of her shoulders. I knew gorging on sugar wasn't the best solution for a missed night of sleep so we could fool around, but I never anticipated this type of response. She's barely responsive, and when she does come around, nothing she mumbles makes any sense.

I'd rather she be mute than mutter the crap she's been spilling the past hour.

"S-she's sick."

I shoot my eyes to the little demon sitting on the blanket Megan laid out for him during one of her lucid moments before shaking my head. "No, she's not. She's fine. Now eat your fucking Wheaties and shut up." My tone isn't as confident as I'm hoping, but it is better than the blank look Megan gives me when she finally opens her eyes. "He's on his way, and you'll want to be awake for this." I lean in close before whispering words I thought I'd never say, "Do you need something? A stiff drink, a valium, a..."

I swish my tongue around my mouth before grinding out through clenched teeth, "... Prozac?"

Megan pulls me away from the ledge I'm about to leap over when she shakes her head. She still looks as dazed as fuck when she sits up in the chair she's been slumped in the past two hours, but the color in her cheeks returns stronger than ever when the creak of a warehouse door pulling open sounds through the empty space.

"Just you!" I scream after yanking Jasper up from the blanket and pressing the switchblade to a vein in his neck. "You were told to come alone," I snarl out when I notice a second shadow bouncing in the lights I set up to blind Nick's entrance.

Even if the snipers I'm sure his brother placed around the warehouse have night vision, they won't be able to see anything through the amount of wattage I'm directing their way.

My mind spirals when a feminine voice mutters, "The message said I was to come too."

"Cleo?" I mutter, certain I'm hearing things.

It wouldn't be the first time.

After holding her hand up to block the blinding rays shadowing her face, Cleo nods. "It also said you'd let Jasper go if I came with Nick." She shifts her eyes from me to Jasper before whispering, "It's okay, Jasper. You're okay. Mommy is right outside."

"That wasn't the deal." I shake my head so fast my brain rattles against my skull before I shift on my feet to face Megan. She looks worried. Rightfully so. I am as pissed as fuck. Bringing Cleo into this changes everything, and I don't mean in a good way. "This wasn't the plan. *She* isn't meant to be here. *She* isn't a part of this." I loosen my grip around Jasper's waist so I can tug at my hair. My brain is throbbing so much, it feels like it's about to seep out of my ears. "Why are you doing this? Why bring her into this?"

Some of my wires cross when portions of my past merge with

the present. Not since a hummed lullaby unearthed the truth have I seen Cleo as Cleo. She is my mother in all meanings of the word, and try as I may, my brain won't acknowledge any different.

With Megan lost of a reply and a psychosis racing for me faster than I can contain it, I shift my focus back to Nick—except he's no longer Nick. He is my father. My tormentor. The man who is to blame for every single fucked-up thing I've done.

"You knew she'd fail, but you still made her do it. You just wanted an excuse to kill her, and my test gave you the green light." My back molars smash together so firmly, they crack. "I'm not letting you do this again. Killing her will be more humane than what you'll put her through. She could die over and over again, but you still won't let her go, will you?"

When I push Jasper out of the way so I can line up my gun with my mother's head, he races to my father's side like he won't be the cause of years of pain. I stumble on unsteady feet when my father tugs Jasper behind him in a protective stance before he attempts to place himself between the bullet earmarked for my mother's head and me.

He's never protected her before.

Not once.

I stare at Nick, confused as to where he came from when he mutters, "Megan..."

"Don't talk to her!" I snarl, my mood not so unhinged I've forgotten how badly he treated her. "She needed your help, but instead of helping her, you chewed her up and spat her out. You cared about no one but yourself." My words dart out of my mouth with a ton of spit. "You could have saved her, you could have saved us, but instead, you put yourself first."

I'm taken aback when my father's face blurs with Nick's when he replies, "You're right. I could of. But I was young—"

"That isn't an excuse!"

"I know. I know," he shouts when his deflection shifts my focus back to Cleo. "But I was never given a chance to fix it."

Both Nick's icy blue eyes and the dead cold eyes of my father snap to mine when I shout, "Don't look at her!"

He licks his dry lips, shifts his eyes away from Megan, then mutters, "She doesn't look well."

"She's sick," Jasper whispers from behind his father's leg at the same time I say, "She's fine! Now. No thanks to you, though."

Nick swallows before bobbing his head up and down. "I'll admit, I could have handled things better back then." I make a 'duh' noise. "But by the time I realized the mistakes I had made, she was gone. No one knew where she was."

As my mind balances on the edge of the sharp cliff of a debilitating psychosis, I mutter, "Because your brother locked her way."

"No." His brisk head shake adds to his short denial. "We had *nothing* to do with it. We didn't know who took her." He says 'we' like his brother is hiding in the shadows. From what I've read about Isaac Holt, he probably is. "But now that she's back, I can fix my mistakes."

I laugh in his face. "It's too late. Look at her." When he jumps to the command in my tone, I work my jaw side to side. I hate the remorse in his eyes when he locks them with Megan. I fucking loathe it. "She can't come back from that."

The pride in my voice doesn't match the seriousness of my reply. Megan is fucked in the head, but there's nothing wrong with that. If we were all born the same way, life would be real boring.

"Lucky for you, she doesn't want to come back from that." I shift my gun from Cleo's head to Nick's. For some stupid reason, he looks relieved that the focus is on him. "But that doesn't mean I'll let you off easily. It's gone too far to pretend nothing happened." I roam my eyes over his body before shifting them to his empty hands he's holding out in front of himself in a non-defensive manner. "Where is it? Where's the device?"

"I'm just reaching for the micro-SD," Nick promises when his digging hand almost sees a bullet hole lodged between his blond brows. "They're all on here. Every image you sent."

"Including..." I swish my tongue around my mouth, hating how dry memories of my past make my throat. "Including the one I sent directly to you?"

Megan's glassy eyes shoot to mine when Nick dips his chin. Even with Nick breaking our invisible connection with unrequired words, they're full of awe and admiration. "And Isaac's security team destroyed any trace of it. No one will *ever* see it." After tossing the SD card to my feet, he adds with a stutter, "N-now you need to let my son go. That was the deal."

I shake my head. Our trip to Ravenshoe was hatched solely to get back the image hours behind a monitor couldn't locate, but that doesn't mean his penance is over. He hurt Megan, and as much as my head screams at me that one man can't be trialed for the injustices of another, I refuse to listen.

Nick isn't my father, but his crimes were just as ruthless. They hurt women I love, and for that alone, they must die—both of them.

My compression of the trigger suspends midway when my name is murmured. It didn't come from Cleo or Nick, nor the woman still bound in the trunk of her sedan parked at the back of the warehouse with hidden tunnels that will conceal our escape for hours. It came from the woman at my side, the one who's usually mute unless she's walking the gallows of hell.

When Megan peers at me with pleading yet almost lifeless eyes, I shake my head. "It's not enough. He isn't sorry—"

"I am."

The lies stop spilling from Nick's mouth when I notch the

trigger almost all the way back. "You're *not* sorry. You can't even say the word!" I nudge my head to Cleo, who's so quiet, I'm beginning to wonder how I ever confused her with my mother. "She knows that better than anyone."

Unlike my father, I didn't pick my targets based on their purity rating. I wanted women like my mother—hotheaded Spaniards who'd fight for equality almost longer than they'd resign to the fact it would never happen with a man as governing as me.

That isn't Cleo. She's demure. Bland. So fucking under her 'master's' command, I doubt any decisions she makes are her own.

She's nothing like Megan.

Megan jumps on queue like a good little pet, but she'll also gut anyone who dares to tell her she's wrong for following my command.

She's not a wallflower. She's a fucking imp, and now that the error I made when I sent a picture of her delicious cunt to another man has been rectified, I can teach her exactly how black the veins weaved around her heart are.

"Are you sad you're not as strong as her?" I'm staring at Cleo, but I'm speaking to my mother. "Or was the 'victim' act your ruse all along?" My brain rattles against my skull when I *tsk* her with a dismissive head shake. "You could have walked away, but you were as sick as him." When strands of dark hair fall into Cleo's eyes when she denies my claim without words, I shout, "Yes, you were, or how did I become this?" I whack the butt of my gun against my temple. "He fucked with my head, but you made me this way because not an ounce of his blood runs through my veins."

"He lied to you, Dexter." My eyes snap to the gravelly tone interrupting our reunion so fast, Nick's son disappears into the shadows edging the warehouse along with Cleo before I can swing my gun in the direction they went.

It's fine, though. Megan's tormentor is still in front of me, and now his brother has joined us for the final showdown.

With Isaac's jaw ticking in sync with the spasm in my top lip, he shifts his narrowed gaze from Nick to me. He tries to wipe the riled expression off his face. He shouldn't have bothered. I can smell the annoyance festering out of him. It is almost as enticing as the fear pumping out of Nick. "Every single thing your father told you was a lie." He holds his hands out in front of himself before gesturing that he's reaching for a piece of paper in the breast pocket of his suit jacket. "You were conceived six months *after* your mother disappeared."

I shake my head. "No—"

"Yes," Isaac argues like I don't have a gun pointed at his little brother's head before he folds out the paper to reveal a missing person's report for a woman who looks oddly similar to my mother. It's dated fifteen months before my father cut me out of my mother's stomach. "This is you," he mutters before he taps on a much smaller image of a dark-haired baby with a lightning-shaped scar down his forehead in the far corner. "And these are your grandparents."

His ruse is over.

"My mother was in foster care. She was a drug addict who ran away so she wouldn't have to abort me."

"No," Isaac argues again, his tone more sympathetic this time around. "Your mother was taken during an exchange program in her final year of high school. She was very much loved and want-ed." He locks his eyes with Megan who appears as unstable as I feel. "As was your mother. And although she was sick, that was only because she didn't have the right people helping her. She could have gotten better, and so can you, Megan. Do you want to get better?"

My vindictive chuckle bounces around the almost desolate

warehouse when Megan shakes her head. I've told her numerous times she no longer has to pretend. She can be anyone she wants to be—even a deranged psychopath.

"What's your game plan now?" I ask at the same time a commotion at my side gains my attention. It isn't marshals barging in with the hope they'll take me down before I kill Nick. It is Megan howling in pain as she folds in two while clutching her stomach.

"What's wrong with h—"

"Nothing! Nothing is wrong with her." With my gun bouncing between Nick and his big brother, I crank my neck back to Megan in just enough time to see her stumble forward at a rate too quick for her feet to keep up with. "Megan..." I growl out a second before she faceplants with the dirty concrete floor.

My pulse rings in my ears when I kick her with my boot, and she doesn't rouse in the slightest.

"She needs help—"

"She's fine. She's just tired."

Strands of blond hair flop into Nick's face when he shakes the mop on his head. "No, she's not. She's bleeding, and her cheeks are really pale."

"What did you do to her?" I scream when my endeavor to roll Megan over sees my boot covered with her blood. Usually, I'd relish the thought of any part of my body wearing her blood, but there's too much coating my boot to believe it's from a little nick to her thigh.

"This wasn't us—"

"Bullshit!" I scream, my mood so unbalanced, I'm torn between dragging Megan to her feet by her hair or falling to my knees and begging God to take me instead. "She was fine until she saw you. You did this to her." With my gun shaking from the shudder rolling through my body, I lower it to Nick's chest so my aim doesn't have to be perfect to take him down before I bob down to roll Megan over.

"What the fuck..." Nick murmurs under his breath when he spots the cause for the redness on my boot.

The cuts in Megan's stomach have oozed through both her bandages and her dress. The murky blood flooding out of her is angry and red, but it has nothing on the rage that fills me when Isaac says, "If you don't get her help, she will die." He ignores the rapid shake of my head. "Her body is going into shock. Most likely sepsis. First dizziness and disorientation, then vomiting..." I recall how Megan ran to the bushes when I forgot to warn her about the deceased bodies in the trunk of the substitute teacher's car. She usually handles gore better than that, but something has been off with her tonight. "Now—"

"Say it again and I will kill you."

Like a man not in fear for his life, Isaac mutters, "Without urgent medical attention, she *will* die."

"No. No. No. No. *No!*" For each screamed denial, I rip at my hair. "She's fine. She'll be fine. She's—"

I stop rambling when Nick mutters, "Not breathing."

He snaps his eyes to mine as quickly as I drop mine to Megan.

Her chest is still.

She's not moving at all.

"Megan..."

I kick her again. My whack is harder than intended, but I need to make sure she's aware now is not the time for games.

"*Now*, Megan!" I shout, conscious she could be playing the ruse we practiced over and over again three nights ago. If my father got to her first, he wouldn't have stopped until he believed she was dead, then he would have revived her.

It was during the revival process she was meant to strike.

"*Megan!*" This shout is desperate. Fully unhinged. "Wake the fuck up."

"She's—"

"No!" I shout, refusing to hear the words Charles said to my father when he took it one step too far with my mother. "She's... she's... she's..." With words eluding me and my mind swamped by a psychosis so dark I doubt I will ever find my way out of it, I shift on my feet to face Nick. "You..." Realizing there's only one way for him to fully understand how much he hurt Megan, I swallow my words and pick up my pace instead.

Halfway across the room, my gun is loaded, and my fists are ready to maim, then out of nowhere, a woman with hair as dark as my mother's and eyes just as molten pops out from behind Isaac. She screams for me to stop, warns me that she will gun me down if I don't, but with my smarts gobbled up by a mental condition no number of apologies could smother, I continue storming for Nick.

I have him by the scruff of his shirt. My fist is careening toward his face, then my campaign is upended by three large bangs.

Pop.

Pop.

Pop.

I sail back with a grunt. My collision with the floor is as brutal as the one Megan took only moments ago. Hot lava spills through me as the coppery taste of blood gurgles in my windpipe, but I don't fight the blackness endeavoring to choke me.

I'll let it take me. I've just got one matter to take care of first.

As pain rips through me, I slant my head, lock my eyes with Megan, then stretch out my arm. Her eyes are open, exposed, and utterly breathtaking but as lifeless as death.

After closing her eyes with the slightest slide of my fingertips, I use some of the blood dripping from a bullet wound in my stomach to mark her forehead with a cross. It's not as aligned as the one my father placed on my mother's head, but surely, it will have the same result.

"Remember that you are dust, and to the dust, you shall return," I garble out between my lungs' gasps for air.

Megan killed for me.

She killed for herself.

But that's all it takes, right?

Two little words and a pledge to do better, and all the bad you've done is washed away and forgotten.

Confident that is the case, I whisper, "Fuck you," between shallow, jaded breaths. "Fuck. You."

They're not the words that will get me into heaven, but that's okay. Hell can't be worse than where I've lived for the past twenty-eight years, and it's most likely empty anyway since all devils are walking the earth alongside me.

EPILOGUE
DEXTER

Ten months later…

*W*hat the fuck is that?

You saw it too?

Of course! How could I miss it?

Pretty fireflies.

I laugh at the immaturity of the final voice. He's the childish, naïve one I'm confident could convince the rest of the rowdy bunch that there's no fun in corruption and that conformity is the jam.

He's also the one who misses Megan the most.

I'm not allowed to think about her, ask about her, or act as if I knew her.

I'm not allowed to do anything except sit in my chair and pray like fuck one of the nursing staff wipes the dribble off my chin before it soaks into my prison jumpsuit.

With my arms and legs being the weight of concrete, and my

head double the heaviness of their combined weights, changing outfits in the middle of the day is a task a braindead idiot can't undertake alone, and since most of the staff here are males, you can be as sure as fuck that I'd sit in soiled undergarments before I'd let one of these fuckers stare at my periwinkler.

My eyes cross when a firefly sits on the tip of my nose. A voice at the very back of the loud horde yells that it isn't real, but I'm too out of my mind to care. I'm doped up on the good stuff. As high as a fucking kite, but despite this, still an inmate at the number one hospital for the criminally insane on this side of the country.

They know a master when they see one.

Well, they would have six-plus months ago. Now my brain is nothing but mush. I'm one prescription away from a permanent vegetative state. I can't even move my legs, much less my cock, which is a real disappointment when the faintest whiff of an inexpensive perfume lingers in the air.

When I roll my head to the side, which is the weight of a bowling ball, the firefly flutters away, and another angelic image takes its place. Skinny, freckled cheeks, ruddy lips, and hair that's almost black enough to seep through the haze making my vision blurry is an enticing image for a man who's been starved of both touch and visual contact for months on end.

She looks like an angel.

A demented angel if she's locked up in here with us.

I don't argue with the voice when the faintest murmur whispers in my ear, "Can you see the fireflies, Dexter?" When I nod, she mutters, "I wonder if they'd still be pretty without their glowing butts?"

I stop hunting one of the many bugs in front of me with my teeth since my arms and legs are restrained to my wheelchair when something jabs me in the neck. It feels oddly similar to the prick of a needle, but before I can determine why the nurse didn't insert my medication via the cannula in my arm, another cool object brushes the same area. It's a tad lower but has the same coolness of the saline they squeeze through the lines each morning to make sure every drop of my medication is administered directly to my veins.

A temporary state of paralysis could be confusing me. I had a lot of issues with muscle spasms and functionality of my limbs the weeks after I was shot. The bitch who mimicked Isaac's cocky strut so well I didn't spot her behind him shot me three times. Two of her bullets embedded in my stomach, her intended zone, but the third one scorched through my forearm.

It is the arm that's signaling a difference in temperature between my wheelchair and me.

"W-w-what—"

"Shh," whispers the voice again before she dabs up the dribble that arrived with my one word, then pivots away from me.

The voice the others forever shove to the back of the pack finally makes it to the front when the scent of recently washed hair wafts into my nostrils. It's fruity and dirty, proving without a doubt that it belongs to a psycho.

I told you, he screams, his voice as loud as the wallops of my heart. *It's her! It's fucking her!*

I try not to let excitement get the better of me, but when my fingers brush the edge of a cool steel material that's sharp enough for the scent of my blood to linger in the air seconds after being nicked by it, it is almost impossible not to scream in hysterics with the other nutters on this half of the asylum.

Little Ms. Skitzo could be making a comeback, but instead of relishing the idea that she isn't dead, all I'm wondering is where has she been the past ten months if not in a shallow grave?

It better not have been with him.

"SHUT UP FOR JUST A MINUTE," I snap at the childish voice stealing my focus from the task at hand. My limbs have been too weighed down with medication the past six months to attempt to pull them out of the restraints holding me hostage to my bed, but tonight, my brain is nowhere near as sludgy. I'm almost lucid—*almost.*

When my wrist pops out of the leather handcuff tethering me to my bed, I shoot my eyes to the door, certain it is seconds away from being kicked open by one of the two guards who monitor the camera in the corner of my room every single night.

Once several minutes pass with the silence of an inmate in solitary confinement, I use my free hand to remove the shackles from my wrist and ankles. The switchblade stuffed into my wrist cuff earlier today would make quick work of the leather straps tethering me down, but with my head nowhere near as murky as it's been the past ten months and my heart throbbing fast enough to dissolve the drugs in my veins at double the speed of normal dispersion, the three-buckle design on each restraint isn't baffling me as it did only yesterday.

With legs dangling off the bed along with the cuffs, I grit my teeth before attempting to bear weight on my feet. They've been so unused the past ten months, my toes are wilted, and the arches of my feet aren't close to natural, but just like I was born to be a killer, my feet were designed to walk, and that's exactly what they do when my ass leaves the mattress with a breathless grunt.

After holding my finger in the air, wordlessly demanding for the voices in my head to be quiet, I press my ear to the door separating my room from the corridor guards roam at all hours of the day and night.

Upon failing to hear a single scuttle of a pair of boots, I push down on the door handle. My mouth falls open like a prepubescent teen seeing his first pair of boobs when the descent of the handle isn't interrupted by a sturdy lock.

Little Ms. Sunshine with the skitzo eyes is back, bigger and badder than ever.

Since I don't have access to shoes, my bare feet padding down the isolated corridor is soundless. No one can hear my escape, not even the guard slumped over the monitor now displaying my empty bed.

He looks like he is sleeping. Only a true psychopath knows he isn't. You can't miss the putrid scent of a man who pissed his pants in the seconds leading to his death. And just the knowledge that he was scared enough to desecrate himself sees me leaving his gun in his tiny cubicle with him. I won't need it. Megan said she'd kill anyone who tried to take me away from her—even myself.

When I reach the end of the corridor, I sling my head to the left before slowly veering it to the right. I was too doped out of my head when I arrived here to pay attention to the exit and entry points. I could be about to walk into a packed staffroom for all I know.

With my cockiness too high for a man who spent the past six months feeding the dragon tattoo on his shoulder, I crack my knuckles and rear up for a fight before veering to the left.

I realize the error of my intuition only two steps later. It isn't the numerous pleas in my head for me to turn around and go the other way forcing me to reconsider. It's a moose on a hill in the far corner of the hospital grounds that is stealing my attention. They're not uncommon around these parts, but it's the fact he's inside the fence that's taller than him that has me switching tactics.

Megan heard my father call me Moose, but she also got the whole story on my nickname's origin when she was curled up on my lap after she killed him.

It really is her.

She isn't dead.

Although she may be when I learn who occupied her time the past ten months.

White air puffs out of my mouth when I push open a door that's rarely unlocked before I sprint across the crispy ground. The sleet was heavy today, and the barbs of ice that stab my feet should slow me down, but they don't. I make it to the hill the moose is on in enough time to watch brilliance being birthed for the second time.

The hem of Megan's floral dress flicks up around her slim thighs when she adds strength to her swing. Her shovel smacks a guard up the side of his head so quickly, the flirty grin he was hitting Megan with before she blinded him with her kill shot is still on his face when his knees buckle beneath him.

Not wanting our reunion tainted by his raspy breaths as his lungs drown in blood, Megan hits him for the second time. This blow is brutal enough to splatter her face and dress with remnants of his brain.

"Nuh-uh," I groggily murmur when her hand shoots up to rub off the blob of brain matter stuck to her right cheek. "If you're responsible for a mess, you've also got to clean it."

Anyone who ever said Megan was stupid needs to eat their words. She's so smart, she knows the person responsible for tidying up her misdemeanor isn't her. It's the man she went on a murderous rampage for. The one who'd still be eating dinner out of a straw and staring at a cardboard box like an endless stream of horror flicks was playing on one of its flaps.

"You made the mess for me, so it's only fair that I clean it."

When I cup her jaw, Megan dumps the shovel onto the no-longer breathing guard before she nuzzles her blood-smeared cheek into my palm. The purr of her breaths as she relishes my touch is almost enough for me to skip a manic episode.

'Almost' being the imperative part of my reply.

Before the timid voice in my head can talk me out of it, I lower my hand to Megan's neck, clamp her throat, then pin her to the fence she precut in preparation for our escape. "Where have you been, Megan? Were you with him? Is that why it took you so long to come get me?"

I tighten my grip when Megan answers in the last way I anticipate. The crazy in her eyes is still there, her delusional personality still paramount, but instead of shaking her head in a way that defies logic, she dips her chin instead.

"You were with him?"

She nods again, and I lose my shit.

I scream and shout and bang my fists on any object I can find, then I tear out enough chunks of hair, the chance of leaving DNA behind at my next crime scene is greatly reduced.

Yet, despite the anarchic rage that takes several long minutes to dispel, not a single hair on Megan's head is ruffled. She remains perfectly untouched, safe, and uninjured because the king's whole objective is to shelter the queen, and shelter her I will.

Even if it kills me.

BONUS EPILOGUE
MEGAN

Four years later...

*a*s sirens wail across acres of rolling turf, I spin in a circle, seeking Dexter in the crowd. If carnage is prevailing, he is usually close by, if not in the midst of it.

The voices screaming obscenities in my head lessen their snarky tones when I spot him crossing the street three police cruisers just whizzed down. Red goop is oozing from his hands, and several blobs have splattered on his black boots.

It's warm out today, but he still chose his usual getup of long pants, a long-sleeve shirt, boots, and a low-riding cap. He has the swagger of the rock star he no longer wants to kill but with a dangerous edge that announces your most wicked thoughts will never be as deviant as the ones that regularly fill his head.

He is as deranged as they come, and he loves us with everything he has.

I was worried that wasn't going to be the case when I first

broke him out of Drakes. Within a second of slotting his backside behind the steering wheel of a truck big enough to carry the cutout of a moose, he steered our borrowed ride to Ravenshoe.

It was only the coo from a basket wedged behind the passenger seat that slowed him down. He thought we had a stow-away rodent. I laughed about the fret on his face for almost a minute before whipping off the blanket keeping our new friend hidden from prying eyes.

"Whose kid is that?" Dexter roared as his eyes darted between the little bundle of blue and me.

I never thought anything would top the expression on his face when he heard me talk for the first time, but my stammered, "Y-You," that night still occasionally pushes through the nightmares that frequent my dreams almost every night.

I thought Dexter knew the cause of my delay. I telepathically spoke to him every day during our mutual incarcerations, but it was only when he double-checked the truth in my eyes did I realize the silly internet towers popping up all over the country most likely skewed my endeavors to communicate with him.

I wasn't with Nick, who is still breathing today solely because he kept my heart pumping until medics arrived. I had severe sepsis from the cuts in my stomach and the punctured lung I endured when we crashed into a tree. I was clinically dead, but with Nick keeping my heart pumping and Dexter marking my forehead to keep the heathens away, my brain didn't suffer any negative side effects from me flatlining.

Well, not any more than it had already suffered from my childhood.

After a four-week stay in a fancy hospital owned by Nick's brother, I was to be transferred to a mental hospital that's adept at handling mothers-to-be without the fetus-harming medication most hospitals for the clinically deranged use.

I was shocked I was pregnant. So much so, I was admitted with only the slightest protest. I broke one guard's nose before shoving a sedative full of murky liquid into a second guard's neck.

I'd still be fighting now if the man in the pricy suit didn't tell me I could hurt my baby with Dexter if I didn't settle down. He promised the new hospital would take care of us both, and they'd do it without harming my infant or me.

Once his honest tone calmed me down, he also explained that my mother lied when she told the bad men I couldn't have babies. That, along with the super-hot baths she made me take every time they visited saved me from an entity who breeds babies for a living.

I'm still supposed to be at Winterville now, my incarceration was for seven years minimum, but with our son born and the diaper delivery guy far too friendly with the loonies every guy wants to bed at least once in their lives, I stuffed my baby with Dexter into a laundry basket and hatched an escape plan.

Since I spent the nine months of my pregnancy strapped to a bed like Dexter, getting him out was going to take more than a handful of compliments. It only took remembering his substitute teacher ruse for me to devise the perfect plan.

People are willing to do almost anything when you're carrying a newborn baby in your arms. They'll even let a stranger inside their fortress home to warm up a bottle.

The guard's willingness to help saw her tied to the boiler in her basement instead of ruining the mattress in her master suite with the blood that's meant to be in her veins.

My thoughts snap back to the present when Dexter gestures for Damien to join us. He's been tackling the fort at a playground only a few hundred miles from Ravenshoe the past thirty minutes.

We only returned stateside earlier this year. Our first three and a half years as a family were spent abroad with Dexter's grandparents Isaac informed him about. They were a nice couple in their late sixties, but they could have been a lot nicer. They said Damien was the devil's spawn, and that he needed to be medicated to make sure the long list of mental illnesses that have run in Dexter's mother's side of the family the past three centuries weren't passed down to Damien.

You can imagine how Dexter handled that situation.

If you can't, you'll be in the dark just as much as me because despite my wish to scratch the old biddy's eyes out, Dexter said Damien was too little to go to work with his father just yet, so I had to take him on a playdate instead.

It was as eventful as Dexter's gory afternoon—and I see that being the case again when Damien's sprint across the glossy grass is cut short by a boy with an ugly face and a fat tummy. He's so eager to chase down the ice cream truck Dexter fetched our raspberry gelatos from, he took a shortcut across the grass instead of following the footpath, which meant he bumped straight into Damien during the process.

"Wait," Dexter snaps out when my first thoughts are to jump to Damien's defense. I'm not going to hurt the little boy. His horrible haircut and chubby thighs reveal his parents are already mistreating him. I am merely going to comfort our son like I do Dexter when the nightmares of his past resurface stronger than ever. "Let's see what he does first."

With his brain having none of the worm holes my father accused mine of having, Damien gets back onto his feet, wipes his grazed knees with his even more grazed hands, hesitantly smiles at his bully, then makes his way to Dexter and me.

I'm proud of his tear-free face.

Dexter seems to be on the other end of the spectrum.

He hates bullies, but even more than that, he hates when the bully is groomed by one several years older than the person they're belittling.

Damien's original accoster was happy to let bygones be bygones, his eyes are still locked on the ice cream truck, but like most spoiled brats around these parts, he isn't at the park alone. He's here with his mother, a socialite I'm confident spends more time on her cell phone than caring for her offspring.

"You need to tell your boy to watch where he's going," she spits out after covering the speaker of the cell phone attached to her ear. After dragging her eyes down my floral dress and wedged sandals, she mutters, "This park is reserved for residents who reside here. It isn't an open free-for-all."

"It's a park," I snap back, shocked by her rudeness. "They're n-not reserved for anyone."

"They're n-not reserved," she mimics with a roll of her eyes. "They are... and that sign over there says so." She points to a sign that states nothing of the sort before muttering, "But I guess you can't understand what it says since you're too stupid to read."

As Dexter dumps our gelatos into the bin at our side, I snarl, "What did you say?"

"You heard what I said. I said you're—"

Dexter doesn't backhand the words out of her mouth. He doesn't even cut her off with an ear-burning string of obscenities. He merely steps between us before he brings out the charm that's had us off law enforcement radars for almost four years. "How about I buy you and your son a gelato to make up for the inconvenience." He waves his hand through the air before raking it through his dark locks no longer hidden by his cap. "It's hot out, and moods get a little erratic when the gauge won't stop rising. It often has us saying things we don't mean."

"I meant it—"

"Oh, I know," Dexter interrupts before he steps even closer to her, so she becomes trapped by his glistening baby blues. "Just like I know your time is far too important to waste handling a situation like *this*." I should be upset when he thrusts his hand at me during the 'this' part of his statement, but I'm not. I recognized his game plan the instant he dumped our gelatos.

His hands are about to be coated with a sticky red substance again—except this time, it will be my taunter's blood dribbling from his palms instead of a sour raspberry sorbet the second imp in my belly has been demanding the past two months.

Dexter gestures for the lady to commence the short walk to the ice cream van before he spins around to face me. Death is dancing in his eyes. He is the most attractive he's ever been.

After winking at an identical murderous gleam brightening my eyes, he bobs down in front of Damien before ruffling his hair. "Daddy needs to go to work now, okay? So we will finish our game of hide and seek tomorrow."

Forever eager to be his father's number one fan, Damien immediately bobs his head. His agreement pleases Dexter greatly, but it has nothing on the excitement that races through me when Dexter removes the key for the basement hanging around his neck to place it into my palm.

I'm not being left out of the festivities this time around.

This key is a front-row ticket to the Wicked Witch's final show.

"Make sure Damien is in bed before you come down," Dexter mutters into my ear before he presses his lips to my temple. "We don't want any unexpected visitors this time around."

Damien wasn't our last unwanted guest. It was our landlord who was reported missing by his daughter-in-law three months ago.

It's only murder if they find a body.

Without one, it's merely a missing person's case.

Facebook: facebook.com/authorshandi

Tiktok: https://www.tiktok.com/@authorshandiboyes

Instagram: instagram.com/authorshandi

Email: authorshandi@gmail.com

Reader's Group: bit.ly/ShandiBookBabes

Website: authorshandi.com

Newsletter: https://www.subscribepage.com/AuthorShandi

If you enjoyed this book, please leave a review.

ALSO BY SHANDI BOYES

Perception Series

Saving Noah (Noah & Emily)

Fighting Jacob (Jacob & Lola)

Taming Nick (Nick & Jenni)

Redeeming Slater (Slater and Kylie)

Saving Emily (Noah & Emily - Novella)

Wrapped Up with Rise Up (Perception Novella - should be read after the
Bound Series)

Enigma

Enigma (Isaac & Isabelle #1)

Unraveling an Enigma (Isaac & Isabelle #2)

Enigma The Mystery Unmasked (Isaac & Isabelle #3)

Enigma: The Final Chapter (Isaac & Isabelle #4)

Beneath The Secrets (Hugo & Ava #1)

Beneath The Sheets(Hugo & Ava #2)

Spy Thy Neighbor (Hunter & Paige)

The Opposite Effect (Brax & Clara)

I Married a Mob Boss(Rico & Blaire)

Second Shot(Hawke & Gemma)

The Way We Are(Ryan & Savannah #1)

The Way We Were(Ryan & Savannah #2)

Sugar and Spice (Cormack & Harlow)

Lady In Waiting (Regan & Alex #1)

Man in Queue (Regan & Alex #2)

Couple on Hold(Regan & Alex #3)

Enigma: The Wedding (Isaac and Isabelle)

Silent Vigilante (Brandon and Melody #1)

Hushed Guardian (Brandon & Melody #2)

Quiet Protector (Brandon & Melody #3)

Enigma: An Isaac Retelling

Twisted Lies (Jae & CJ)

Bound Series

Chains (Marcus & Cleo #1)

Links(Marcus & Cleo #2)

Bound(Marcus & Cleo #3)

Restrain(Marcus & Cleo #4)

The Misfits

Russian Mob Chronicles

Nikolai: A Mafia Prince Romance (Nikolai & Justine #1)

Nikolai: Taking Back What's Mine (Nikolai & Justine #2)

Nikolai: What's Left of Me(Nikolai & Justine #3)

Nikolai: Mine to Protect(Nikolai & Justine #4)

Asher: My Russian Revenge (Asher & Zariah)

Nikolai: Through the Devil's Eyes(Nikolai & Justine #5)

Trey (Trey & K)

The Italian Cartel

Dimitri

Roxanne

Reign

Mafia Ties (Novella)

Maddox

Demi

Rocco

Clover

Smith

RomCom Standalones

Just Playin' (Elvis & Willow)

Ain't Happenin' (Lorenzo & Skylar)

The Drop Zone (Colby & Jamie)

Very Unlikely (Brand New Couple)

Short Stories - Newsletter Downloads

Christmas Trio (Wesley, Andrew & Mallory -- short story)

Falling For A Stranger (Short Story)

Coming Soon

Jack Carson

Printed in Great Britain
by Amazon

23149447R10183